A NOVEL

BUT NOT
WARRIORS

A NOVEL

BUT NOT WARRIORS

Jack Williamson

LYNX
BOOKS

Library of Congress Cataloging-in-Publication Data

Williamson, Jack, 1924–
   But not warriors / Jack Williamson.—1st ed.
      p.   cm.
   ISBN 1-55802-388-7
   1. World War, 1939–1945—Fiction. I. Title.
PS3573.I45628B87 1989
813′.54—dc19   89–2386
                                             CIP

First Edition

This book is published by Lynx Books, a division of Lynx Communications, Inc., 41 Madison Avenue, New York, New York, 10010. The name ''Lynx'' and the logo consisting of a stylized head of a lynx are trademarks of Lynx Communications, Inc.

Printed in the United States of America

0 9 8 7 6 5 4 3 2 1

To Mary, Jean-Ann, Patty,
Louise, Marge, Barbara,
Jeri and Ann, the all-girl
orchestra whose comments
made this a better book.

"My center is giving way
My right is pushed back
Situation excellent,
I am attacking."

—FIELD MARSHAL FERDINAND FOCH
Second Battle of the Marne, 1918

A NOVEL

BUT NOT WARRIORS

THE
☆ WARRIORS ☆

THE kids in Piebald called them "the one-eyed army."

Not that impaired vision was their only affliction.

Every unit stationed at the prisoner-of-war camp outside town had been mustered *into* World War II in worse shape than a lot of front-line outfits were mustered *out.*

Limited Service. Not fit for combat.

The 575th, for one, had four officers and 136 enlisted men and, among them, there were only 227 eyeballs that performed reasonably well or even aimed consistently in matching directions.

Their service records, in dispassionate clinical jargon, cataloged a depressing inventory of disfigurements and diminished capacities, singling out debilitating orthopedic misalignments, departed and abused extremities, obstructed orifices, and malfunctioning systems. The "bad backs" were exceeded in number only by fallen arches, but the latter, of course, could be multiplied by two per complainer.

If Blackie Sifko beckoned to you with the little finger of his right hand, it was because that was the only finger he had on that hand, having left the remainder in some coal-mining machinery several hundred feet under his hometown in West Virginia.

"Sheee-it," he said, chuckling during a crap game one night in the latrine. "Five assholes in this fuckin' game an' only eighteen fingers." An illustrative if somewhat exaggerated report.

PFC Garnett liked to horrify newcomers by wedging his glass

eye out when no one was looking and popping it into his mouth. Then he would suddenly clap a hand to the red-rimmed cavity and begin hacking and gagging furiously, bending over double and hopping around, finally spitting the glistening orb back into his palm in feigned relief. While his audience gawked, dumbfounded, he worked the eye back into place, cursing and complaining all the while as if this was some sort of intercranial slippage problem he was faced with continually.

Anberger warned him over and over again, "One of these days you gonna swaller that thing," but Garnett would just slap his knee and laugh like all get out. Anberger shook his head. That Garnett. Anberger had seen glass eyes before. Josie Sue Beckam had one, the girl who worked in the filling station back home, but he'd never seen anybody fart around with one the way Garnett did.

And he didn't see how Garnett could stand the taste, either. Whatever it was it tasted like.

Not all the infirmities were as apparent as missing fingers or eyeballs. A lot of the men, they agreed solemnly among themselves, *looked* perfectly normal. Private Lawler, for one, was merely underweight, albeit grossly so.

"I got a dog at home weighs more'n him," Blackie insisted. "An' that's a fact."

Big Sam Claybin was "mostly jus' old." He was thirty-eight. PFC Houghton had a congenital skin disease, his red, peeling countenance leading the others to call him Chief, as in Indian chief. Houghton was one of the assistant cooks, and there were continuing complaints and unappetizing comments made about the likelihood of his flaking off into the food. But nothing was ever done about it and Houghton stayed on in the mess hall, scratching and grinning among the pots and pans.

With the exception of the officers, all of the company had come straight out of the hills and hollows of West Virginia and Harlan County, Kentucky. Loose-jointed, rough-edged mountain folk, most of them had been "brung up" in soot-covered cabins above the coal tipple or even farther up the fork where "the electric" hadn't been put in yet.

"W'all got one leg shorter'n the other," Dalt Cooper liked to brag, "from walkin' along them ridges."

Cooper was a big gangling red-faced youth, prematurely bald, and when he grinned, he displayed a mouthful of opaque, sparkling white government-issue teeth. His "cutters," he called them. His cutters and his "runners." That's what he called his G.I. shoes, the dress browns and the rough high-top field boots. Never, Cooper said, until the day he was drafted, had he ever in his life owned two pairs of shoes at the same time. In that regard he was not alone in the company.

They all stood around with their weight on one leg, spit frequently, and injected the phrase "by God" at least once into every other sentence.

The stalwarts of the 575th were little different physically from thousands of similarly incapacitated civilians swept up in the early desperation following Pearl Harbor. They were the dregs of the nation's volume-oriented Selective Service System, the exhaust fumes of America's fighting machine.

"Limited Service" was a broad, loosely interpreted classification enfolding a scramble of draftees judged incapable of meeting the demands of battle but healthy enough for rear-echelon service. They could type reports, carry hospital bedpans, drive trucks, and stand guard duty. One ragged cut above 4-F, the stay-at-home mark, they were lined up in alphabetical order, given G.I. haircuts and inoculations, dressed in soldier costumes, and marched away to obscurity.

By category, by official government decree, they were never to see or hear the violence of combat.

That supposition, in the case of the 575th, did not take into account Captain Cadwallader Aloysius Maxwell.

Captain Maxwell, "by jumpin' Christ," was going to take "this bunch of no-good sonsabitches" overseas.

THEIR ☆ LEADER ☆

D ESCRIBING Captain Maxwell to newcomers was a popular amusement at Piebald.

"Ornery sumbitch. Fuckin' ole goat playin' soldier." That was a typical opening at the PX over a pitcher of 3.2 beer. "Rougher'n a outhouse cob."

In the more genteel atmosphere of the officers' club, he had been termed "a Roman general born two thousand years too late," "the all-time personification of antiquated military rectums," and, in a letter sent home by a young lieutenant with a literary bent, "an aging gunfighter stalking the company area, eyes and brass glittering, looking for someone to draw on."

He was tall, thin, and angular, graying, scarred, and fifty-four years old, a hook-nosed Lincolnesque figure with a square, slightly overshot jaw and coal black eyes squinted deep into an eroded, leathery visage.

"Blunt . . . stubborn . . . rude . . . given to excessive use of alcohol . . . obsessed with orders into combat." All of these words and phrases appeared regularly in his periodic fitness reports where, though recommendations for promotion were conspicuously absent, he invariably was adjudged a competent officer.

The consensus was that he was "a goddam hard-ass."

Plus all those other things, too.

He was the son of an itinerant evangelical preacher who had rattled back and forth across the prairie states in a rickety horse-drawn wagon with his wife, a Bible, four raffia collection baskets, and a moldering yellow tent. He was born in that tent one night during a paralyzing thunder and lightning storm in Tonganoxie, Kansas. His name was selected next morning from a list of "Common Christian Names" in the back of a borrowed dictionary: Cadwallader (Welsh: arranger of battle) Aloysius (Latin/Germanic: famous warrior). Together they spelled "combat."

"That ain't a fit name for a little boy, Jess."

"That's his given name. I'm givin' it to him."

The good Reverend Maxwell, when he wished to be, was a man of few words.

"The sickness" made the preacher's only offspring a teenage orphan in the early 1900s. Consigned to the care of a maiden aunt, brimming with the hot, impatient juices of youth, he spent his next allotted decade searching diligently, but found no frontiers to tame. There were no savages to fight, no pirate ships to sail, no wagonloads of gold to get through the pass.

And then, just for him, along came World War I.

His commission in 1917 was the result of his graduation seven years earlier from a second-rate military school in Pinckney, Missouri. Stammer Military Academy was regarded by the townspeople, and perhaps by his desperate aunt when she deposited him there, as more of a penal institution for unmanageable adolescents than a fountain of learning. But if his piece of parchment from Stammer didn't mark him as a leader of men, the army didn't ask him to stand aside while they checked.

There was a war on and Uncle Sam needed everybody.

"Sign your name an' get in line over there."

Similar urgencies bounced Maxwell precipitously from shavetail to first lieutenant to captain, and to command of a Third Division company of combat engineers. After an agonizing year-long delay in the States, his regiment finally marched ashore in France on October 3, 1918. It was his thirtieth birthday.

"Y'left . . . Y'left . . . Y'had a good home but y'left, right, left, right!"

He could still hear the shrill keening of the sea gulls wheeling overhead and the confident rhythmic clunk of heavy boots on the wooden docks at Le Havre. Somewhere to the north lay the enemy, and just one hundred miles or so beyond those wooded hills was Paris. That heady day was the nicest birthday present he could have chosen for himself.

As it turned out, however, that was also the day the Germans asked President Wilson for an armistice.

"What the Sam Hill's all the racket about?"

"What's all the *racket* about? It's all done, Cap'm. The goddam krauts have surrendered!"

The war was over. And Captain Maxwell had missed it.

The hostilities sputtered on for a few days, stopped, started again, and finally dwindled to an uncertain conclusion with the regiment still bivouacked on the docks next to the big gray troop transport that had brought them there.

Since they were closest to the gangplanks, their provisions and equipment still crated, they were faced around one morning, marched back aboard the ship, and sent home. The last American doughboys to get to Europe, they were the very first to leave.

He had never forgiven the Germans or President Wilson.

There were prizes to be had, nonetheless. They arrived in New York to a tumultuous welcome, fireboats cannonading joyous white plumes of water into the sky, steam whistles and sirens shrieking, delirious throngs mobbing the docks, hurling hats and confetti. They were "The first Yanks home from the war," never having heard a shot fired by either side or seen a German uniform, let alone a French girl.

There were prizes to be had, nonetheless.

"Welcome home, Captain!"

"Hey, soldier! Buy you a drink?"

"Cap'm! Come join us!"

There were willing, wide-eyed women to be embraced, plaudits to be accepted. Whatever the ironies of the situation, the men took what came their way. It was not a time for restraint and perspective.

Caught up in the country's charged emotions, he impulsively signed up for another three years and, just as quickly, realized his mistake. He was demoted to peacetime rank of second lieutenant and assigned to a colorless supply depot in New Jersey, overseeing a listless detachment of idlers and social misfits.

Overnight, the marching bands, the adoring crowds, the flags and bunting disappeared. All at once, a man still in uniform was viewed with, at best, tolerance, and no one wanted to hear war stories anymore.

At the first opportunity he took his discharge. The bespectacled sergeant who signed him out had five hash marks on his sleeve and part of one ear missing.

"You wanta sign up for the Reserve, Lieutenant?"

"What the hell for?"

The sergeant grunted and shrugged. "I dunno. Protect your commission, I guess."

He signed the paper without reading it. A hell of a lot of difference it made; there weren't going to be any more wars.

A blurred kaleidoscope of cheap hotels and women, saloons and card rooms took him quickly through his mustering-out pay. Except for some extra clothing in a cardboard suitcase, his only material possession was a nickel-plated six-gun with a staghorn handle, won in a crap game in a New Jersey alley.

He hopped a freight.

Drifting south through a series of mindless part-time jobs and lucky to find them, he arrived via boxcar one evening in New Orleans, where pure chance appeared to have turned things his way. The fat red-faced man on the next bar stool had been in the Third Division, too. More important, he was the head security guard on one of the docks there.

"You look like maybe you could use a job. A shave and a bath, too, if you don't mind me sayin'. I could get you on the payroll if you like."

The captain was back in uniform.

His employment terminated just four nights later, however, after he shot out the rear tires and back window of a Checker cab that blundered through his gate in the fog.

The taxi, in addition to its terrified Cajun driver, contained the principal owner of that particular freight terminal, who was unused to his help addressing him as a "no-good son of a bitch" while trying to push a cocked six-shooter up his nose.

His pay, minus the allowance for the uniform, came to $4.10. He blew it that same morning in a Toulouse Street whorehouse. The next empty boxcar just happened to be headed north.

It was the era of Prohibition—a time of rigid rules and laws. It had been for four years. He and that divisive constitutional amendment would seem to have been made for each other, but he couldn't get comfortable with either side. On the one hand, he was an advocate of such rules and their enforcement. On the other, he was driven by the thrill of the contest and by disdain for the makers of rules. He tried both sides.

He offered his services to the Treasury Department as an undercover agent . . . or tried to.

"I'm sorry, Mr. Maxwell, but Agent Bemis is still tied up." She acted like she might catch something if she looked at him. "I can't tell you when he'll be free to speak with you. He's very busy."

He had been waiting in the hot, stuffy little office for two hours. He took the wilted *Collier's* magazine he'd been thumbing through, rolled it into a tight cylinder, and handed it to her.

"You tell Agent Bemis to choose either end of this, insert it in his ass, and sit down." And he turned and walked out, leaving the door open.

Frankie "The Shoes" Agajanian was more receptive. Frankie was running *real whiskey* south from the Canadian border into Syracuse.

On that side of the fence there was excitement and good money to be made. Fifty dollars a week or more, depending on the ebb and flow of the supply line, just for sitting in the front seat of a truck with a shotgun between his knees.

One moonless night on a deserted stretch of Lake Ontario shoreline, the Armenian's trucks rendezvoused with a two-lunger diesel rust bucket stacked to its gunwales with Canadian whiskey. Midway through the transfer from boat to trucks, the dark treeline behind them blossomed suddenly into a glaring half-circle of light.

"All right! Freeze! Everybody!"

Feds or hijackers? He was standing at the end of a splintery wharf, next to the idling boat, with two cases of booze in his arms.

Suddenly a twelve-gauge Winchester boomed defiantly in the night and was answered immediately by a crackle of small-arms fire from the trees. The windscreen in the boat's pilothouse exploded in a burst of glass fragments and he heard a curse in French as the skipper hauled back on the throttle and spun the wheel madly away from the wharf.

"Shit!"

He dropped the two cases of whiskey and leaped blindly for the cluttered deck, banging his left knee hard on an iron winch as he landed. Behind him there were shouts and more gunfire.

And then suddenly silence . . . except for the boat's engine—*t'put, t'put, t'put, t'put*—taking them out into the darkness on the lake.

He never found out the fate of his colleagues.

Two nights later, his knee swollen and throbbing, he limped back across the border into Detroit. He had almost a hundred dollars in his pocket and, rolled up in a ragged sweater the skipper had given him, his old six-shooter with the yellowing staghorn grips. He had been a lot worse off.

A block from the bridge he saw a woman standing alone under a dim streetlight. It was one o'clock in the morning. She said her name was Lucille.

She was a little leery when she first saw him coming down the sidewalk. His clothes looked as if he'd slept in them, and his left pants leg was torn below the knee. He was limping, as if he'd been in a fight. Maybe he'd been rolled, in which case she wasn't interested.

She smiled at him, though, just to see how things would go, and he smiled back at her.

Later on, she realized it wasn't a smile at all. It was just the way he stretched his lips across his teeth sometimes.

Lucille had a cop friend, a big Polack, who had a friend who owned a speakeasy on the East Side. A twenty-five-dollar thank-you to the cop got Maxwell a job there as a bartender.

It turned out to be a poor investment. The money was good, but after the excitement and mobility of the Armenian's booze convoy, Maxwell tired quickly of the day-after-day confinement behind the bar, the drunks, and the stale air, and the constant hooting and honking of the five-piece jazz combo on the little stage in the corner.

For another thank-you, the cop came up with a second friend who sold him a Buick roadster with a hasty cover-up paint job, a patched cloth top, isinglass windows, and yellow wooden spokes in the wheels. He left town the next morning, pointed west so the sun wouldn't be in his eyes, with his six-shooter, a hundred and forty dollars, and no destination in mind.

He tried selling encyclopedias in Peoria.

"You ought to buy a set, lady. Lots of good stuff in there."

"Oh, yeah? Like what?"

In Saint Louis he signed on as a deckhand on a paddle-wheel steamboat and left town that same day without ever stepping onto the gangplank.

Outside El Paso, a big chuckhole in the road snapped the Buick's front axle. Two Apaches on horseback ran a rope through the back bumper and, for a couple of bottles of beer, dragged the car a quarter-mile through the dirt to a blacksmith's shop.

In the twenties, El Paso was hardly what you'd call a boom-town. Scattered across a mud bank on the north side of the Rio Grande, it had just sort of materialized there. The conquistadors founded it while passing through on their way to somewhere else. As soon as the axle was fixed, Maxwell followed the conquistadors.

He was driving north through the heat in California's San Joaquin Valley when he happened to glance at the thermometer in the Buick's circular hood ornament. It was bright red all the way to the top.

At that instant, the radiator expired with a magnificent eruption of rust, steam, and boiling water.

He was on the outskirts of Delgado, an uninspired little cotton-picking town in the yellow-brown flatlands north of Fresno. A Mexican on a high-wheeled John Deere tractor towed him into a Richfield station.

Delgado, it turned out, was looking to hire a constable. He

saw the hand-lettered notice pasted inside the station's cracked front window, flanked by a faded rodeo poster and a couple of curlicues of encrusted flypaper. It didn't look like much of a job.

"How much to fix the radiator?"

The grease-smeared attendant studied it carefully, then tugged his oilcloth beanie off and scratched his head.

"Two dollars. Plus another two bits to scrape all them butterflies and yellow jackets out of it."

That was seventy cents more than the captain had in his pocket. He worked up a grin for the attendant.

"Were you in the war, buddy?"

The man shook his head dolefully. He tapped himself on the belly. "Got a bad heart. Couldn't go." He smiled back. "Wanted to."

Goddam slacker.

The captain went over to the cracked window and read the handbill again. Constable. From the station, you could see the whole town, a flat dirt street with all the stores on one side and the railroad tracks on the other.

"Jumpin' Jesus Christ." He walked up the road and found the mayor behind the counter in the feed store.

His first impression was correct. It wasn't much of a job.

"Eighteen dollars a month," the mayor said, "plus a room and free meals at the Sentosa, acrost the street from the jailhouse. There ain't a whole hell of a lot to do here, 'cept'n on Saturday nights when the cotton pickers come in. They get all liquored up over at the Columbia Bar and Grill."

Barely a month later, His Honor the mayor came home from his feed store in the middle of the day and found his chief law-enforcement officer and Mrs. His Honor a'copula on his front room divan. His big dumb Chesapeake Bay retriever was sitting right there watching them, grinning like an idiot and wagging his tail appreciatively.

The attendant at the Richfield station said the previous constable had been fired for the same violation.

Maxwell drifted on up to Oakland. Process server, taxicab driver, night manager of a tattered Seventh Street hotel. In the next thirty-six months, he found and then lost or walked away from a dozen meaningless jobs, looking for something he couldn't identify. He had been out of the army for nine wasted years when, one night in a West Oakland beer hall, he met a Southern Pacific Railroad cop who gave him a job chasing hoboes out of empty boxcars.

It was a job he was thoroughly familiar with from the opposite side of the big sliding doors.

He liked it, not just busting heads particularly, but being in charge again, having a sector of responsibility, being someone the bindle stiffs had to respect and, whenever possible, avoid.

One rainy night, he was picking his way across the slippery crisscross of tracks in the dark, heading back to his motel room, when he caught the flare of a match inside an open boxcar. The beam of his heavy six-cell flashlight picked out two bums trying to shrink back into a far corner, a half-consumed bottle of cheap muscatel on the floor between them.

"Come out of there, you no-good sonsabitches!"

When his command was not immediately heeded, he started in after them, unlimbering the sawed-off baseball bat stuck in his belt.

He was halfway in, balanced precariously on the iron edge of the doorway, when—*bang!*—without warning, the whole string of boxcars was snatched forward by a switch engine, flipping him end over end back out into the night.

He woke up in the emergency room at Highland Hospital with a concussion, a busted collarbone . . . and no job. It was 1930; the country had slipped into the Great Depression and no job stayed vacant waiting for a man to get out of bed.

When he recovered, he found work of sorts in a sleazy, unheated bail bonds office across the street from the Oakland City Hall. He wasn't even a bail bondsman. He hung around the jail and police station night and day and was paid 10 percent of any commissions he managed to bring in—10 percent of 10 percent. There wasn't any salary and, with a lot of people out of work, there weren't that many making bail, either.

One night by chance he encountered Jean, the only child of a Michigan prison chaplain. She was thirty-two, a lover of fine music and genteel company, and he was a decade older, tuned to jukeboxes and brassy women. For no reason he could remember, they married, and the unlikely product of this injudicious union was a blond, blue-eyed little snippet they incongruously christened Patience.

Still searching for savages to fight, pirate ships, and wagonloads of gold, the captain found instead a job as a night dispatcher for an ambulance company.

Then the devil spun the wheel once more and the arrow stopped on the name Pearl Harbor.

Jackpot.

Early the next morning, the army recruiting sergeant arrived at his windowless office in the basement of the Oakland City Hall to find a tall, gaunt man with a hooked nose impatiently pacing back and forth in front of the locked door. He had a dilapidated overnight bag in one hand and a large, dog-eared manila envelope in the other.

"Good morning, sir," the sergeant said cautiously.

Startled, the man stopped and wheeled around. His lips twisted into a distorted grin as he thrust the big envelope forward. Printed boldly in the upper left corner were the words "National Reserve, Army of the United States."

He stepped back a pace to let the sergeant get the door open, then followed him into the darkened office, his lips stretched tight across his teeth.

"We're going to get those little yellow bastards now," he declared. He gestured with his overnight bag. "I'm ready to go, Sergeant. Right now. You just find me an outfit with some balls."

(The 136 enlisted men of the 575th had, among them, 270 testicles.)

THE
☆ BATTLEFIELD ☆

CAPTAIN Maxwell's preposterous target was locked firmly in his sights: he was going to transform this unfortunate assemblage of the halt and hard-of-hearing into a guts-and-nuts fighting outfit the likes of which this army had never seen. And he was then *personally* going to march them straight into the middle of the war, wherever he managed to find it.

His temporary staging area, as he regarded it, was Piebald, an hour's jeep ride into the thorny Arizona desert south of Tucson. Named after the faceless, dried-out little town adjoining it, Piebald was one of a number of little-known prisoner-of-war camps scattered across the United States and Canada.

Here, imprisoned behind double rows of high, heavy wire-mesh fences topped with tangled coils of barbed wire, were nearly two thousand battle-hardened veterans of Hitler's vaunted Afrika Korps and, carefully segregated in an adjacent stockade, twice that number of Il Duce's finest.

There were those among the captain's colleagues, fellow officers among his own and other units at the camp, who thought Piebald, to say nothing of the 575th, an unlikely starting mark for anyone's road to battle stars and glory. He chose to ignore their views, and them, too, whenever possible.

His limping, myopic troops were even less supportive.

"My *ay-keeng* ass!"

While the rest of Piebald slept, the 575th lit up the desert night with tracer bullets ricocheting off stumps, rocks, and abandoned automobile bodies. While the sane sought shade during the suffocating 118-degree summer heat, the 575th lurched, spraddle-legged and sweating, through twenty-five-mile forced marches across the unforgiving brush- and cactus-strewn landscape, groaning beneath the burden of stove-hot steel helmets, heavy weapons, and oversize field packs.

"Take me home, Mother; I've seen it all now."

"What's he think this is, the fuckin' marines?"

"Fuckin' marines couldn't hack it."

No less than three times a week, sunshine or sandstorm, they charged, bayonets and store teeth bared, into an array of straw-filled burlap bags propped up on wooden tripods.

"Jab! Jab! Jab! Slash! Bash! Crash! Recover!"

Buck Sergeant Bleeker, his summer uniform creased and bleached by "Reg'lar Army" laundries, trotted along behind them, screeching, nipping at their heels like a short-legged hound dog.

"You don't move it, Anberger, I'm gonna shove that bayonet up your ass!"

There were endless drills with dummy hand grenades, tear gas, and simulated land mines. Blindfolded, they fumbled through the disassembly and reassembly of rifles, pistols, and machine guns. They suffered night and daytime compass exercises and agonized over demanding map-reading problems using a grid superimposed on a life-size photo of a Hollywood bathing beauty.

"Meet y'all on top of one of them hills."

"How 'bout down in that gully instead?"

"Sheee-it. That's prob'ly a fuckin' swamp."

They practiced house-to-house fighting, using the mess hall, barracks, and latrine in their company area. They practiced knife fighting, alley fighting, and fighting with nightsticks, and every morning after breakfast they endured a desperate run through a maniacal obstacle course, spurred on by Bleeker's shrill threats and the relentless sweep second hand on the captain's stopwatch.

"The last man through"—the captain let them dwell upon

the identity of the guilty one—"took eight seconds over ten minutes! You can thank *him* for no passes into town tonight!"

"Ho-leee . . ."

Every Tuesday, every Thursday, as certain as the hot sun rising from behind the mesa, it was belly down at the firing range behind camp—the company's cooks and clerks, too—banging away with the big-butt World War I Springfields and Enfields at paper targets two hundred yards across the rocky wash.

"Ready on the right? Ready on the left? Ready on the firing line!"

"I ain't never been able to see outa my right eye, Sergeant."

"Scrooch yer ass aroun' an' shoot lef'-handed, then."

"The flag is down! Commence firing!"

At four o'clock one chilled Sunday morning, they were routed from their blankets by a squawking bugle call and, gummy-eyed and protesting, herded into waiting trucks.

"You think the *enemy* is going to wait for you to eat *breakfast*?" the captain scoffed.

A kidney-jolting two hours later they arrived at the gates of Fort Cochise, an infantry training center scratched out amid the snakes and rocks on the Mexican border. There, looking sideways at one another in disbelief, they were directed to crawl out of a shallow trench, rifles cradled in front of them, and squirm across fifty yards of open ground under a snapping blanket of live machine-gun bullets.

"This here's a infiltration course," Sergeant Crawford told them kindly. "It's s'posed to teach you dumb asses confidence, not to mess your drawers under fire."

"Confidence, my ass."

"You got nothin' to worry about," a grinning instructor assured them. "The goddam bullets will be six inches over your heads."

Blackie Sifko stopped halfway across to tip his helmet back with his all-purpose little finger. "This is s'posed to be a *guard* company, ain't it? How'd the fuckin' prisoners get holt of a machine gun?"

When Cooper crawled up behind him and paused to spit out some sand, he inadvertently spit out his cutters, too.

"Gitcher ass movin' out there, Sifko! Keep yer interval, Cooper!"

Muttering, Cooper scooped up his bridgework, crammed it back into his mouth, sand and all, and struggled forward again, trying not to clamp down on his grating gums. It was easy enough for Bleeker to holler. The sawed-off little sumbitch wasn't out here with bullets buzzin' down the crack of *his* ass.

"Feee-*yew*! Kibby, you cocksucker! Did you fart?"

It was a good bet. Kibby was noted for his flatulence.

The men of the other two guard companies at Piebald—the officers and enlisted personnel of the support units there, too— found the 575th's regimen amusing.

Some of the best entertainment in camp was considered to be the captain's inspection of the guard detail when it was the 575th's turn to man the gates and guard towers.

Ever larger groups of off-duty personnel, often a number of their officers, too—even a few nurses from the base hospital— just *happened* to find themselves in the vicinity at the appointed hour. Grinning, nudging one another in anticipation, they gathered in clusters at semi-discreet distances, their irreverent commentary just out of the captain's earshot as they waited for the show to commence.

"O-pen rrraanks! . . . Hhharch!"

The desperately shined and ironed detail blossomed into an expanded formation, hurrying to realign their ranks. The captain stood ten paces in front of them, hovering over them like a dark cloud of doom. The onlookers shifted about for better vantage points, snickering, unable to contain their delight.

"Go get 'em, Iron Nuts."

"Sic 'em, Cap'm."

The captain was, of course, aware of his audience, but he showed no sign. Grim-faced, his eyes steel darts, he stomped down the lines of sweating, khaki-clad mannequins, halting in front of each to glare at weapon and owner alike in search of imperfection.

Sergeant Crawford always took pains to warn any new man in the detail. "When he grabs for your rifle, let it go . . . fast . . . or the butt'll swing aroun' and crack you right in the jewels."

The captain didn't *take* the rifle out of a man's hands to inspect it, he *exploded* it out with an open-handed smack that reverberated across the tiny adjoining parade ground and echoed off the surrounding buildings.

Furiously, he pinwheeled the cumbersome weapon from one knotty fist to the other—*pop! slap! whack!*—eyeballing trigger guard, breech and bore, thrusting it back as rudely as he had taken it. And he demanded that it be retrieved from *him* with equal vigor.

"When an officer takes your piece to *inspect* it," he would bellow at some quaking unfortunate, snatching the rifle away a second time, "you don't stand there walling your eyes around like a ruptured *jackass*! You understand that?"

"Yes, sir." Faintly. Not understanding it at all.

"You stare him right in the *eye*! Like you're telling him to go straight to *hell*! And when he hands it *back*"—the heavy weapon rebounding forward, knocking the victim back a half-step—"you don't just hold out your lily-white hands for it . . . you take it away from him!" *Smack!* . . . yanking it free once again. "Like you got a pair of balls!"

From the onlookers came muted applause.

"Tell him, Cap'm Max."

"Get on the ball, you sorry yardbirds."

"Ho-leee . . . ! How'd you like to be in that outfit?"

Baby-faced Private Donaldson was the only one known to have snuffed the captain's fireworks in mid-bombardment. The first time his rifle was jerked from his trembling grasp, he promptly burst into tears. Terrified.

The captain stood there looking at him for a long moment, then turned without a word and stalked away from the formation, dangling Donaldson's rifle from one hand by its leather sling. Like a lady's handbag.

Donaldson was afraid to ask for it back. He had to borrow a rifle to stand guard duty.

Whatever the occasional setbacks, the captain had no doubt

of his ultimate triumph, his dispatch to the fighting front. The only question in his mind was when.

Constantly he assured all who would listen of the company's readiness for combat, and petitioned through channels for orders to ship out. "Ad nauseam," according to Lieutenant Colonel Ratnekof, the post commander. And it didn't take much of a hint to suggest the coveted orders were near at hand. Nearly every night, following the flag-lowering ceremony, the 575th was treated to the latest bulletin, clue, or rumor which, according to their commanding officer, signaled imminent departure for Europe or the Pacific.

His prognostications were received by the ranks with some skepticism.

"Bullshit."

The muttered, scarcely audible response wafted from one nonbeliever to the next. "Anybody sees this outfit overseas'll figure we already *lost* the fuckin' war."

One evening the omen was a small crate of training manuals sent by error to the 575th's supply room. He held one pamphlet aloft, like a battle flag, and read the title page to them.

"The care ... and operation ... of the 81mm mortar!" He looked up from the booklet, his eyes narrowing, his silence emphasizing the significance of the moment. *"That,* in case it hasn't occurred to you, is an infantry *combat* weapon. Figure it out for yourself."

"Bulllll-shit." Like the murmur of the wind through the telephone wires.

Another sure indicator was replacement of the company's antiquated Springfield and Enfield rifles with the new Garand M-1. Then there was the directive from headquarters that all personnel be instructed in "enemy aircraft recognition."

"You think they're expecting enemy aircraft over *here*?" A disdainful sweep of a long arm ridiculed that notion. "We are going over *there*!"

"Bulllll-shit." Like ventriloquists, without moving their lips.

Each morning, the bugle seemed to summon them out of the darkness a little earlier. They stumbled down the barracks steps in damp, protesting, ragged clumps to stand reveille, stuffing in their shirttails, blinking, smacking their lips, trying to work up enough foul-tasting saliva to spit.

And the captain was out there waiting for them, pacing back and forth in the glare of the floodlight over the orderly-room steps, the wide, ironed-flat brim of his old campaign hat tilted aggressively forward. His left hand brushed the butt of the long-barreled nonregulation six-gun slung beneath one bony hip.

It was a new day.

And they were going to war.

CHAPTER ONE

☆ ☆

DRAFTED!

How the hell could he be drafted? He'd have to be the first eighteen-year-old drafted in the whole county. In the whole damn *country* maybe.

He couldn't be *drafted*; he was going to join the *marines*, for God's sake.

Aug snatched the folded sheet of paper from the top of his dresser and, switching hands with it as he got into his windbreaker, read through it again in a mocking singsong. By now he knew it almost word for word: " 'The President of the United States to,' " and his name was typed in there, " 'Jarold (NMI) Rustyanek. Greeting.' "

Balls.

He felt the frustration welling up again, constricting his stomach, just as it had when he'd opened the mailbox and seen the buff-colored official government envelope lying in there all by itself. The army, for God's sake. You didn't have to open the stupid envelope to know what it was.

" 'Having submitted yourself to a local board composed of your neighbors,' " including Willis Bilmeister's old man, it should have read, " 'you are hereby notified that you have now been selected . . .' "

He'd been telling everybody—Mary Jane Mendenhall, Boner, Angie, *everybody*—he was going to join the marines. *Drafted*, for God's sake. He scowled at his reflection in the mirror. The stupid army didn't have him yet. If Angie didn't come through—

Angie had *better* come through—maybe he'd . . . drop something on his foot or break his leg or something. He pulled his shirt collar open wider and tentatively jabbed at his collarbone with the handle of his heavy wooden hairbrush. He winced. That would hurt. Only thing was, if he flunked out of the army, could he get into the marines? Nicky Luna got out of it with bad ears. Aug looked at himself in the mirror, screwed up his face, and tried to look deaf. "Hunh?—What?" That ought to be easy enough. If he said he couldn't hear, how could they prove he could? Then he could just go into the marine recruiting place and . . . hear perfectly. He'd think of something. He picked up the draft notice and stuffed it into a pocket. Boner wanted to see it.

When Aug called to tell him, Boner had said "Bullshit," as if he couldn't believe it. But that was Boner's response to almost everything these days, ever since he'd started going to that welding school down in Richmond. "Bunch of bullshit." He had also suggested kicking the crap out of Willis Bilmeister. Boner was the physical sort. He was almost a year older than Aug, but *he* wasn't getting drafted. Or Willis Bilmeister, either. You could bet your shorts on that.

The strong smell of cabbage came up at Aug as he left his room and started down the stairway. His mother and sister were in the kitchen doing the dishes, and he paused at the foot of the stairs and raised his voice to be heard over the clatter. "I'm going! I might be back late!"

"Where you going?" His mother stuck her head out of the kitchen, a gravy boat and a damp towel in her hands.

"I told you. To Boner's."

His mother grimaced. She would never get used to that name. "Well, don't be late; you know how your father is."

Aug grunted and rolled his eyes. He was maybe going off to fight a war, for God's sake, and his father didn't want him staying out late. He let the screen door bang shut behind him as he went down the front steps.

It was just starting to get dark. Across the street, Old Lady Pereira was sitting in her rusty porch swing with that mangy orange cat on her lap. She watched, wagging her head in disapproval, as he sauntered over to the big red Buick and climbed in, doing his best to look nonchalant. There weren't too many Buicks on Santos Street. Not new ones, anyway.

He sat there for a moment behind the shiny black steering wheel, letting his eyes wander over the plush interior, drawing in the new-car smell. Mmmm. He scrunched down into the luxurious leather and brushed his fingertips over the glittering chrome on the horn ring, the dashboard, and the push buttons on the built-in Philco radio.

Everyone in town knew the Buick. Chickenshit red. That's what the kids called its unusual creamy-red paint job. That's because George Sushiwara had paid for the car, the story went, with money he got selling chicken manure.

Others referred to it less charitably now as "that Jap car." Aug shrugged. It didn't bother him.

The Sushiwaras owned a small chicken ranch out on Kimber, north of town. Or they used to. The government had herded them onto a bus one morning, a few weeks after Pearl Harbor, and shipped them off somewhere with a lot of other Japanese-Americans.

One of the notices was still tacked up in the post office.

Instructions
To All Persons Of
JAPANESE
Ancestry

Two suitcases apiece. That's about all they could take with them. "The size and number of packages," the notice read, "is limited to that which can be carried by the individual or family group."

Enemy aliens. "Dirty Japs." That's what everybody started calling them. There were stories in the *Argus-Sentinel* about coded radio messages being intercepted and lights flashing from the hills above the beaches at night. What a crock. George Sushiwara was born at General Hospital, for God's sake, over on Melba Street. Mrs. Sushiwara was from Santa Rosa, sixteen miles away.

Ben Madruga bought all of their chickens for twenty-five dollars.

"You can sell 'em to me for twenty-five bucks or just go away an' leave 'em. Up to you." Aug was standing right there. There wasn't time to look for another buyer, and Ben Madruga knew it.

Aug had worked for the Sushiwaras for more than a year, ever since high school, cleaning sheds, feeding the chickens and sorting eggs, carrying buckets to fill the big mason jars upended in the watering dishes. It wasn't much of a job, but it was better than working at the feed mill.

The Sushiwaras had treated him pretty decent. They had a son twelve years old. Jimmy, everyone said, "wasn't quite right in the head." Screwy. That's what they meant. Jimmy was no dummy; he got good grades in school, but every now and then his mind wandered off somewhere and he wouldn't know anybody, not even his parents. The other kids razzed him because he wore a white shirt and necktie to school and carried his homework in a black leather briefcase, like schoolchildren used to do in Japan.

Aug had spent a lot of time with Jimmy during the past summer, talking with him, playing catch. He wasn't a bad little fart. Once or twice, when Aug and Boner went fishing up on the Russian River, they took Jimmy along. Jimmy liked to fish.

When the red Buick arrived on Nick Marolda's car lot, it was the last new Buick Nick or anybody else was going to see for a long time, but of course nobody knew that. Mr. Sushiwara had put less than a thousand miles on it when he was told he and his family would have to move out, into this camp, and he couldn't take the car with him. Ben Madruga offered him two hundred dollars for it.

"You won't get a better offer, I'll tell you that." He turned his head and spit a squirt of brown tobacco juice. "Not in the time you got left, you won't."

Mr. Sushiwara came over that night to ask if Aug could look after it for him, drive it now and then, and take care of it until the war was over, or until they let the Japanese-Americans come home.

Aug's father wasn't entirely sympathetic. The day after Pearl Harbor, he'd pinned his World War I Victory Medal on his sweater and started wearing it down at the shop. The way he saw it was "They ought to ship all them little yellow monkeys back where they come from."

"A lot of them, most of them," Aug told him, "came from right around here."

"That's okay. It ain't right what they done."

Grudgingly, however, he told Mr. Sushiwara he could "bring the damn thing over and put it up on blocks," if he wanted to, out behind the garage.

Mr. Sushiwara was very polite. "I am most grateful for your generous offer, but"—he gestured toward Aug and smiled apologetically—"if it would not be too much of an imposition, I would prefer that Aug drive the car once in a while. It would be much better for it."

The night before they were sent off, somebody drove by the Sushiwaras' house and shot a hole in their front room window.

So here he was, eighteen years old, with a brand-new chickenshit red four-door Buick sedan. The deluxe model with chrome hubcaps. Aug looked at himself in the rearview mirror and patted down a wayward curl. He turned the key in the ignition and stepped on the starter button. Old Lady Pereira was still wagging her head as he backed out of the driveway.

It wasn't that dark yet, but he switched on the headlights anyway. And turned on the radio. A soft blue light glowed behind the dial. Slowly, the slurred, mellow tone of Russ Morgan's trombone faded in, surrounding him, swelling until it filled the inside of the car.

He turned left at the end of the block. It was only a short walk to Boner's place, but he would never have considered leaving the Buick home in the driveway. Leaving the Buick and Mary Jane Mendenhall behind would be the worst part about going away.

No. The worst part would be the stupid army, with its dumb-looking uniform, and letting Willis Bilmeister think he'd gotten the best of him. Willis and his peckerhead old man. Aug didn't like that part at all.

Willis Bilmeister's father was manager of the Regal, the brand-new movie theater downtown. Willis could go to the movies any time he wanted, and take his friends, too, for nothing. Willis didn't have that many friends, but there was no denying the appeal of free movies, so a lot of the kids had begun buttering up to him. Even Mary Jane Mendenhall started going to Saturday matinees with him. Mary Jane was head cheerleader at school. She had red hair, two footballs under her sweater, and could be asked out any time she chose to be by any boy she selected.

Willis told everyone they were going steady, but Mary Jane said, uh-uh, they weren't either; she just liked going to the movies. And besides, she told Betty Scoonover, in the dark you couldn't see Willis's pimples.

Just a month or so earlier, Aug and Boner had gone to a matinee and ended up a couple of rows behind Willis and Mary Jane. Aug had sneaked a tin peashooter in, and every time Willis started to put his arm up on the seat behind Mary Jane, Aug plinked him in the ear with a dried kernel of corn.

Mary Jane started laughing, and Willis got mad and got his father, and Old Man Bilmeister threw Aug *and* Boner out.

"You're always in here causing trouble," he told Aug. "If you can't behave yourself, you can just leave. Get out. And stay out." He started up the aisle, then turned back and pointed at Boner.

"And that goes for your friends, too."

In the back alley, there was a big wooden fan built into the wall of the theater to draw cool air inside. By coincidence, the very same day the two of them got thrown out, a dead cat—a *really dead* cat—apparently flung himself into the fan in a fit of despondency. It took almost four days to get all the pieces of the cat out from under the seats and get rid of the stench, even with the fan going full blast, several gallons of disinfectant slopped around, and all the doors open.

You couldn't show movies, of course, with all that. Old Man Bilmeister was pretty upset.

It was only a week later when Aug unexpectedly acquired the big red Buick and Mary Jane stopped going to the movies with Willis and started going for rides with Aug. Willis, everybody said, was pretty upset about that.

And all of a sudden here comes the stupid draft notice.

Old Man Bilmeister was also head of the local draft board.

Aug punched a button on the radio, then another, changing stations without really listening. How was he going to get even? Glue the doors of the theater closed? Screw up the electricity? Do something to Willis?

Something *good*. He had a reputation to maintain.

Constable Vervais, for one, would verify that. Over the years, his old Pontiac patrol car had had more than one cup of sugar poured into its gas tank and a sackful of potatoes pounded up its exhaust pipe. So would Old Lady Bunker, the librarian, who wouldn't care if she never heard another marble going 'round and 'round, *boing, boing, boing*, in the bowl-shaped chandelier over her desk. So would red-nosed Joe Marble, the undertaker, who had had to console the bereaved relatives of old Gino Petracelli when the alarm clock went off in his casket during the eulogy.

A *lot* of people in town would bear witness to Aug's reputation. A lot of people wouldn't be all that sad to see him drafted. They wouldn't even care if he went into the marines.

In high school, whenever *anything* had suddenly gone wrong—with the bell system, the school bus, the showers in the girls' locker room, anything *strange*—Miss Longnecker, the principal, had what had proved to be a highly efficient system for apprehending the perpetrator, if any.

She would nail Aug.

If Aug could prove his innocence beyond reasonable doubt, which required an airtight case by the defense, *then* Miss Longnecker would begin looking for other causes.

Aug, everyone agreed, had been pretty much of a flop as a practicing scholar. His older sister Marian had breezed right through high school, an exemplary student, class secretary all four years, editor of the *Hatchet*, excellent grades, "a delightful girl," everyone said.

Aug, on the other hand, had sort of dawdled along, amusing his friends, charming the teachers, and displaying what Miss

Longnecker called "a general lack of application toward his studies and a misdirected sense of humor."

Actually, she liked Aug. But that didn't stop her from expelling him twice, once for electrocuting Mr. Griffith and, the year before, for sticking a pipe bomb into the toilet tank in the women teachers' bathroom.

It wasn't really a bomb. Well, maybe it was, he conceded, kind of. He had taken a cardboard tube from a roll of toilet paper, stuffed it full of black powder from the chemistry lab, sealed it up tight, and coated it with melted wax, so the water wouldn't get to it. Then he poked the frayed end of an old extension cord in one end, dropped the device into the tank, and ran the wire out the window and into the boys' room next door.

One noon hour just before Easter vacation, Old Lady Hawley was sitting on the throne contemplating her next Latin class when he plugged in his end of the wire.

The resulting bang was a lot louder on Aug's side of the wall than he had figured. He could only imagine what it was like on Mrs. Hawley's side, where the explosion broke the toilet tank into three pieces. She was jumping around yelling, with her pants down around her ankles and water all over the place, while Old Man George was trying to get past her into the booth and turn it off. Two weeks later, linoleum was still coming up out in the hallway.

The following year, it had been Mr. Griffith's turn to join in the fun. He taught physics, and the subject in class that memorable afternoon was static electricity.

Almost every year when Mr. Griffith got around to that chapter of the book, somebody in class would come up with the original and highly amusing idea of attaching the static electricity machine to the doorknob, so Mr. Griffith would get a little shock, sort of, when he came into the classroom. Mr. Griffith had come to expect it. He liked to tell about it in the teachers' room, so everyone would know what a good sport he was.

It was Junior Bemis who got the idea of giving him a real jolt by hooking up the antiquated Ford coil he'd found in the supply room. Aug, of course, had to go Junior one better. He proposed wiring the doorknob right into a wall socket.

Some members of the class—everybody but Aug, as a matter of fact—regarded this idea as a little extreme, if not potentially homicidal. This was exactly the kind of support and encouragement that Aug thrived on.

When Mr. Griffith came prancing down the hallway with his apple and half-pint of milk and reached for the doorknob that afternoon, this big blue bolt of electricity came out and shook hands with him. According to his tremulous testimony shortly thereafter, it "practically" knocked him flat in the corridor.

If the whole school hadn't been miserably underwired, he sniffled, if physics, Spanish, and homemaking hadn't all been on the same thirty-amp fuse, he would certainly have suffered an early demise. He was only forty-seven.

And Aug, as Miss Longnecker sternly emphasized to the quickly apprehended defendant, could have been facing something a lot more serious than just being expelled for the second time in two years.

He might have stayed expelled, too, if it hadn't been for his father. Mr. Rustyanek showed up next morning in his blue serge suit to express sincere concern for Mr. Griffith's well-being and Miss Longnecker's digestion, and to plead for one final reprieve for his incorrigible heir. The phrase he used, actually, was "that stupid kid of mine."

There were only a few weeks left before graduation. It ended up kind of a probation thing. Mr. Griffith gave him an F in physics.

Why hadn't he gone down and joined the marines when he first got the idea?

Because driving Mary Jane around town in the Buick was an even better idea.

Aug punched another button on the radio, thinking seriously for the first time about Angie's plan. It sounded weird, but it was better than any plans *he* had.

Angie Zarsczynski was in her first year as a student nurse down in San Francisco. She had the hots for Aug. She'd had the hots for him ever since the fourth grade. She had often told him that. Angie was a plain talker.

"I could fix it for you, if you want," she told him, "so you'd flunk the physical."

"Fix it how?"

"Like they'd think you were going to have a heart attack. I could get you these pills."

"What kinda pills? You're gonna give me a heart attack?"

"What do you think, I'm dumb? They speed up your pulse rate, make your heart go like a son of a bitch—bip-bip-bip-bip-bip." Angie had always talked like one of the guys, which was her only similarity to them. A tall, robust young woman, she had huge boobs and a butt like a bass fiddle.

Angie had graduated from high school with grades worse than Aug's, and he wasn't altogether confident about her prescribing pills. Even aspirin. But he *was* certain about not wanting to get drafted.

"They won't screw me up or anything, will they? What are they called?"

"I forget. What do you care? You're not going to sell them."

Wouldn't that be a shot? Willis and his old man would pee all over themselves if the army sent him home. If the pills worked, he'd have to do something real nice for Angie. Practicing, he groaned and clapped his hand over his heart, as if he was experiencing great difficulty.

The big Buick rocked majestically across the railroad tracks. Aug turned into the graveled street to the right and, a block farther down, pulled up in front of Boner's house. Angie's old green Chevy was in the driveway. There was a light on upstairs, over the garage in back where Boner had his room. Aug got out of the Buick, closed the door carefully—cuh-*lunk*—and took a few steps backward to give the car a final appraising look.

As he went up the outside stairs, he heard Boner's radio going and Angie laughing loudly at something. Angie had a laugh like two dogs barking at a cat.

"Hey, Aug." Boner was seated at his rickety old card table, Angie opposite him, next to the bed in the only other chair. There was a black bottle of rum, unopened, on the table between them. Aug gave Boner the thumbs-up sign and nodded at Angie. "You get those pills?"

"Something better than that, maybe."

Angie patted the bed next to her chair. "You'll see. Sit down. We gotta have our going-away drink first."

"Maybe I'm not goin' away. Yet."

"Maybe you're not." She grinned and held up a large, flat package wrapped in Christmas paper.

"What's that?"

"Sit down, sit down. You'll see." She was still wearing her gray and white student nurse's uniform, the translucent material stretched tight across her breasts and bottom.

Boner laughed and said, "Hey, let's see that ole draft notice."

Aug pulled the crumpled paper from his pocket and smoothed it out on the card table, frowning as he bent forward to read it once more.

"C'mon, let's see it."

Boner took the notice and, narrowing his eyes, studied it intently, his lips moving slowly as he sounded out the words. Angie got up and moved around behind him, resting one breast on his shoulder as she leaned forward to read.

She frowned. "Shouldn't 'greeting' have an *s* on the end of it? 'Greeting.' That's a dumb way to start."

Boner held the paper up to the light, as if to verify Old Man Bilmeister's signature. "Buncha bullshit." He tossed the notice back onto the table. It slid over the edge, did a couple of side-slips, and ducked under his dresser, kicking up a smidge of dust from the linoleum floor. Aug made no move to retrieve it.

All three of them had been friends since their first day at grammar school.

Boner had his nickname hung onto him in the sixth grade, where he had managed to develop the hots for Miss Gallegas, a shapely and attractive young woman fresh out of teachers' college in Berkeley.

Boner was large all over for a boy his age. One day in class, Miss Gallegas had him stand to read a couple of paragraphs about the Euphrates River, and she noticed this big bulge in the front of his cords, like a piece of hoe handle. Right there in front of the class, she asked him what he had in his pocket.

And he told her. A boner.

Miss Gallegas was only twenty-one and pretty much untraveled. She had never heard the word before. By the time they got it fairly well defined and very nearly identified, Boner grinning and sliding his feet around, the rest of the class, all the boys anyway, were banging on their desks and laughing so hard that Miss Barnes, the principal, came down the hall to see what all the racket was about.

Miss Gallegas ended up running out of the room in tears.

From then on, Boner was his name. There weren't a lot of people in town who could even remember his real name. Hardly anyone but his mother called him Norman.

His father ran the Mohawk station out on East Alvarado. Boner used to pump gas there on weekends and after school when he didn't have practice. He wasn't the smartest kid in school, but he could knock a baseball clean out of Sonoma County if he caught it solid. Cap Taylor, the football coach, claimed Boner had won a lot of games for the old orange and black just by falling on people. People on the other team.

There was a locker in the Trojan gym, its door all caved in, that was still called "Boner's Locker." After they lost the football game that year with Napa, he'd smacked it one with his fist, rendering its door largely inoperable.

Boner grinned. "I been thinking. Maybe we should go down there tonight and glue all the doors of his movie house shut?"

Aug grunted. "I already thought of that. That's no good."

"How about if we shoot out the windows in the box office?"

"Hey, I'll go," Angie said. "I could get my dad's pistol." Aug and Boner gave her sideways glances, but they both knew that, given any encouragement, Angie would do what she promised.

"Down, girl," Aug told her.

Two years earlier, Boner had bought an old .45 automatic at the pawnshop in Sonoma. He'd gone in to look for a wrist-watch with a sweep second hand, seen the pistol, and on a whim, bought it for nine dollars, most of his summer-job earnings. That was a lot of money.

They had never fired it—maybe it *wouldn't* fire—just posed with it in front of Boner's mirror, pretending they were Jimmy

Cagney or Humphrey Bogart or somebody. They'd fantasized about going downtown late some night in Boner's Model A and shooting out the front window in Homer Fogel's grocery store. Shoot out the window and vanish in the night. Phantom raiders.

They had disliked Homer Fogel ever since they were little kids. He was forever running them out of his store, afraid they were going to cop a couple of grapes or a stick of licorice, or sneak a peek at the *Spicy Westerns* in the magazine rack. On Halloween, he always coated the window with something, some kind of slippery stuff, so the kids couldn't write on it with soap.

But shooting out his window was just fantasy. They had never really considered it.

"Let's have our drink." Angie returned to her chair and pulled two bottles of Coke from a paper sack on the floor. "Where's your bottle opener?"

"On the dresser."

She began pawing through the jumble of sports magazines, toilet articles, and unmatched socks atop the old dresser. "*Where* on the dresser?"

"Right there somewhere."

"Well . . . found it. Jeez, why don't you . . . ?"

Boner sighed. From his chair, he twisted around to reach for the bottom drawer of the dresser, pulled it open with some difficulty, and withdrew a large, smudged glass mixing bowl, which he plopped onto the card table. Without ceremony, he unscrewed the metal cap from the bottle of rum and began pouring the dark liquid into the bowl, softly whistling an unidentifiable tune between his teeth.

Angie popped the caps off the Coke bottles and dropped heavily onto her chair. When the last of the liquor had lolloped in, she leaned forward, a bottle in either hand, and began pouring the Coke into the bowl as Boner stirred the mixture vigorously with the eraser end of a yellow pencil. Aug pulled the table closer to the bed, leaning on his forearms to better observe the ritual.

Boner removed the pencil from the bowl, dipped a stubby

index finger in, and tasted the mix carefully. He closed his eyes, assessing the formula.

"Another Coke."

Angie produced a third bottle, uncapped it, and handed it over. She dug into the sack again, withdrew some straws, and passed them around. Two apiece.

When the third Coke had been stirred in to Boner's satisfaction, he laid the pencil aside, picked up his straws, and raised them in salute to Aug.

"Here's to the soldier boy."

Aug gave him the finger. "I'm going into the *marines*."

He pulled the table still closer. Together they stuck their straws into the bowl, leaned forward in unison, and at a signal from Angie, began sucking up the heavy mixture furiously, in deep drafts, cheeks hollowed, eyes wide, swallowing as fast as they could until not another rattling drop could be vacuumed up into their straws.

"Hot *damn!*" Boner stood up, patting his distended abdomen. Aug and Angie grinned at each other foolishly. In approximately thirty seconds, they had each swallowed the equivalent of at least five, maybe six, generously proportioned "Cuba libers," as Angie called them.

Aug waited for the liquor to hit him, though he knew it would take a while. Vaguely unsatisfied, he looked around, hoping Boner might have a second bottle somewhere.

It wasn't much of a place, just the one cramped, dimly lighted room with the painted-over dresser, a wobbly nightstand, and the creaky, sway-backed bed. The card table and the two unmatched chairs were the only remaining pieces of furniture. There wasn't any bathroom. Boner went before he came up to bed after supper or, if duty called during the night, slid the window open next to his bed and peed onto his mother's hydrangea bush.

Boner belched loudly and chuckled, patting his stomach again.

"When you gotta go play soldier, Aug?"

"Wednesday."

"Jeez. They don't give you much time to get ready."

Aug didn't have that many arrangements to make. Reluctantly, he had continued to work at the chicken ranch after the Sushiwaras left. Ben Madruga had negotiated some sort of arrangement for use of the chicken sheds, too, and Mr. Sushiwara had asked Aug if he would stay on just to keep an eye on the house. Aug hadn't wanted to. He didn't like Ben Madruga. But he felt he owed Mr. Sushiwara something extra for use of the Buick.

But Aug's enthusiasm for after-hours caretaking faded quickly—after all, it was easy to reason the Sushiwaras might never return—and the once neat little house and garden already had the look of abandonment.

He had quit his job there just this morning. When he told Madruga about the draft notice, the man only grunted and walked away without comment. Aug hadn't expected a gold watch.

"Wha' time on Wednesday?" Boner's words were already beginning to slur. Angie sat without moving, her elbows still on the table, a dreamy, wide smile spreading slowly across her face.

Aug wriggled off the bed onto the floor and, on his hands and knees, peered under the dresser in search of the draft notice. There was a wadded-up sock under there, plus a soiled paper plate and what appeared to be a long-expired apple core. Boner was no great shakes at housekeeping. Aug slid the draft notice out and looked at it.

"Six in the morning." He looked again. He was beginning to feel the effect of the liquor himself. "Six-ten. Early."

"Buncha bullshit." Grinning vacantly, Boner drifted over to the bed and fell across it on his back, his arms outstretched, the springs shrieking in protest. He belched again, louder this time, and began struggling to sit up. He made it on his third try, a damp lock of hair tumbling down over his eyes, his face steamy red from exertion and liquor. Angie reached out and pushed lightly on his chest, and he fell back, laughing—"Hunh-hunh-hunh"—like an old jalopy jerking ahead with a faulty clutch.

"Boy, you're a cheap date," Angie observed. "You get drunk

easy." It was true. Boner could get swacked on two glasses of Par-T-Pak cola.

Aug felt a sudden warmth, half liquor, half not, as he regarded the motionless form stretched out across the bed.

Big, friendly, easygoing Boner. Everybody liked Boner. And now, all of a sudden, it looked like he was going to be making a lot of money. A whole lot of money.

He'd been going to this welding school, driving down there in his beat-up Model A with Bert Rooney. The people at the school were saying he and Bert could both get on at the yard in Richmond if they wanted to, building liberty ships. Defense jobs. Eighty, eighty-five dollars a week, counting overtime.

Eighty-five a week? Were they kidding? Aug's dad didn't bring home that much in two weeks from the shoe store.

Besides that, defense jobs would keep them out of the army. Aug had been kidding Boner about that for the last week or so.

"American boys fighting in foxholes halfway around the world, defending their country, for God's sake, and what about you? You're going to be sitting it out at home, getting rich, playing stink finger with all the girls. If they don't shoot you after all the ships you weld up sink."

Boner said he wasn't afraid to go fight; he didn't care. But Aug said, "Oh, no, you just stay home and count your money. Somebody else'll protect your big fat butt."

And now maybe that somebody else was going to be Aug.

Eighty-five dollars a week. That was a hunk of money. Aug wondered if he'd make eighty-five a *month* in the army.

If he went.

Angie sat up straight and made her eyebrows go up and down several times, as if she was trying to focus her eyes. "What do your folks think about you getting drafted?"

She closed her eyes and put her head back, rolling her shoulders around to loosen them up. Aug watched her breasts roll around, too, under the thin cloth of her uniform.

"My mother thinks it's God's will. My father thinks it's great. He'd sign up himself if they'd let him run everything."

Anton Rustyanek—"Roost-ya-nek; it's Hungarian"—labored ten hours a day, six days a week, at his modest little shoe repair shop on Peralta Street, selling new shoes and, more frequently, patching up old ones. He also stocked a few leather belts and wallets, rawhide boot laces, gray wool work socks in the larger sizes, and, incongruously, a small selection of Hillerich & Bradsby baseball bats. He was a San Francisco Seals fan.

A heavy square wooden sign with the one word "Shoes" hung over the sidewalk in front of his store. Its plainly fashioned white-on-black lettering was indicative of both the merchandise and proprietor within.

Aug's father had an uninvolved formula for the proper functioning of the judicial system, which he voiced frequently, in conjunction with other improvements that could be expected "if I was runnin' this country: Be good . . . or be dead."

That was it, the complete platform. Good . . . or dead. Same penalty for bank robbery and traffic tickets. It would simplify the whole court procedure, require fewer decisions, "and get rid of a lot of other nonsense at the same time."

Aug's mother was a practicing Catholic and a housewife. In that order. Their two-story frame house on Santos Street was full of medallions and pictures of Jesus and Mary, and miniature religious statues, many of the latter with tiny pink light bulbs inside. Aug didn't go to church anymore, but his mother and his sister Marian, a year older than he, went every Sunday morning, attended special masses during the week, Altar Society meetings, and—every Saturday afternoon at four o'clock sharp—confession.

Aug couldn't imagine what either one of them, especially his sister, could have to confess every week. Seconds on dessert, maybe.

His father didn't go to church, either, "but too damn much of my money does," he complained. There were many spirited discussions at the supper table on that subject and on the need of a church building that big and expensive in a town that small. It was a big church, no denying it.

"And what about you?" Angie pushed her chair back and stood up unsteadily, one hand keeping touch with the card table.

"What do you think about going off to war?" She grinned. "If you pass the physical, of course."

Aug tossed his head noncommittally. How did he feel? "It's somebody telling me I *gotta* go. Willis Bilmeister and his old man. I was going to go down and join up—honest—the marines. First chance I got."

"How come the marines?"

"You might as well get a good-looking uniform." Mary Jane Mendenhall just *loved* marine uniforms.

From the bed came a thunderous, drawn-out snore.

Aug's cheeks were definitely beginning to feel numb. He sat down at the table. Angie sat down, too, looking directly into his eyes, smiling at him, as if anticipating whatever was coming next. Angie. She never got really swacked, no matter how much they drunk. Drank. Aug aimed an elbow at the edge of the table, missed, and ended up leaning on one knee, pretending that was what he had meant to do all along.

Angie laughed. "You look like that statue at the library, *The Thinker.*" She mimicked Aug's pose. "*The Stewed Thinker.*"

Aug straightened up. "I'm not drunk." He wasn't. Not entirely. He looked toward the bed. "That Boner, now, he's drunk."

Boner stopped snoring suddenly, as if considering the charge, then went back at it even louder.

Aug looked at the dented alarm clock click-clacking loudly on the nightstand next to the bed. Quarter after nine. He had a little buzz on, no doubt about it, but he wasn't going to be drunk. No drunker, anyway. He got up from his chair again and stretched cautiously, leaning far over to one side, then the other, like a ball player getting ready to bat. He gestured at the flat package on the floor next to Angie's chair.

"C'mon, tell me. What's that?"

Angie reached down for it and handed it to him.

"It's just a little going-away gift, or a stay-at-home gift, I guess. I couldn't find anything to wrap it in but Christmas paper." She made a little move with her head. "Just to show you how I . . ." Her eyes, for God's sake, were starting to water.

Aug took the package self-consciously, hefting it, turning it over in his hands, unable to guess at its content.

"What is it, a girlie calendar?"

Angie shrugged expansively, obviously pleased with herself. "Open it."

Aug pulled the loose wrapping away, revealing a sturdy manila envelope. He looked at Angie quizzically, turning the envelope over, and opened the flap at one end, then withdrew a large photographic negative. He looked at Angie again, then back at the negative.

"What the hell is this?"

"It's an X ray, dummy." She took it from Aug. "It's a picture of your bad back." She held the X ray up to the single light bulb dangling from the ceiling and pointed at it. "See that? Right there?" She took a deep breath, closed her eyes, and chanted, "This is a classic example of a spondyl . . . olis . . . thesis," as if she were reciting in nursing school and wasn't dead sure about her answer.

"What are you talking about?" Aug peered at the negative again, unable to make any sense of the shadowy image.

"Spon-dyl-olis-*the*-sis," Angie began again. "That is subluxation—"

"Jesus, Angie—"

"Don't interrupt. Subluxation—slippage"—she half turned to indicate the small of her back—"of one vertebra over another. A bad back, in other words." She lowered the negative and grinned broadly. "A *very* bad back. Bad enough to keep you . . . out of the army."

"You're kidding." He took the negative from her and gestured with it. "What's this got to do with me?"

Angie made a face and waggled her head in dismay. "Don't be dumb, Aug. They give you a physical, right? All you have to do is show them this thing, walk hunched over a little bit, and limp. And if some doctor touches you . . . around here"—she showed Aug the spot—"you yell your butt off. Ex-*scroosh*-iating pain."

She handed the X ray to Aug and patted him confidently on

the shoulder. "You'll see. You'll be back on the noon bus. Four-F."

Four-F? Wouldn't that be something? Wouldn't that frost Willis Bilmeister and his old man? He held the negative up to the light, trying to comprehend all that it represented.

"Where'd you get this?"

"Where'd you think? I swiped it." Angie made a noncommittal gesture with her hands. "I borrowed it. I'll put it back . . . when you're through with it."

"You really think this would work?" Angie, for God's sake, was only a first-year student, and for all Aug knew, this could be an X ray of a goat. He raised the negative to the light again. "Who's D. L. Gravestock?"

Angie looked over Aug's shoulder. "The owner of those bones, I guess." She dismissed the question. "The technician who took the X ray, maybe. Who knows?"

Aug turned the picture over uncertainly and looked briefly at the other side, his expression revealing his doubts. "Could they tell this isn't me, that it's someone else?"

"How could they without another X ray for comparison?"

Aug held the picture up once more, frowning. "I don't see anything here that looks like a"—he looked at Angie—"like a . . . you know, a cock. This is some *guy's* X ray, isn't it?"

Angie shook her head sadly. "That wouldn't show up on an X ray, dummy." She glanced at Boner's recumbent form. "Most people's wouldn't."

"I don't know." Aug dropped the negative to his side. "I'll really get my tail in a sling if they figure out—"

"Come on. What's the worst they could do to you? Stick you in the army? One of the doctors at the hospital says they put hundreds of guys through there every day. More than that, maybe. Thousands. They just pinch every butt that goes by to make sure it's warm." She patted Aug on the shoulder maternally. "Trust me."

Aug thought about it for a moment, turning the X ray over and over in his hands. He turned to Angie and grinned, suddenly warming to the idea. "What the heck, nothing to lose, right? It'll be a real shot. If it works, I'll buy you a beer. Hell, I'll buy you a case of beer."

"If it works, I'll think of something better than that."

Aug picked up the draft notice and slid it into the envelope with the X ray. "I'm pooped. I think I'll head for home." He glanced over at Boner, who, for no apparent reason, had stopped snoring. "What about him?"

"What about him? He's home in bed, isn't he? Go on home. Maybe I'll undress him. I'd rather undress you."

Aug blushed. "Yeah, well . . . I'd better go home and practice limping." He grinned and held up the big envelope. "Hey. Thanks, Angie."

Angie moved a step closer and kissed him.

A muffled groan came from the bed.

"Wait . . . minute," Boner mumbled. The bedsprings screeched in anguish as he struggled to turn over on his side. He managed only to thrash his way to the edge of the bed and ended up, with a jarring thump, sitting upright on the floor. His head lolled back, and a contented grin stretched across his face. "All start sucking . . . same time."

Aug waved the envelope at Angie and went out the door. As he started down the stairs, he heard Boner begin snoring again. It sounded like the noise their straws had made at the bottom of the mixing bowl. Only louder.

CHAPTER
☆ TWO ☆

ALL his life, wherever he went it seemed, Lieutenant Flowers's rosy cheeks, blue eyes, and wavy blond hair had led inevitably to his being tagged Daisy—Daisy Flowers.

He had arrived at Piebald only that morning on his first duty assignment and had reported in promptly at the 575th's orderly room.

First Sergeant Garrison took his cigar out of his mouth and gave Flowers the look he reserved for shavetail lieutenants fresh out of ROTC. It was a heavy-lidded look, preceded by a moment of silence, that suggested he had one final comment but had decided not to make it.

"Lieutenant Michaels's O.D. an' Cap'm Maxwell's off post," he mumbled. He returned the wet cigar to his mouth and rolled it to the other side. "He wants you should take over retreat tonight."

Retreat!

Second Lieutenant Meredith Flowers, barely twenty-one, fresh out of Indiana State College, had never *stood* retreat, let alone led the ceremony. Half panicked, he scurried back to his room in bachelor officers' quarters to riffle through his stack of manuals.

Daisy had grown up in the river country south of Caldwell, Idaho, the youngest of three sons of a middling-successful potato farmer and his wife. Mrs. Flowers had been a piano teacher, and while the other two boys sought and found local fame as high school athletes, Daisy turned instead to his mother's piano.

Under her gentle tutelage, despite a nagging inner-ear problem, he had acquired skills sufficient to win a music scholarship from Carnegie Tech.

The day he was to leave for college, he struggled out of the house carrying a heavy trunk, stepped on a baseball bat left lying on the porch, and fell down the front steps, fracturing his left wrist.

Willing it not to be broken, refusing to consider the possibility that it might be, he had convinced his parents it was only a sprain and had gone off to Pittsburgh anyway. Untended, the wrist mended stiff as a stick, and it soon became apparent the concertos he longed to play would never materialize. The university generously let him keep his scholarship for the balance of the term, and the following year he transferred to Indiana State to major in social sciences.

He joined ROTC in his junior year in the hope that the military uniform would impress a certain shapely young woman. It didn't work out. He was called up a week after he graduated and, luck of the draw, assigned to Piebald and the 575th.

Retreat, the traditional evening flag-lowering exercise, was required of all off-duty personnel at Piebald, each unit in its own company area. Because the flagpole was out of sight, down at the main gate, the rites were directed by bugle calls wafted through scratchy, poorly wired loudspeakers scattered across the camp.

The sound system was not the best. The speakers were poorly wired and aimed in haphazard directions, and—particularly on windy days—it required close attention to hear and properly identify the muffled notes blown by the bugler.

Lieutenant Flowers had been classified Limited Service—not because of his stiffened wrist but because of the inner-ear problem. It was windy that evening, and nervously taking his place before the assembled company, he missed the initial bugle call entirely.

Nearly everyone else in the company, standing at ease in platoon formation, heard it.

Sergeant Bleeker, positioned just six paces in front of the lieutenant, coughed discreetly and came to attention. When that produced no response, he tried "parade rest." But Daisy remained at ease, adrift on cloud twelve, beaming at the grins he could see blossoming through the ranks. *Look at that. Obviously a happy organization.*

The wind shifted slightly.

He caught the opening notes of the second bugle call and, mistaking it for the first, crisply called the company to "Ten-*shun*! . . . P'raaade *rest*!" With a pardonable sense of pride, he performed a smart about-face and assumed the stance himself, back straight, feet spread precisely, hands clasped tightly at the small of his back.

Second Lieutenant Meredith Allen Flowers, thank you, was in command.

Over the rooftops beyond the PX, the motor pool, hospital, and chapel, Old Glory started down the pole, and everyone else at Piebald was at salute.

Behind the lieutenant's back, the troops were having some difficulty restraining themselves. "Sergeant Bleeker," Garnett guffawed later, "was havin' a shit fit."

When the bugle call faded, Daisy brought his heels together sharply, about-faced again, and brought the company to "ten-*shun*" with a snap he was certain his commanding officer would have applauded had he been there. Confidently, he waited for the first notes of the bugle call to follow.

They waited. They waited, standing at attention, for what seemed like an exceptionally long time.

Tilting his head to one side, straining to hear, Daisy felt the first tiny tug of doubt. Some of the men and their platoon sergeants, too, appeared to be suppressing grins. Sergeant Bleeker, on the other hand, was looking progressively more upset. For no particular reason, Daisy wondered suddenly if his fly could be open. He resisted the urge to look down.

Then through the loudspeakers came the distorted, indistinct notes of the bugle again.

It was mess call.

"Pre-*sent* . . . *hhharms*!" As the rifles came up in salute, he wheeled, faced in the general direction of the main gate, and snapped his right hand to his brow. While the rest of Piebald crowded into their respective mess halls for the evening meal, the 575th stood saluting, mercifully hidden by their own bar-racks.

For all of his lack of experience with the military, Second Lieutenant Meredith Flowers was no moron. Instinctively he knew something was not quite right with that bugle call. It didn't *sound* right. But how could that be? When it died away, he dropped his hand, glanced down quickly—it was buttoned—and turned hesitantly to face the company again.

"*Two!*"

His mind went blank. Two? *That's not it; that's what we used to say in Boy Scouts*. He started to salute again and then dropped his hand a second time, his cheeks flaming. Some of the men brought their rifles down; others started to bring them down, stopped halfway, and brought them up again. All of them gaped at him questioningly. Daisy was certain he heard a groan from Sergeant Bleeker.

What *was* the command? It came to him.

"Order . . . arms."

He mumbled the words, avoiding Sergeant Bleeker's eyes, then lamely added, "Dismissed."

Damn.

Shoulders sagging in defeat, desolate in his embarrassment, he stood there watching the men drift away, pummeling each other in ill-concealed delight.

"Take me home, Mother! I've seen it all now!"

"Ho-lee!"

"Fuckin' cooks oughta be happy. First time we ever saluted supper."

First thing next morning, Sergeant Bleeker appeared at the orderly room with a request for transfer.

First Sergeant Garrison never even showed it to the captain.

CHAPTER THREE

☆ CHAPTER THREE ☆

THERE was a door or a window open somewhere.

Like everyone else in line, Aug was stark naked. He shivered as chilled early-morning air currents snaked across the polished floor from somewhere behind him and wrapped themselves around his knees, raising goose bumps all over him.

Outside, San Francisco was drizzly, cold, and windy, a mixed exhalation of industrial gases, salt air, and Chinese cooking. Inside the cavernous induction station, except for the intermittent tendrils of cold air, it was overheated and stuffy and smelled like Lifebuoy soap and fresh paint.

The scuffed rough-plaster walls and high old-fashioned ceilings were water-stained and grimy, in varied shades of faded ocher, but the smooth linoleum floor had been newly painted a glossy red-brown, with oversize white footprints added to guide the naked draftees as they shuffled dispiritedly from one hallway to another.

Aug had to pee. Bad.

He'd had to when he arrived at the draft board office that morning, but the building had been locked, of course, and, figuring he could wait, he had just put it out of his mind and climbed aboard the bus with the others. He couldn't wait now. He shifted from one foot to the other and back again, wondering what the penalty was for leaving the line.

The knock-kneed legs and pimpled buttocks in front of him moved forward a few paces and Aug followed, maintaining a modest interval. Perversely, he avoided stepping on the painted footprints. The pain in his bladder had gone from dull ache to demand. He turned to look around once more. There had to be a toilet around there somewhere.

" 'Scold. Goddam draft somewhere."

The ginger-haired black man behind him was six or eight years older than he, Aug estimated. His watery eyeballs were red-veined and yellow, and he seemed to be constantly scratching himself, but his most overwhelming characteristic was his bad breath. Aug moved away a half-step as the putrefied odor washed over him.

"There's a draft everywhere," he responded. "That's why we're all here." He grinned, inviting an appreciative response, but the man just looked at him sullenly and turned away, muttering something. Aug shrugged. Screw him, anyway. Unlike most of the younger candidates in line, the man made no attempt to cover his genitals with the sheaf of papers they all carried. He hadn't been circumcised. Neither had Aug.

Aug was getting desperate. He really had to pee. The kidney on his right side was beginning to swell. He bent forward a little to ease the pain.

The line began moving again, for an unusually long distance this time, thirty or forty feet, as if a large number of draftees had suddenly been diverted elsewhere, rushed off naked to repel an enemy assault, or culled out en masse for some coincidental abomination making them all unfit for service.

There hadn't been any medical examinations thus far, just a growing collection of paperwork they could just as easily have carried fully clothed. Aug had tried to show his X ray to the first official-looking person he encountered, a bald heavyset man with no neck who was handing out more papers, but No-Neck had cut him off with a disinterested waggle of his head and waved him on. Healthy, spastic, blind, or leprous, take your papers and keep moving.

The line ambled forward another eight or ten feet, turned a corner, and . . . Aug spotted what appeared to be the open doorway of a rest room. A moment later, the exquisite roar of a high-pressure toilet flushing answered his prayer, nearly triggering a reflex response from his distended bladder. A red-faced man in a white jacket emerged, buttoning his fly, and hurried away.

He turned to the black man behind him. "I've gotta take a leak."

He quick-stepped up the line to the doorway, ducked inside, and—thank God!—hurried over to the single urinal on the far wall. Shifting his X ray and paperwork under one arm, he took hasty aim and let go.

"Ooooh"—eyes closed—"Gaaahd!" Like water from a fire hose cannonading against the stained white porcelain, dull pain evaporating from his bladder, engulfing both kidneys, fading, the strong odor of hot urine coming up from the concave receptacle, he let it rush unimpeded all the way up from his heels, just opened the valve and let it surge for what seemed like a full blessed minute or more.

They could take him into the damn army, send him anywhere they wanted to. He didn't care; it felt so good.

There was a pale pink cake of disinfectant and a sodden cigarette butt in the drain. With the lessening stream, he chased the discarded butt away from the pink disk and back again. On the wall above the fixture, someone had penciled, "In case of air raid, get under urinal. It hasn't been hit yet."

On the way out, he noticed the small metal sign on the door: Staff Only.

The line had made another substantial move while he was gone, and, looking to his left, he saw the black man about to enter the next open doorway. He hurried to catch up and stepped back into place. Readying his X ray, he remembered Angie's instructions to limp as he went through the door.

Side by side across the back wall were six urinals with men standing spread-legged in front of them. A technician in a white jacket thrust a small glass jar into Aug's hand.

"Fill it up."

Aug looked at him dumbly, then down at the jar, then back at the technician. The man returned his gaze warily, his eyebrows drawing together, as if sensing trouble.

"A specimen." He gestured toward the bank of urinals, then at the jar. "Urine. Piss in it."

Without hope, Aug moved away. In front of him, another draftee stepped back with a brimming container, and Aug hesitantly took his place. Transferring the papers and X ray back under his arm again, he took the proper stance, sighed heavily, and draped his penis over the lip of the spotless glass bottle.

The ceiling, part of it, had recently been covered with squares of white acoustical tile. The tile two up and three over from the far corner had already worked loose. The ceiling over the urinals was fourteen tiles wide. Aug jiggled his penis a little and sighed again, pessimistically.

The black man stepped up to Aug's left and filled his jar without difficulty. Venting his surplus into the urinal, he turned his head to regard Aug, looked down at the still-empty container, and, without expression, up at Aug again. He half opened his mouth, as if to comment, but changed his mind, turned, and walked away.

Others stepped up to Aug's right and left, performed as instructed, peed some more, and moved on. Aug tried to stand nonchalantly, as if he had just arrived, but he felt the questioning stares. He thought about asking one of them to pee in his bottle.

Squaring his shoulders, he gave his full attention to the objective. He closed his eyes and contrived vivid images of towering waterfalls, tumbling mountain streams, gushing garden hoses, and fountains, each picture bolstered by loud sound effects, water gurgling, splashing over the rocks, cascading into a bathtub.

He visualized water pouring out of the pipe into Old Man Denton's duck pond. Nothing. *Come on!*

Finally, squinting his eyes and contracting every muscle, he was able to dribble a scant half-inch into the bottom of the jar. He looked at it. There wasn't going to be any more if he stood there for an hour. Apprehensively, he carried the meager sample back to the man in the white jacket.

"This is the best you can do, for crissake?"

Others turned to look, snickering, as the man in white held the near-empty bottle high and jiggled it disdainfully. He snatched a yellow slip from Aug's sheaf of papers and, muttering his disgust, wrapped it around the container and snapped a rubber band over it. He jerked his head—"Go on"—and waved Aug toward the line moving through the doorway on the opposite side of the room.

Aug fantasized turning a bucketful over the man's head.

The naked column snaked into an open area as spacious as the main floor of a large department store, the high ceiling supported by big pillars. To either side of the painted footprints, head-high buff-colored plywood partitions had been set up, smudged by the fingers of the multitudes who had passed earlier. A short, bulbous-nosed man in an overstuffed white jacket directed the draftees one at a time into vacated cubicles.

"Up there, third on the left. You"—he pointed at Aug—"in there."

A slender Chinese, white-jacketed like the rest of the staff and wearing thick horn-rim glasses, stood bent over a small table, drawing blood from the arm of a draftee seated with his back to Aug. Without looking up, the Chinese gestured toward an empty chair on the opposite side of the table. Aug sat down. The seat of the chair felt damp, as if the previous occupant had been perspiring.

The Chinese—a doctor or a technician, Aug couldn't tell which—pulled the big syringe out of the other man's arm, stuck a cotton ball where the needle had been, and said, "Bend your arm." Discarding the used needle onto a white metal tray, he took a slip of blue paper from the man, secured it around the barrel of the syringe with a rubber band, and set the tube in a wooden rack. Without another word, he turned to Aug, roughly wrapped a length of rubber tubing around his upper arm, and dabbed at the crook of his elbow with a damp ball of cotton.

"Make a fist."

Aug complied as the man poised a fresh needle and syringe above his arm, looking for a suitable target.

"Ouch."

It didn't hurt that much. Aug just felt the need to make conversation. It produced none. The rubber tubing was snapped off, and Aug watched the glass barrel of the syringe fill with dark red blood.

"I always thought I had blue blood."

He made no comment, and there was no change in his expression. The man had a dark mole on his cheek. Two long hairs were growing out of it.

When the syringe was full, the Chinese pulled the needle out, put a ball of cotton where it had been, said, "Bend your arm," and turned to discard the needle. The new arrival in the other chair, Aug noted, was keeping his head turned, not wanting to look.

Minus 25cc's of blood and a second piece of paper, Aug went out to rejoin the line.

In the next cubicle he was directed to, he found a scholarly-looking gentleman in a herringbone tweed suit seated behind a yellow wooden desk, writing industriously. He looked up as Aug entered, smiled cordially, and waved him to the empty chair in front of the desk.

"Be with you in a moment."

There was a white paper towel on the seat of the chair. Aug wondered if it was changed for each interview. The man was writing at the bottom of some kind of form. He wrote very carefully, neatly, with a large bright-orange fountain pen. He had a high forehead crossed by a few wisps of hair and wore gold-rimmed spectacles.

"Well." He finished writing and set the paper aside. "How are you?" He picked up a green pencil and began drumming it on the desktop, looking at Aug intently.

Aug shrugged. "Okay. I guess."

The man shifted his attention to Aug's lap and, without saying anything, stared directly at him there until Aug self-consciously started to cross his legs, stopped, and then went ahead and crossed them. With that the man raised his eyes and smiled cheerfully. He kept drumming the pencil on the desk.

"Do you like girls?" Tap-tap-tap.

Aug shrugged again, tilting his head as if he were considering the matter. "I guess. Sure, I like them all right." What kind of a question was that?

"Mm-hm." Tap-tap-tap. "Do you have sex with girls very often?"

Aug flushed and tried to suppress a grin. How often was often? He spread his hands and shrugged again. "I guess. Yeah, once in a while. Couple of times a week, maybe."

"Twice a week?"

"Well"—Aug gulped and twisted around in the chair—"not every week."

Actually, he had had almost no field experience in the activity referred to. Though he pretended otherwise, Aug was not altogether sure of himself in the company of women.

His sex life had been limited to some undefined groping in the back row at the movies, one startling episode in his father's '39 Ford coupe, and a gin-dampened nonperformance one night at a seedy whorehouse in Napa where he and Boner and Bert Rooney had gone to celebrate their high school commencement.

It was his first and only experience in a brothel. The madam, a short, fat brunette in a dark blue housecoat, had brought the girls out. They were all remarkably unattractive. Aug picked out the ugliest one in line, reasoning that, being that ugly, she had to be good. It had not turned out to be a useful formula.

The man smiled at him and doodled something on a piece of paper.

"You were limping when you came in. Do you have some sort of injury?"

Well, finally. Bingo. Aug started to hand him the X-ray envelope, but the psychologist waved it away. "You can discuss that with a doctor. Are you anxious about going into the army? Does the thought frighten you?"

Aug shifted his position in the chair, uncrossing, then recrossing his legs.

"Actually, I was thinking about joining the marines. I'm not scared to go into the army, but I'd just as soon not if I don't have to. As far as I'm concerned—"

The psychologist stopped him with a wave of his hand. "Let me see your papers. No . . . this one." He drew one of the papers out of Aug's hand, scribbled something on it, and handed it back to him. He smiled jovially, said thank you, and waved him out.

Back in line, Aug looked to see what was written on the paper, but he couldn't make it out. The first word looked like "nonmal." *Normal*—that was it. Normal something. Off to one side, there was a short column of abbreviations with a bold check mark next to "Psy Stbl," whatever that meant. The man had acted as if he knew all the answers before he asked the questions.

"You. In there."

The next cubicle was wide enough for three doctors to work side by side, each with his own naked prospect to check out. With scarcely a wasted motion, they poked and prodded, peered into and explored the cavities, tapped, twisted, and manipulated, all the while keeping up a running conversation with one another on subjects having nothing at all to do with what they were about.

The entire examination consumed perhaps five minutes. Eyes, ears, nose, throat, and rectum. *Stamp!* USDA choice. Next.

The doctor at the center station jotted something on a piece of paper, handed the paper back to the man he'd been examining, and slapped him lightly on the shoulder. "Go get 'em, tiger."

He looked at Aug and beckoned.

Aug swallowed.

Hunching over ever so slightly and adopting what he hoped was a convincing expression of anguish, he limped painfully toward his fate.

"Hiya, champ." The doctor was about forty, Aug guessed, trim, with a crew cut. "You're not looking too spry this morning. Let's have the paperwork. What's this?"

"It's my X ray. I've got a bad back." He sighed forlornly.

The doctor raised his eyebrows in mild surprise and exchanged glances with the doctor on his right. He turned the big envelope over and looked at it for a moment, then tossed it onto a small table with the other papers.

"Well, long as you're here, let's see what other damage we can find." He pointed. "Face that way. Spread the feet." Expertly, he hooked a little finger behind Aug's testicles. "Turn your head. Cough."

Aug coughed.

"Again. Harder." Aug coughed harder.

Brusquely, efficiently, the doctor started through the checklist, probing, flexing, jabbing. But not on the back. Aug was primed to yell on cue, but the doctor stayed away from his back.

"Stretch your arms out . . . all the way, both of them. Is that the best you can straighten your right arm?"

"It's a little crooked. I fell out of a tree and broke my elbow when I was a little kid."

"It's more than a *little* crooked. Are you right-handed?"

"Yes."

"Well, boss, that's not too good. I guess we'll have to put you down for Limited Service."

"What's Limited Service?"

"That means no Medal of Honor, champ. Stateside stuff." He began writing on one of Aug's papers.

Aug looked at his elbow. He had come here to claim a disability, to escape the draft. But now this doctor was saying he wasn't *fit* to go to war. His manhood was being questioned.

"It doesn't give me any trouble."

"Mm-hm." The doctor finished writing and returned his pen to his jacket pocket. "Okay, let's have a look at the back. What's wrong with it?"

"A couple of my vertebrae are goofed up." Vertebrae? Verte . . . ? Aug couldn't remember what you called more than one of them.

The doctor touched him light on the lower back, just lightly enough that Aug decided it didn't deserve an all-out yell. He murmured a protest and squirmed a little, however, just to get the problem established.

"Mm-hm." The doctor reached for the X ray, and Aug tensed as he pulled it out of the envelope and held it up to inspect it.

"Jesus."

Hot dog. Good ole Angie. Limited Service, nothing. He wondered when the bus was leaving for home.

"That's the worst spondylolisthesis I've ever seen."

"I know."

Instantly Aug wished he hadn't said that. The doctor looked at him appraisingly, then back at the X ray.

"You must be in considerable pain."

Aug shrugged, his face a picture of courageous suffering. "I've learned to live with it."

The doctor was looking at the lower left corner of the negative. "Who's D. L. Gravestock?"

"That's who took the X ray, I guess. I don't know." Why did he keep staring at the thing? Why didn't he just give him the slip to go home? Aug interlaced his fingers and looked up at the ceiling. It was beginning to feel warm in there.

"Hey, Fred." The doctor waved one of his colleagues over. "Lyle. Take a look at this." Aug swallowed and shifted his weight from one foot to the other.

The other two doctors squinted at the negative.

"Jesus H. Christ."

"Son of a bitch. That's a dandy."

"Yeah," Aug's doctor agreed, "but what do you think about this?" He pointed at another area of the picture. The other two leaned closer again.

"Hmmm." The one called Lyle looked over at Aug, then back at the X ray. "That is interesting."

Aug's doctor turned toward him with a grave expression.

"We've got some distressing news here, champ." The other two doctors looked equally concerned.

"What's that?" Aug looked from one face to another. "What's the matter?"

"You have a problem"—the doctor indicated the X ray—"potentially more serious than just a couple of slipped vertebrae."

"I do?" Aug swallowed noisily. Even if it wasn't his X ray, he couldn't help feeling concerned.

The doctor nodded, showing him the negative. "You see this light area . . . right here?" He pointed at the lower center of the picture. "That is a calcified fibroid tumor." He paused, giving Aug time to absorb the information. "But the worst part is where it's located."

Aug was genuinely distressed.

The doctors looked equally distressed.

All three of them exploded into laughter.

"It's in your *uterus*, you simple idiot! Where the hell did you get this X ray?"

Aug groaned and closed his eyes as the hoots of laughter swept over him, pounding into him like storm waves beating upon a broken seawall, overwhelming him, dragging him down into their depths.

That dumb Angie.

"Raise your right hand and repeat after me: 'I do solemnly swear . . . that I will bear true faith and allegiance . . . to the United States of America . . . that I will serve them honestly and faithfully . . . against all their enemies . . . and that I will obey the orders of the President of the United States . . .' "

He knew it wouldn't make any difference, but all the time he was saying it, Aug kept his fingers crossed.

CHAPTER FOUR

☆ CHAPTER FOUR ☆

As the final tinny notes of the bugle faded away in the loud-speaker system, Buck Sergeant Bleeker drew himself up to his full five feet eight, threw his head back like a banty rooster, and shrilled, "Orrr-*derrr* . . . hhharms!"

The polished rifles came down as one, heavy butts smacking into the dust next to boots glistening in the late-afternoon sun.

The captain returned Bleeker's salute, his eyes traversing the three platoons standing like khaki statues. Out of the side of his mouth he barked, "At ease!" It came out like the flat report of a .45 automatic, and the men slumped immediately from their rigid poses of attention, shuffling uneasily from one foot to the other. Their expressions suggested they knew what was coming next.

The captain slowly unbuttoned a shirt pocket, continuing to move his eyes across the ranks, and withdrew a folded sheet of paper. Before opening it, he carefully, deliberately rebuttoned the pocket flap. Without expression, he held the paper high as if providing indisputable testimony of the truth he was about to reveal. He opened the first fold, the second, the third, held the now fully exposed sheet in front of him, and began to read in loud, measured tones, projecting his voice as if he were addressing an entire battalion.

"Subject—Assignment Personnel. To—commanding officer, Five hundred seventy-fifth MPEG Guard Company, Piebald, Arizona. One . . ." He raised his eyes before continuing. "Company will prepare for arrival, twenty-nine April 'forty-three. Enlisted personnel to bring table of organization to"—he looked up for one triumphant moment before delivering the final words—"full strength!"

Without reading further, he dropped his hands to his sides. "They're bringing this outfit to"—once again he emphasized the words—"full . . . strength. You wonder why? Why they're filling up the ranks? It's pretty damn easy to figure out." His eyes searched for anyone not able to figure it out.

"You're going to be marching up a gangplank. Be ready for it!"

Abruptly, he turned to Sergeant Bleeker. "Dismiss 'em." He returned Bleeker's salute, turned on his heel, and stalked away.

Then, from the ranks, from those who had heard similar pronouncements almost daily for three months, from those who knew full well God was not about to let a man with a back or an eye or a knee this bad be sent into combat, came the barely audible response, wafting from one platoon to another: "Bulllllll . . . shit."

The line in front stopped, moved forward a few steps, and telescoped inward again. Standing in line seemed to be the army's number one maneuver.

At the first counter inside the big warehouse, each draftee was issued two voluminous olive-drab barracks bags. *Everything* went into the heavy canvas bags, which were slung, one from each shoulder, on wide web straps.

Aug's arms hurt, both of them. Their second stop, after piling off the bus at the reception center, had been the dispensary— first the barbershop, then the dispensary—and his upper arms throbbed with gnawing, paralyzing pain that was aggravated by the slightest muscular contraction, as if the inescapable, seemingly endless series of inoculations had left swarms of needles broken off inside, too deeply embedded in the bone to ever be retrieved.

Smallpox, tetanus, typhoid. Who could count?

"Wait'll they stick that screwdriver in yer arm!"

The swaggering veterans of two or three days' service clustered around the entrance of the dispensary to torment the newly arrived rookies.

A screwdriver in your arm. Aug had thought they were kidding.

In front of him, Mozetti, Angelo M., 39120283, accepted a narrow folded cap and two coarse olive-drab neckties and disdainfully flung them into one of his bags without looking at them.

A half-head shorter than Aug, Mozetti was built like a gallon wine jug from the neck down, all chest and trunk and no waist, with a matched set of impressively bowed legs beneath. When he waved his arms, which he did continually, whatever the point to be made, the difference in their lengths was not apparent. His left arm was two full inches shorter than his right, the result, he said, of "always jackin' off right-handed"—delicacy, Aug had noted early on, was not one of Mozetti's burdens.

Angelo Mozetti had been summoned, protesting, from the cool green vineyards north of Napa where his family, he said, had been bottling "Dago Red" for four generations. The impressive diamond ring he wore on the little finger of his left hand, coupled with a gold Rolex on his wrist, led Aug to suspect that the Mozetti family had a better product than just cheap table wine.

The line moved up a few paces.

Counter to counter, there was no discernible logic in the sequence. Olive-drab wool shirts, trousers, and brass-buttoned dress jacket—"That's your *blouse*, Mac." A drawstring bag containing a bar of yellow soap, a toothbrush, and a plastic safety razor.

"Where's the goddam blades?" Mozetti was pawing through the little bag. "There's no toothpaste, either."

"Buy 'em at the PX."

"The hell with that. If the army wants me to shave, they can give me goddam razor blades."

The soldier behind the counter shrugged, uninterested, and waved Mozetti on. He tossed an identical toilet kit at Aug, his mind elsewhere.

The barracks bags grew steadily heavier. Khaki socks, undershorts, and sleeveless undershirts; a ponderous olive-drab wool overcoat with brass buttons; a stiff rubberized raincoat; green fatigues, work uniforms with baggy pants and jacket and a floppy hat; stiff canvas leggings with brass hooks up the sides and dangling laces.

They came to the bedding counter. Mozetti found this, too, lacking.

"Where's the sheets?"

"No sheets."

"What do you mean, no sheets? You expect me to sleep under *these*?" He hefted the two rough wool blankets, glaring at the man behind the counter.

"You're in the army, Mac. Ain't no fuckin' hotel."

"A fucking . . . fuckup," Mozetti sputtered, unable to find more suitable words. With his arms and hands full, he had only his mouth left for talking, and that was like asking him to walk without moving his feet.

Muttering anatomically oriented suggestions for disposition of the bedding, he moved on, bumping into the man in front of him as he glared back over his shoulder at the PFC behind the counter.

Unperturbed, the PFC pivoted, grabbed once, twice, a third time, and rotated back without moving his feet. Two heavy blankets, a pillowcase, and a mattress cover thudded into Aug's chest.

Aug winced. He might have groaned aloud if he hadn't been sure that would brighten the man's day. Without comment, he crammed the bedding into one of his bags and followed Mozetti, who was still muttering to himself.

It was stuffy in the warehouse. There were windows along the nearest wall, glassed-in slots high up under the eaves, the kind that didn't open. By now everyone in line was sweating—not the uniformed clerks behind the counters, just the "customers" in their civvies—and the perspiration made its own contribution to the odor of mothballs, canvas, wool, waterproofing paste, and leather. Aug's neck and back itched, the result of snippets of hair that had escaped down his collar during the earlier brief assault in the barbershop.

Old Man Parry would like to have seen that barbershop, he

thought. It took Old Man Parry almost an hour to cut your hair, what with talking about his arthritis, his six-year-old Chevy with only seven thousand miles on it, what time he had gone into the house that morning to urinate, and the state of his wife's genitals. Thirty-five cents for a haircut and the day's gossip.

Aug's father always got mad when Dan Parry was shaving him—and hooked his little finger in the corner of his dad's mouth to stretch the skin tight.

His dad would sit up in the chair and tell him off—really angry. And next time he came in for a shave, Old Man Parry would do it again.

Dan Parry would have dropped his bridge seeing those army barbers go to work with their clippers, standing there up to their ankles in hair, skinning ducktails and pompadours off in maybe sixty seconds.

"You'll be sorrr-eeee!" The grinning "veterans" outside the barbershop.

"I take a nine triple-A."

Mozetti was standing, legs spread, on an elevated platform, his stocking feet in a pair of shiny metal measuring brackets adjustable for length and width. Another bored PFC stood below him lazily chewing gum, manipulating the brackets to conform loosely to the feet within them.

Very loosely.

The PFC turned his head to one side and called out, "Nine and a half . . . B." A moment later, a pair of heavy high-top shoes, their laces tied together, crashed unceremoniously onto an adjacent counter.

"Nine and a half . . . B!" Mozetti was incredulous. "I can't wear those fucking things! Not if I stuff *newspapers* in 'em!"

The PFC didn't miss a beat with his gum. "You'll spread into 'em." He tapped Mozetti on one ankle, indicating he should step down and move on.

The soldier dispensing the footwear was equally unsympathetic. "You don't want 'em"—he shrugged—"go barefoot." He grinned widely, displaying two shiny gold incisors. "Or write to your congressman, if you want." He turned away to replenish his shelves.

Mozetti picked up the shoes and stared at them in disbelief. For a moment, he looked as if he might employ them as weapons.

"You sonsabitches! You don't give a shit if I ruin my feet!"

They didn't even glance in his direction. Mozetti was right: they *didn't* care if he ruined his feet. And they probably got son-of-a-bitched ten times an hour. Aug stepped up to take his turn in the brackets.

He wondered if he should tell the PFC his father fitted shoes. He supposed not.

"I'd like a leather heel, something in a brown oxford."

Click! Click! Click! "Ten and a half . . . C!" An answered clump on the counter. "Next."

Ten and a half C? Aug grinned at the absurdity. He could put *both* feet in one of them. Shaking his head, he picked up the thick-soled lumps of leather, slipped back into his own low-cut shoes, and followed Mozetti.

The line reached the end of the warehouse. The scalped, sore-armed, and overladen inductees squeezed awkwardly through a narrow door leading outside, their bulging barracks bags throwing them off balance with each faltering step forward.

It had stopped raining. The late-afternoon sun filtering through a stand of twisted cypress trees transformed the dark foliage into clumps of orange and green velvet. The air felt fresh and clean, the smell of rain mixed with a hint of salt from the ocean somewhere beyond the trees.

"Fall in! Over here!"

A handful of square-jawed, incredibly neat-looking soldiers, lean and hard in starched, close-fitting uniforms, were systematically pushing and prodding stumbling bodies into a semblance of ranks.

"Line up! Move it!"

Ten men to a line, four lines deep. As each unit of forty was formed, a new platoon was begun and another marched away, a never-ending supply of replacements struggling out of the warehouse into the sunlight.

Mozetti and Aug ended up side by side in the second rank. In front of them, a tall, skinny youth with sagging trousers shrugged out of his straps and dropped his heavy barracks bags onto the ground with obvious relief.

"Get them bags up outa that dirt!"

Three brilliant yellow stripes on his sharply creased sleeves, three brightly colored ribbons above his left breast pocket. The flat-brimmed campaign hat cocked over his forehead looked brand-new and spotless, his brass belt buckle gleamed, and his shoes glittered like wet cherries. He carried a short leather baton in one hand, like a riding crop, slapping it into his open palm—*pop!*—for emphasis.

"Get 'em up!" *Pop!*

Offended, the tall youth bent to retrieve his bags and sighed deeply.

Mozetti grunted and mumbled something unintelligible.

The sergeant looked like a B-movie actor, Aug decided, caught up in his role, posturing in front of a mirror. But he looked like a mean son of a gun, too.

Next to the tall youth, a slight, somewhat effeminate recruit with thick glasses and a receding hairline stood slump-shouldered with his bags dragging in the dirt on either side like pregnant pontoons.

Pop! "Cinch up on them straps, soldier!"

The young man twisted unsteadily in the straps, staggered by the weight of the bags, and began fumbling with one of the buckles. Aug stepped forward to give him a hand.

Pop! "Somebody tell you to help that man?"

The leather baton pointed at Aug like a sword, and Aug shrugged and stepped back, his face flaming.

"Fucking asshole," Mozetti muttered.

The sergeant commenced pacing back and forth, eyeing the unit belligerently, smacking his open palm with the baton.

"When you're told to put your bags down"—*pop!*—"you put 'em down! When you're told to pick 'em up"—*pop!*—"you pick 'em up! When you're told to fart"—*pop!*—"you fart! When I don't tell you to do nothin' "—he glared straight at Aug—*pop!* —"you do nothin'!"

He stopped pacing and looked to the right . . . to the left. Not a sound.

"My name . . . is Sergeant!" He gave them a moment to absorb that information. "Your name . . . is Fifth Platoon, M Company! M"—*pop!*—"like in 'morons'!" He looked for a response to that. There was none.

"You're gonna *march* over to the barracks, get rid of that civilian crap you're wearin', an' get into *uniform!*" Pop! "Then you're gonna march over an' get your *brains* tested!" *Pop!* "Lookin' this bunch over. . ." He looked them over. "That shouldn't take very long!" *Pop!* "Any questions?"

He gave them a full two seconds to think of one.

"P'toon . . . tennns-*hut*!"

All of them understood they were to do *something*. Indeed, some of the group even came to a version of attention. The remainder stirred into a variety of positions somewhat different from their previous stances, shuffling their feet and looking at one another for inspiration.

We did just what he hoped we would, Aug decided, *screwed up. He likes that.* All part of the show with new inductees.

The sergeant shook his head slowly, his voice conveying his disgust. "How the *hell* do they expect us to win this war? You tell me." No one offered a solution.

The presentation went back into full volume.

"When you hear somebody yell, 'tennns-*hut*,' you jump!" *Pop!* "You hear?" Everyone heard. "You stick your hands down at your sides . . . like this!" He demonstrated. "Heels together! Eyes front an' center!" *Pop!* "You got that?" They all got that. "Awright." He looked at them menacingly. "P'tooon . . . tennns-*hut*!"

Aug immediately shot his hands down to his sides, stiffening to rigid attention as both of his barracks bags dropped like stones into the dirt.

For several seconds the sergeant just looked at him, his eyes narrowing. Then he stepped slowly past the skinny youth in the front rank to stand directly in front of Aug, staring him straight in the eye, hard. When he finally spoke, his voice was low and strained.

"Just what the hell are you up to, citizen?"

"Just standing at attention, Sergeant." He kept his eyes

straight ahead and bit his lip. He heard a strained noise from Mozetti. He sounded as if he was having trouble breathing.

The sergeant's eyes squeezed to mere slits. "What's your name?"

"Fifth Platoon, M Company." Another muffled moan from Mozetti. "Like in 'morons.' "

The sergeant's face was a mottled red. He pointed his baton at Aug's barracks bags. "Pick up them bags."

Aug picked them up and slipped the straps over his shoulders. The sergeant put his face close to Aug's and kept his voice low and slow. "I'm gonna keep an eye on you, turd bird. You understand? One more wise-ass move outa you an' you're gonna be swimming in it up to your balls."

He stared at Aug for another long moment, then turned and walked stiff-legged back to his center-stage position. He glared at Aug again, then turned to look over the whole platoon and stiffened to attention himself.

"P-toon . . . tennns-*hut*!"

They were already at attention, but they shifted their feet again, some of them, willing to overlook the error.

"Riiight . . . ffface!"

With some hesitation and a few false starts, they found the approximate compass point.

"Forrr*ward* . . . hhharch!" Barracks bags swinging, they lurched forward—if not as one, at least with everyone moving in the same general direction. A precision drill team they were not.

"Hut! . . . Hut! . . . Hut! Toop! Threep! Fooor! Get in step, goddammit! Your left! Your left! . . . Jesus."

The reception center at Monterey, California, was one of the army's permanent installations, a choice peacetime post. The center's function was to receive and process newly inducted personnel and to move them out as expeditiously as possible to the units that needed them. Everywhere there was the look of squared-away olive-drab order, purpose, and tradition. The broad streets were paved and in good repair, pleasantly landscaped with trees and shrubbery. The barracks were roomy, reasonably comfortable one-story buildings with shaded porches.

The grounds sloped gently in the direction of downtown Monterey and the ocean, and there were no signs of the customary training facilities, rifle ranges, or obstacle courses.

"You'll be sorrreee!" A handful of soldiers lounging against a barracks called out to the platoon as it plodded doggedly up the street. The plodders tried to pretend they hadn't heard.

"I'm *already* sorry," Mozetti grumbled.

"Column left . . . *hhharch*! Jesus." Mindful of his earlier problems with phrases military, the sergeant resorted to waving his arms and pointing. "Turn left . . . in there!" He directed them into a small open area in front of a vacant barracks. "I never *seen* such goddam . . ."

Without further guidance, they halted. One or two started to drop their barracks bags but remembered in time and painfully hunched them back into place. The sergeant climbed midway up the wide front steps and turned to address them.

"This here's your barracks! Remember the number . . . B-fifteen! If you forget it, you can sleep under a tree! Go in an' throw your gear on a bunk . . . *Not yet, goddammit!* When I *tell* you! An' put on your O.D.'s."

The slight bespectacled youth whose bags still drooped close to the ground raised a tentative hand.

"What are O.D.'s?"

The sergeant gave him a disgusted look. "O.D. stands for 'olive-drab.' " He gestured at his own immaculate uniform. "What I'm wearin'. G.I. stands for 'government issue'. That's you. S.O.L. stands for 'shit outa luck,' an' that's what you're gonna be if you're not out here in the street, in uniform, ten seconds after I blow this whistle!"

He looked at his wristwatch. "You got eighteen minutes! Any questions?" He gave them a second and a half this time. "Fall out!" A contemptuous wave of his hand conveyed his meaning, and enough of them broke for the steps, the remainder soon figured it out.

The interior of the barracks was a long, shadowed room with a low ceiling and windows on either side. It was crowded with three rows of long metal cots running the length of the building. Each cot had a pillow rolled up in a bare mattress at one end, exposing the springs. There were enough cots for the new platoon and some left over.

Aug appropriated the one immediately to the left of the door, and Mozetti and the slight bespectacled youth—his name was Kaplowitz—took the two next to it.

The rest of the group quickly spread throughout the room, calling out to new friends, dumping their barracks bags heavily on the polished brown linoleum floor. Temporarily free of the sergeant's restraints, they reverted to nervous wisecracks and laughter as they dug through their bags for the required items of uniform.

"Whatta we put on? Everything in here's O.D."

"Same as he's wearing, he said."

"There ain't nothin' in here with sergeant's stripes."

"Hey, what about those pretty ribbons on his shirt? Whatta you suppose they're for?"

"Gonorrhea, syphilis, and crabs." Mozetti's contribution drew the loudest laughter.

Every garment, they discovered, concealed a collection of clothing tags, little squares of white cardboard pinned to crotch, armpits, shoulders, cuffs, fly, and waistband, signifying each seam had been inspected and approved for shipment.

Kaplowitz giggled as he made a neat pile of tags and pins on his mattress. "Do you suppose, if they're good, clothing inspectors get promoted from crotch to collar?"

"Other way around," someone said, "with WAC uniforms."

More laughter. Most of them were half naked now, hesitantly fitting themselves, piece by piece, into the unfamiliar uniform, transforming themselves from individuals to indistinguishable segments of sameness. Same socks, same underwear, same shirts and pants, their civvies tied up in bundles now to be disposed of.

Mozetti shrugged into his shirt and was pricked sharply—"Goddammit!"—in the back of his neck. He found the lurking clothing tag beneath the collar flap.

As Aug pulled on the sturdy wool trousers, he stopped, suddenly reminded of his father and a trip they had taken to San Francisco together when he was about five.

His parents had bought him a pair of wool trousers at the dry goods store on Main Street, his first long pants. They were for church and other special occasions. He hated them. The rough material scratched his sensitive legs unbearably, and he avoided wearing the pants whenever possible. But one of the requirements of the trip to San Francisco was that he dress up, and as badly as he wanted to go, he had debated turning the trip down rather than putting on the scratchy trousers.

He had solved the problem by wearing his red and white striped cotton pajama pants underneath the wool, a satisfying solution not discovered by his father until they were on the ferryboat departing Sausalito. His sister had teased him about it for a long time.

He smiled, wondering what the sergeant's reaction would be to pajamas under the uniform.

That was the one item they hadn't been issued.

"What do you think this brain-testing crap is that stupid bastard was talking about?" Mozetti was sitting on the edge of his bunk, bent over, trying to lace his clumsy shoes tighter. He had put on two pairs of socks, but his feet still slid around inside.

Aug shrugged. "More paperwork and another line to stand in."

"It's a written aptitude and IQ test."

They turned. It was the tall, skinny youth who had been in the front rank. "It's a comprehensive examination to determine where you're best suited to serve. You can state a preference"— he smiled knowingly—"but you're going to go wherever they want to send you."

Ignoring him, Mozetti went back to his shoelaces. "Air Corps, that's what I'm putting in for, the fucking ground crew for long-distance bombers, the kind they park a million miles from where the war is." He gave the laces a final tug. "Don't volunteer for anything. That's what my old man said. He was in the last war. Keep your head down and a tight asshole. And don't volunteer for *anything.*"

"How about draft board maintenance?" the skinny youth

offered, trying hard to be included, "or Gray Ladies guard duty? That should be pretty good." Nobody responded.

Throughout the barracks now, the metamorphosis was nearly complete, newly emerged soldiers smoothing out wrinkles, tugging at shirt cuffs, unconsciously squaring their shoulders, standing a little straighter. Kaplowitz was trying to undo a mangled knot in his necktie. He giggled.

Here and there, a few men made halfhearted attempts to spread blankets over their cots. Others were trying to rearrange the tumbled gear remaining in their barracks bags, making wisecracks, trying to appear anything but nervous. One by one they drifted outside to await the sergeant's whistle, putting their hands in their pockets and taking them out again, their heavy shoes making loud, clumping noises.

Together Aug, Mozetti, and Kaplowitz moved toward the door.

Their way was blocked by a young man just coming through the entrance. Still in his civvies, barracks bags slung from his shoulders, he was perspiring heavily and breathing hard, as if he had run all the way from the supply warehouse. He kept blinking as he tried to peer around them into the barracks.

"Is this B-thirteen?"

"No." Kaplowitz started to direct him toward the next barracks, but Aug stopped him with a move of his hand. He gave the lost recruit a stern look.

"Where are you from, citizen?"

The young man awkwardly came to attention, as best he could with the bulky bags on his shoulders.

"Sacramento, sir"—blinking rapidly. "I had to go to the bathroom."

Aug's gaze was unwavering, unforgiving.

"Mm-hm. Well, you're late, and we're taking this bunch over to get their brains tested." He jerked a thumb over his shoulder. "Pick out a bunk in there and get into your O.D.'s."

Kaplowitz giggled. "Same thing we're wearing."

A sudden inspiration. Aug pointed at the cots they had just walked away from.

"You see those three bunks there?"

"Yes, sir."

"Get them made up—and *neatly*, you understand?—before we get back."

The young man's "Yes, sir!" was unhesitating, resolute, the kind of response you can count on in battle.

The whistle blew, and Aug, Mozetti, and Kaplowitz went down the stairs to join the platoon.

CHAPTER
☆ **FIVE** ☆

APPROACHING from the north on the tar-patched, two-lane highway, passersby came upon the prisoner-of-war camp at Piebald without warning.

Topping a rise in the undulating olive-green carpet of greasewood and cactus, they suddenly saw it spread out in the haze below them, an indistinct crosshatch of white-painted building blocks with green tarpaper roofs in a sparse forest of utility poles.

The single splash of vivid color, as the road dipped down and around the camp, was the huge orange and white checkered water tank squatting ponderously amid the brush and rocks on the steep grade.

At the main gate, a long-dead giant saguaro pitted with abandoned owl holes tilted precariously to one side, a reluctant centerpiece in the rock and cactus garden in front of the sentry shack. To the right, below the frontage road leading past the headquarters building, a stringy P had been traced in yellow rocks against a dusty background of red-brown lava. Excluding the drunken saguaro and rock garden, it was the only landscaping in evidence.

Inside, just beyond the gate, a tall flagpole and a vintage cannon on splintered wheels were encircled by the inevitable border of whitewashed rocks. Inexplicably, the cannon was aimed at the center of the camp rather than away from it, as if to protect the outside world from the goings-on there.

Hospital, chapel, motor pool, theater, PX, warehouses, barracks, mess halls, and latrines—beyond them a small parade ground and the tall, grim fences of the stockade.

It was not a scene to lift the heart and soul.

Ten miles out that afternoon, from his seat under the tarpaulin arched over the rear of the big army truck, Aug's view was limited to a narrow vista of pavement and parched desert landscape retreating rapidly to the rear.

The view was further obscured by a battered floor lamp teetering unsteadily at the tailgate between the wooden bench seats on either side. Its scrawny stand, scratched and dented, was made of cheap, imitation brass, the bottom of its torn, bright red shade trimmed with a loosened fringe of gold-colored tassels. With each lurch of the truck on the uneven roadway, the lamp jerked violently back and forth, its tassels dancing about obscenely.

It belonged to Aug.

He had bought it for a dollar from a drunken Pima Indian who staggered onto the station platform at Warlock, where they were waiting for the truck from camp. It was an impulsive show of bravado in front of the others, and he had expected it to end right there. He hadn't intended it to find its way into the truck, but the driver, a stubby, freckle-faced young man who wore his folded cloth cap almost sideways on his head, had slammed the tailgate behind them, then tossed the lamp in, and Aug had shrugged and let it stay.

Its purchase had drawn mixed reviews.

"You can't take that with you," Private Crowder had warned.

The draftees boarded the train at the reception center in California. Private Crowder, an emaciated, stiff-backed youth with a sallow, pimpled complexion, had been given custody of a bulky envelope containing their orders and service records. This awesome assignment had frozen his face into an expression of officious disapproval. He carried the envelope everywhere, to meals, to the toilet, as if it contained the date and location of the invasion of Europe.

Kaplowitz, seated next to Aug in the truck, had hung back from the business on the platform, a smile twitching at his lips, the better to observe it through his thick-lensed glasses. After only a week, the army, he confided, had already exceeded his expectations. Kaplowitz was going to write a novel.

At home, he told Aug, he had always had his head in a book. This was partly due to the necessity of putting his head all the way in in order to see it; his right eye corrected to only 20/40, and that was his good eye. His most distinguishing characteristic in his present company, however, was that he was here, in the army, because he was "intellectually curious"—curious enough to have turned down a student deferment that would have kept him safely tucked away at San Francisco State College for the duration.

Mozetti found that news curious, that anyone who didn't have to be there would be.

Of the others in the contingent—nine had made the trip from California—only Cloony drew Aug's special attention. He had huge, puffy hands, an outsize, overshot lower jaw, and a massive, jutting forehead. His close-set eyes seldom seemed to focus on anything, but three times that morning he had told Aug how pretty it was, the barren scene outside the train windows. He sat by the tailgate now, opposite Mozetti, with a half-smile on his face, the jostling of the truck making it appear he was secretly chuckling to himself about something.

They had no idea where they were going, only to "someplace in Arizona" where they were to be military police. Secretly Aug rather liked the sound of that. He saw himself sauntering down the sidewalk somewhere, a pistol and nightstick at his belt, looking at his reflection in the store windows, catching the admiring glances of the pretty girls passing by.

He rolled his shoulders back, squaring them, and sat up a little straighter. *Military police officer.* He wondered what Constable Vervais back home would think about that. "Back home" was only eleven days back, but it had already faded into the past.

Mozetti cocked one foot atop the tailgate and surveyed the desert behind them. "Where's all the fuckin' buffalo?"

Cloony turned to help him look.

"The American bison," Crowder corrected, "was never indigenous—"

Mozetti gave him the finger. "Up yours, Crowder."

Kaplowitz giggled.

The highway suddenly ducked down beneath them on the descent to camp, and Mozetti leaned far out over the tailgate for a better view. "Hey! We're somewhere." A second look changed his mind. "No, we're not. We're no-fuckin'-where."

With a series of jerks and roars, the big truck was abruptly double-clutched into lower gears and, scarcely slowing its pace, swung sharply right toward the main gate, churning up an impenetrable cloud of dust as the wheels left the pavement. The floor lamp crashed into Mozetti as barracks bags and bodies were flung violently to one side.

"Hey! Dumb asshole up there!" Similar compliments addressed the driver as the draftees struggled to regain their seats.

"Who's drivin' this goddam thing?"

"Nobody. Stupid jerk fell out back there."

The sentry at the gate ducked back into the little guard shack as the truck careened past, then stepped out again and did a double take at the lamp swinging out over the tailgate. Noting this, Mozetti gave Aug the thumbs-up sign and grinned. Aug grinned back at him and nodded. A dollar well spent.

The introductory view of their new home was not inspiring: boxlike buildings squared away in the center of precise rectangles formed by intersecting roads, the latter plastered down with drain oil from the motor pool in a losing effort to defeat the dust. Aug read the signboard outside the post theater as they sped past. He grunted. A Van Johnson movie.

A work detail dressed in green fatigue uniforms yelled at them derisively from the side of the road, "You'll be sorr-reee!," a greeting they had heard over and over again from the moment they reached the reception center in California.

Kaplowitz giggled. "I can't wait to you'll-be-sorr-reee somebody."

Mozetti snorted. "You're never gonna find anybody sorrier than us."

The truck made another hard turn, then another, to the left this time, accelerated, then braked hard and slid nose down to a halt in front of the 575th's orderly room. The pursuing plume of dust promptly caught up, enveloping the space below the tarpaulin, half choking them and obliterating whatever view they might have had of their new home.

"Je-*sus Christ*!"

"Dumb shit up there!"

As the dust cloud began to dissipate, Aug saw a huge figure in a bleached summer uniform materialize slowly at the tailgate like a corpulent genie from within an enchanted cloud of drifting dust. The six bright yellow stripes on his sleeve, three above and three below the diamond-shaped lozenge, identified him as a first sergeant.

His face and body might have been fashioned from an over-inflated pink balloon, dangerously cinched in and overflowing at collar and beltline. His thick lips were folded loosely around an equally fat cigar, his eyes, blinking rapidly in the dust, mere slits in the folds of fat there.

First Sergeant Orville Garrison. Regular Army.

Sergeant Garrison's attention was caught immediately by the outrageous floor lamp, its garish shade knocked askew, leaning toward him over the tailgate. The cigar rolled from one side of his mouth to the other. He looked slowly from Mozetti to Cloony, as if daring either of them to acknowledge ownership. Mozetti grinned cheerfully and shrugged.

The sergeant made an almost imperceptible move with his head. "Out."

The word was barely audible, muffled by the cigar.

"You guys go ahead," Aug said. "I think I'll go on back to California." The sergeant's eyes found him and remained there a moment, studying him.

The recruits reached for their barracks bags, jammed into the narrow floor space between the bench seats, and began backing out, climbing awkwardly over the high tailgate, dragging their heavy baggage with them.

Kaplowitz missed a step, blurted "Yike!," and snatched at the teetering lamp for support. He negotiated a desperate wingover in midair, clawing for altitude, and smacked into the dirt flat on his back. His bags and the lamp fell on top of him, the bawdy red shade mercifully covering his head.

Aug looked at the sergeant and shook his head sadly. "I'd ground him. That's the worst landing I've ever seen." Mozetti laughed and popped his hands together.

The sergeant looked Aug over once again, then slowly removed his cigar and, grunting with the effort, stooped and raised the near edge of the lampshade, revealing Kaplowitz's stricken face.

"What's your name, boy?" It was more of a sigh than spoken words.

"Aaakglipts."

Kaplowitz's spectacles hung from one dirt-covered ear. His eyes were wide, his mouth opening and closing like a beached flounder's.

Shaking his head and wheezing, the sergeant carefully replaced the lampshade and straightened up painfully, his face reddened by the unaccustomed calisthenics. He looked at Aug and Mozetti accusingly, as if blaming them for his troubles.

"His name is Kaplowitz, Sergeant. I've got all their records right here."

Crowder was perched above them, one leg over the tailgate, the big manila envelope raised in one hand. Behind him, Cloony was trying to get an unobstructed view of the scene, a confused look on his face.

"I'd say he just knocked the wind out of himself," Crowder added helpfully.

"No shit," Mozetti commented.

The sergeant looked at Mozetti, then up at Crowder and Cloony. Stooping once more, he grabbed a handful of Kaplowitz's shirt and heaved him to his feet, where he teetered like a dislodged tenpin with Aug and Mozetti steadying him on either side.

Garrison withdrew his sodden cigar and aimed it at Crowder and Cloony. "Both of you," he wheezed. "Down here." The cigar went back into his mouth.

The orderly-room door banged open and Aug looked up to see a skinny PFC—even skinnier than Crowder—clatter down the steps with a clipboard in his hand, doing his very best to look important. It wasn't an easy impersonation. His khaki uniform hung on him like a sack. Little wisps of red hair peeked out from under his cloth cap like tufts of stuffing coming out of a mattress.

"Awright," he said, "who's got the . . . ?" Spotting the manila envelope, he stepped forward and took it abruptly from Crowder. "My name's Lawler," he announced, as if they had all been waiting for that news. "Company clerk."

"Didn't think it was General Marshall," Mozetti muttered, and Kaplowitz, struggling back from the dead, managed a wheezing giggle.

Lawler opened the envelope and, puffing his cheeks out, exhaled noisily. His pained expression reflected the terrible burden of responsibility. As he started to extract the paperwork, Sergeant Garrison reached out and plucked the big envelope from his fingers.

"You don't need nothin' but the roster, Billy," he mumbled. He peered inside, withdrew a single sheet of paper, and handed it over.

PFC Billy Lawler, company clerk, cleared his throat, struggling to regain his official posture. With great care, he affixed the sheet of paper to his clipboard and cleared his throat again.

"Say 'yo' when I call out your name." His voice was louder than it needed to be. *Cloony!*"

Cloony looked down at the ground, shuffling his feet and grinning. "What's 'yo' mean?"

Billy turned to the first sergeant, rolling his eyes theatrically. "It means you're here."

"Seems like you could see that," Cloony said.

Mozetti snorted and clapped his hands together again in delight. Billy glared at him, then returned to his list, shaking his head.

"Crowder!"

"Yo!"

"Kap . . . Kap . . ." Reading was not Billy Lawler's strong suit.

"Kaplowitz."

"Well, answer your name when it's called."

"Here," Kaplowitz said. "Yo." Kaplowitz looked at Aug and grinned delightedly.

Sergeant Garrison was going through the service records. He looked at Kaplowitz, down at the paperwork, then back at Kaplowitz again and extracted one of the sheets from the rest.

Billy Lawler continued with the roster.

"Muh . . . Moz . . . M'zetti!"

"Yeah." The sergeant's cigar rolled to the other side of his mouth and Mozetti added, "Present."

"Rust . . . Rusty . . ."

"Roost-ya-nek. Here." The first sergeant glanced up again.

"Awright," Lawler said, glancing sideways at Garrison as if fearful he might be interrupted. "Y'all go on back to the supply room, other end of this here building, an' get you some blankets, mattress covers, helmets, and rifles."

Rifles?

To *shoot* people. Aug looked at the others, but none of them seemed to have attached any particular significance to the moment. For the first time since he'd been inducted, it occurred to him that he had gotten himself involved in a *war*.

"Then go over yonder to that barracks"—Billy pointed—"an' find you an empty bunk."

Sergeant Garrison held up one huge hand. "Take your gear into the barracks,"—Aug had to lean forward to catch the muffled words—"then go on back to the supply room and get the other stuff." The sentence trailed away to an unintelligible murmur, as if the overstuffed sergeant had suddenly lost interest, his train of thought, or both.

Billy glanced at Garrison, apparently uncertain himself if the sergeant had finished. There being no more noises emanating from the mountain, Billy drew himself up and said, "Dismissed!"

They stooped to pick up their belongings and started away, the heavy canvas duffel bags swinging at their sides like huge pendulums.

"Hold it! Right *there*!"

Aug turned, staggering, with the rest of them. At the top of the orderly-room steps, feet spread wide, his flat-brimmed campaign hat tilted forward just above his eyes, stood an officer. The sun glistened off the captain's bars on his collar. The staghorn butt of a big six-shooter hung just below his left hip.

"Hot dog," Mozetti muttered, "it's Hopalong Cassidy."

The captain walked slowly down the steps and over to the battered floor lamp, still lying in the dust. He gestured at it with one bony thumb as he looked at Sergeant Garrison.

"What the goddam hell is this?"

Aug figured Crowder would squeal on him anyway.

"It's mine."

The captain jerked his head in Aug's direction, frowning and pursing his lips as if he were appraising this newly arrived problem and how best to deal with it.

"It's a going-away gift from my mother," Aug added, then immediately wished he hadn't.

Kaplowitz giggled.

The captain's lips stretched across tobacco-stained teeth in a grimace Aug mistook only momentarily for a grin. The captain took a step closer, impaling him with a cold stare.

He looked Aug up and down. "Nobody taught you to say 'sir' yet? Stand at *attention* when you're addressing an officer, soldier!"

Here we go again.

Aug straightened and brought his hands smartly down to his sides. Both barracks bags slipped off his shoulders and tumbled into the dirt. A self-conscious grin tugged at the corners of his mouth.

The captain's eyes narrowed. "You think something's *funny*?" Aug thought it best not to reply.

Gnarled hands on his hips, his jaw jutting forward, the captain stared Aug straight in the eye, then swung his gaze to include them all. "You may have been sissy-assed civilians *yesterday*, but starting right now you're in the *army*! And you're going to *act* like it. You're *soldiers*. You're not playing parlor games now. You're going over there—somewhere—and shoot some asses off! You're going over there to *fight*!" This news drew some startled expressions.

Aug opened his mouth, then changed his mind and closed it.

The captain returned to him.

"What's your name, soldier?"

"Rustyanek."

Captain Maxwell's eyes narrowed to menacing slits, gun ports in an armored turret. He looked over at the fallen floor lamp, back to Aug again, and turned to Sergeant Garrison. "Sergeant, see if you can find this civilian something to laugh about for a few days."

He gave Aug another hard look, then wheeled abruptly and marched back up the steps into the orderly room.

Sergeant Garrison sighed, his sagging face a picture of sadness. He took the cigar out of his mouth, providing an only slightly improved air passage.

"What *is* your name," he asked Aug.

"Roost-ya-nek." What did they want him to do, make one up? "It's Hungarian."

The first sergeant looked away and sighed again, his eyes tiny sparkles in folds of fat as he thumbed through the paperwork, looking for a corresponding name.

"Rooster Neck?"

Kaplowitz giggled.

Aug shrugged. "Close enough."

"Report to me in fatigues," the sergeant mumbled, still sorting through the papers. "Work clothes . . . soon as you get your stuff squared away." He waved them all toward the barracks.

Ponderously, the sergeant began the process of turning toward the orderly-room steps. He stopped and, glancing at Billy Lawler, tilted his head toward the floor lamp still lying in the dust.

"Get rid of that thing, Billy. I don't ever want to see it again."

Slowly, painfully, Garrison struggled up the steps and squeezed past the screen door into the orderly room. The captain was waiting for him, standing impatiently in the doorway of his tiny office

"Well, Sergeant? What do you think?"

Garrison removed his cigar and, turning it over in his pudgy fingers, studied the soggy mass carefully. "One fuckup—two, probably. One brownnoser and one . . ." He failed to come up with an appropriate description for Cloony and gave up. "The rest of them . . ." He shrugged.

"You think any of 'em can shoot?"

The sergeant again looked over the one service record he'd extracted from the rest.

"I don't know," he mumbled, "but one of 'em can type."

CHAPTER SIX

☆ ☆

"LOOKIT there, Rooster. Damn, if that don't look just like mine."

"If that looked like yours," Aug snorted, "they'd put you in Special Services. Or in a carnival."

Hodge grunted and held the peeled potato up for closer inspection, turning it to one side and then the other. The way he'd carved it, Aug conceded, it *did* kind of look like a dong. Except that it was bent in the middle and almost a foot long.

One whole side of Hodge's head was marbled scar tissue. Most of his left ear was gone, and his left shoulder was slightly drawn up, which caused his hand on that side to hide some, up his cuff, when he stood at attention.

It was the result of a fifty-five-gallon drum exploding, up in the woods behind his home, while he had his head down next to it, stoking the fire.

His father told the sheriff they were drying the drum out to use it for a water barrel.

Aug reached for another misshapen potato. "Here." He tossed it to Hodge. "This one looks like a pair of balls."

They had been peeling spuds, sitting on the back steps behind the mess hall for nearly two hours. It seemed to Aug that he'd been on KP, latrine duty, or some other work detail for six weeks, ever since his arrival at Piebald.

"Rooster Neck, you're a first-class fuckup," Sergeant Bleeker had advised him. "You don't get straightnin' up, by God, I'm gonna personally run your ass right up the flagpole. You hear? You *hear*?"

"Hear *what*, Sergeant?" Aug had turned as if looking for the source of whatever it was Bleeker was hearing.

It was simple diversion. Or survival, maybe.

"You shouldn't tease that dumb little shit like that," Mozetti counseled, only half meaning it. "Man's got a brain like a mop." But irritating Buck Sergeant Bleeker had become Aug's career objective.

He had achieved a career high just that morning with the platoon's response to Bleeker's break-of-day wake-up call.

"Awright! On your feet! Hit the floor! Snap shit!"

The little sergeant had come screeching down the aisle in his customary manner, snapping on the barracks lights, blowing his whistle, kicking bunks, snatching blankets off recumbent bodies. "Let's go, goddammit! Gitcher ass outside!"

Aug had sat up in his cot, put his head back, and yelled, "Say good morning to the sergeant, boys!"

And as one, as he had carefully guided, bribed, rehearsed them—pleaded with them—for three nights running, both floors of the barracks had chanted back in unison.

"Good . . . *morn*ing . . . ass . . . hole!"

That was *good*. That was better even than the ants and honey in Bleeker's footlocker, far better than the Mexican hot pepper in the coffee cup or the boot polish in the toothpaste. Aug picked up another potato and smiled, savoring the triumphs.

Hodge pridefully finished peeling and shaping the testicles and, impaling them with a wooden match dug out of a pocket, attached them to the back end of the potato penis.

"By God, Rooster. That's like starin' at m'self in the mirror. An' that's a fact."

They looked up to find Second Lieutenant Michaels standing there regarding Hodge's handiwork.

"I wouldn't worry about it," Michaels said. "In cold weather, mine shrinks up like that, too."

And he turned and walked on.

Hodge grinned and slapped his knee. He liked Michaels. "*His* shrinks up like that, too. Y'hear that?"

"That lieutenant," Hodge said fondly, "completely don't give a shit. An' that's fer damn sure, Rooster."

Rooster. First Sergeant Garrison's initial mispronunciation of Rustyanek had immediately been shortened and adopted by the company as Aug's second nickname. He didn't mind. In fact, he sort of liked it.

The nickname "Aug" was the product of a lively family argument eighteen years earlier over what to christen the first man-child born in town to the Rustyanek clan, even though his father had insisted it was nobody else's goddam business.

Grandmother Karel had made up her mind he was going to be a priest, and she came up with the name Gregory. She had known a nice priest by that name, she said, back in Kecskemét.

Aug's father said the hell with that, including the name Gregory.

Aug's mother had held out for a while for Bernard, in honor of her eldest brother. But his father said that reminded him of one of those fat dogs with a keg of liquor under its chin, and as a matter of fact, so did her brother.

After a series of negotiations, his parents finally settled on the name Gerald. But when his uncle Yuro came up to the Pear Street hospital for a visit, the day after Aug was born, Old Lady Sanford, who worked at the desk downstairs, asked him, "How come the family named him Harold?"

"It's not Harold," Uncle Yuro told her firmly, "it's Gerald."

Old Lady Sanford said, "Oh." And when Uncle Yuro went upstairs, she took her pencil and erased the H and made it a J.

And that's how come, according to the records at the Sonoma County Courthouse—and now the army's—his first name was listed as Jarold. When Aug's father found out about it, he was going to make them change it, but his mother said he should just leave it alone. She thought Jarold was kind of swanky for a town that small.

Meanwhile, during the initial name-the-baby debate, his uncle Nick had suggested, "Why not call him August? That's when the little bugger was born." The rest of the family started calling him that, sort of as a joke and then, over the years, just kept it up. When he got old enough to go out and play, the kids in the neighborhood shortened it to Aug. Nobody ever called him Jarold.

Hodge was still admiring his genital sculpture.

"Maybe," he speculated, "we could get Cleary to serve this to Bleeker. Jus' like it is."

Cleary was mess sergeant.

"C'mon, Hodge." Aug got up from the steps and tossed the last of the peeled potatoes into one of the big stainless-steel tubs sitting next to them. "Let's get this mess inside before Cleary forgets what's for supper."

"He wouldn't never forget the taters." Hodge shook his head firmly. "Cleary puts taters in the fuckin' fruit salad."

He tenderly laid his creation inside one of the tubs and, with a protesting groan, got up to help Aug carry them inside.

"We oughta save us a mess of them peelin's," he said, "an' get some white lightnin' started."

"Can you make that out of potato peels?" Aug had heard a lot about "mountain dew," but had never tasted any.

"Sheee-it." Hodge waved the question aside. "You make it with peelin's, corncobs, door hinges, whatever you got. Damn revenooers kicked a still apart up behind this old coot's place one time an' found a dead squirrel floatin' aroun' in there." He waggled his head appreciatively. "By God, that was *good* squeezin's."

Half dragging the two tubs between them, they struggled through the back door into the mess hall kitchen.

A skinny, dark-haired youth called to Aug from the sink.

"Hey! *Professore! Cosa fa?*"

Aug grinned at the little Italian P.O.W. and shrugged. *"Niente. Lavorare."*

Amador Batinelli had been a private in the Italian army for three years, since he was sixteen. Like many of his fellow *soldatis*, he had been delighted to be captured by the Americans during an obscure, short-lived battle west of Algiers. He worked happily now, and safely, in the 575th mess hall, freed from the tedium in the compound each day to wash and scour pots and pans.

He called Aug *professore* because Aug was trying, without a great deal of success, to teach him English. In turn, Aug had picked up a few halting words of Italian.

"Hey, Batinelli." Aug helped Hodge set the tubs down and called the Italian over with a move of his head. Batinelli came away from the sink, smiling broadly, wiping his hands on a towel.

"*Sì?*"

Aug pointed. Seated alone at a table at the far end of the mess hall was Sergeant Bleeker. Bleeker had his head down, gnawing at a bologna and cheese sandwich.

"*Verrry* important man," Aug said.

Batinelli's face went blank. "*Non capisco.*"

Aug indicated Bleeker again. "Very *importante.*"

Batinelli looked at Bleeker, then back at Aug. "*Sì?*"

"*Sì.* Sergeant Ass . . . hole."

"Sar-geant . . ."

"Asshole."

"Az-ho."

"*Hole.* Ass-*hole.*"

Batinelli grinned. "*Sì.* Sar-geant . . . Az-hole."

"*Primo. Very* good." Aug motioned toward Bleeker and pantomimed Batinelli walking over and saluting him. " 'Good *morning*, Sergeant Asshole.' " He pointed at Batinelli. "You. 'Good morning, Sergeant Asshole.' "

"Good Mor-neeng." Obviously, Batinelli understood the merit in buttering up Sergeant Asshole, but that was a lot of words to handle. He made a couple of halfhearted attempts, then grinned and shrugged, pointing at himself. "No fuck-eeng good."

Aug laughed and clapped him on the shoulder.

"You got *that* one down perfect, Batinelli." He shrugged. "Another day, maybe."

"*Rooster!*"

Mess Sergeant Cleary jerked a thumb toward the rear of the kitchen. "Hop on a mop. Goddam floors look like a pigpen around here."

Cleary was a huge man, built in the classic proportions of army mess sergeants—jowls, fat protruding lips, and potbelly.

Aug turned as directed. *"È questo il libro rosso?"* he muttered.

Batinelli looked confused. Sergeant Cleary's face flamed. He took a menacing step forward.

"You cussin' me out in guinea?"

"Just practicing my Italian, Sergeant." Aug turned to find the mop, a faint smile tugging at his lips. "All I said was, 'Is this the red book?' " It didn't matter what the words were; it was the way you said them that counted.

Chaplain Appleton was startled to be confronted by Blackie Sifko as he hurried down the steps of the chapel. It was his first experience, being saluted with just a thumb and little finger.

"Good morning, soldier . . . afternoon." The chaplain had a date to play Ping-Pong with one of the nurses from the hospital, and he hoped this fellow with the crooked smile wasn't going to keep him.

"Afternoon, Cap'm." It was a first for Blackie, too. He wasn't certain how you addressed a preacher with captain's bars on his shoulders. "I jus' thought you orter know you got a Eye-tie up on your roof." He pointed up with his little finger.

"An eye tie?" The chaplain looked up at the front of the chapel. What was this fellow talking about?

"What are you saying? An eye tie?" It suddenly came to him. "You mean an Eye-tal . . . an Italian?" Blackie nodded. "Up on the roof?"

"Stark naked," Blackie said. He followed the distraught chaplain out into the middle of the road where the roof of the chapel could be better observed.

"My God."

The fellow was absolutely correct. There *was* a naked person up on the roof. With a bottle in his hand, singing loudly.

He looked at Blackie accusingly. "How did he get up there?"

Blackie shrugged expansively. "Beats the . . . uh, beats me. I was jus' comin' from the hospital, gettin' my penicillin shot, when I seen him up there."

Chaplain Appleton chose to ignore the reference to the penicillin shot. He didn't think he wanted to know what it was for.

Up on the roof, the soloist was struggling to his feet, teetering on the sharp ridge.

"How do you know he's Italian?" It perhaps was not the most pressing problem to solve at the moment, but there was nothing the chaplain could see—and he could see *everything*—that suggested foreign citizenship.

"Sheee-it," Blackie chuckled. "Beg your pardon." He glanced quickly away from the chaplain's frown. "That's ole Maggiori, what pours beer at the PX."

It was apparent that "ole Maggiori" had poured himself a few, too. He had managed to climb to his feet now and, swaying from side to side, arms outflung like a fledgling tightrope performer, he made his way along the ridge to the steeple and leaned heavily against it. He was carefully negotiating the crossing of one ankle over the other when he discovered his audience in the road below.

He was delighted. With a wide grin, bending forward at the waist, he raised his bottle in salute. Blackie recognized it as a bottle of Three Feathers.

"Hey!" Maggiori called down to them. *"Buon giorno! Cosa si fa?"* It had been a wonderful idea, climbing up here for the view. It was a fine day, and the hot sun felt good on his freckled skin. Inside the tiny access door leading back into the steeple, he could see his shorts and undershirt draped over the top rung of the ladder. He had pulled his shoes and socks off after climbing out onto the roof, and they had immediately slid down the steep slope and dropped out of sight on the far side. He shrugged. *"Cosa mi importa?"*

"How are we going to get him down from there?" the chaplain groaned. He pressed both hands to his mouth and craned his head back as he watched Maggiori tilt another generous dose from the bottle.

Blackie wasn't buying any of that "we" getting him down. He wasn't climbing up there after that crazy bastard.

One of the onlookers down there, Maggiori could make out fuzzily, was a man of the cloth. The one waving his arms.

"Quando ce un'altra messa?" he yelled down to him. As long as he was here, he might as well attend the next service. Receiving no reply, he shrugged, drained the final portion from the bottle, and tossed it end over end into the air behind him. Glittering in the sunlight, it bounced once near the edge of the roof, then somersaulted off in the general direction of his shoes and socks.

"If it was Cap'm Maxwell," Blackie offered, "he'd prob'ly knock the sumbitch off'n there with a fire hose."

The fire department. Long ladders! Of course!

Chaplain Appleton fled up the stairs into the chapel.

While he was shouting into the telephone, trying to convince a skeptical sergeant at the fire station that this really *was* the chaplain and there really *was* a naked Italian up on the roof, Maggiori tired of his perch. The hot shingles were beginning to burn his feet, and besides, he had to drain his bladder. Scratching his testicles industriously, he contemplated a golden arc from the steeple to the road below, then thought better of it.

The soldiers from the fire station met him, bare ass first, as he reached the bottom of the ladder.

CHAPTER SEVEN

☆ ☆

COLONEL Ratnekof looked thoroughly pissed off.

"Captain, I have a report here from the base hospital concerning destruction of a window and—"

"Yes, sir. I'm aware of it."

"You're aware of it." The colonel stopped pacing and looked up from the paperwork in his hands. "Good. You're aware that a full can of *beer* ... was apparently fired from the flagpole cannon yesterday evening and—"

"Yes, sir. One of the replacements from California. On the cannon detail."

"And what is *his* story?"

"He denies it."

"It was that wise-ass what's-his-name," the captain muttered to himself. When he got back to the company, he was going to land all over that smart-alecky son of a bitch.

"According to this report," Colonel Ratnekof said, resuming his pacing, "the *projectile* shattered a window, destroyed a wooden rack of urine specimens, and scattered glass, paperwork"—he looked up—"and gonorrhea cultures all over the laboratory."

"Yes, sir. It's just that proving the beer can came out of the cannon is—"

"The cannon was pointed right at the goddam hospital, for crissake! The lab technician heard the boom and ..."

The captain grimaced. "Yes, sir."

The colonel dropped the paperwork onto his desk and sat

down in his chair. Outside his window, the sun was beginning to fade, the shadows lengthening.

"Captain, you and that unit of yours are getting to be a royal pain in the ass. And don't give me that 'Who, me?' look. The gang fight at the PX last week and, the week before, that warrant officer getting beat up in town, damn near killed . . ."

The Oso County sheriff had called the 575th to see if the captain would stage an inspection "to see if any of your men maybe were in a fight last night."

The captain, the sheriff reported, had sounded insulted. "Any of my men been in a *fight*? This is a rough outfit, Sheriff. Probably every son of a bitch in this outfit was in a fight last night."

They never did identify the guilty parties. Nobody liked warrant officers anyway.

"Colonel, we're the only combat-ready outfit in—"

"Look." The colonel pointed a finger, his face growing red. "Knock off that 'combat-ready' crap. That bunch of cripples isn't ever going to see combat and you know it. You and I aren't going to, either. Nobody in this whole goddam camp is. And you know what? That's fine with me. I *like* it here. My wife likes it here. It won't offend me at all if I stay right here until the goddam war is over."

"That's your choice, Colonel. Mine is to—"

"I *know* what your choice is. The whole *camp* knows. You keep sending in those ridiculous requests for transfer, for shipment overseas, and you know what? I approve and forward every one of them. I hope you *do* make it. Life here might be a hell of a lot easier."

The captain clamped his mouth shut. The supercilious no-good son of a bitch.

"But in the meantime, Captain, while you're waiting for your invitation from General Marshall, I would consider it a personal favor—I would *strongly suggest*—that you and that bunch of troublemakers find a way to stay the hell out of my hair! Do I make myself clear?"

He did.

Seething, the captain stomped out of the headquarters building, climbed into his jeep, and headed back toward the company area. On his way past the cannon, he noticed someone had faced it around to point out toward the main gate. He turned left at the chapel and to the right again at the PX. Up ahead, across the parade ground, lay the grim, high fences of the compound. It was already growing dark. The 575th had the duty tonight.

In both compounds, for the Germans and Italians alike, the prisoners were divided into companies, each unit with a double row of barracks, four on a side, facing in on a latrine and a combination mess hall and recreation room. He could see a spirited volleyball game going on in the Italians' enclosure.

As the captain's jeep went past, Private Gino Quartarolli walked into B Company's mess hall and asked Cattaneo, the cook, for some empty tins to clean his paintbrushes in. Quartarolli was assigned to maintenance inside the compound.

Cattaneo, who wasn't all that fond of Quartarolli, asked him what he was doing in the kitchen with a can of paint thinner, and Quartarolli told him he was planning to pour it into the spaghetti sauce to improve the taste.

They had had previous discussions about the content and appeal of Cattaneo's spaghetti sauce.

Quartarolli, who came from a village outside Livorno, was of the opinion that properly made sauce must include minced beef, tomatoes, and mushrooms, just like his mother, her mother and their *nonne* before that had always made it.

Cattaneo insisted the only way to prepare it—and that's the way *he* prepared it—was with eggs, diced ham, cheese, and lots of garlic. It wasn't much to get excited about, unless you were Italian.

That distinction became part of the discussion, too, this evening. Quartarolli, sniffing disdainfully, introduced the theory that Cattaneo wasn't really an Italian. The island of Sardegna, he pointed out, gesturing with his can of paint thinner, was as close to North Africa as it was to Italy. Certainly, Capo Carbonero was, where Cattaneo came from, and that, he said, accounted for his peculiar eating habits. He was an *African*.

Cattaneo countered with picturesque references to the Quartarolli family eating fungus dug from beneath cow manure and rotting tree stumps, and climaxed his presentation with a straight right frying pan to Quartarolli's chops.

Quartarolli set his can of paint thinner aside, snatched up a trimming knife, and prepared for surgery on Cattaneo, while the rest of the kitchen crew selected heavy pots and implements, chose sides, and enthusiastically joined the dispute. Quartarolli managed only two swipes, with no incisions, before it became apparent to everyone that he had chosen a poor resting place for his paint thinner, a very hot stove.

The can exploded like a mini napalm bomb.

Up in Tower Eight, just beyond the fence, Private Cloony was sitting on an upended apple box, his head bent over a pad of lined notepaper illuminated by a flashlight clamped beneath one arm.

"Its ben verry hot," he wrote, his pencil stub advancing in fits and jerks along the ruled lines, "but we got to march aroun any how." He took a deep breath and continued. "The captain says wer gong oversees iny day now."

Gradually Cloony became aware of the escalating noise level below the tower. Raising his head, he heard muffled shouts and what sounded like breaking glass and crockery, and the crump of heavy objects falling. Confused by this intrusion on his thought processes, he turned slowly and peered over the rough sill of the open window, his pencil still poised over the notepad.

At that instant, like an untidy projectile flung from a catapult, a writhing tangle of bodies hurtled through the screen door at the rear of B Company's mess hall, crashed heavily onto the porch, and in a welter of kicks, swinging fists, and shouted invective, bumped down the steps into the dirt.

Cloony was unsure what he should do. He reached for his rifle but stopped, mouth gaping, as another participant caromed out through one of the mess hall windows in a starburst of splintered wood and glass.

A dense black cloud of smoke began boiling out of the shattered window, and from the surrounding barracks in the compound, men came running, their excited shouts echoing off the buildings, mingling with the growing crackle of flames now evident within the mess hall.

Cloony turned away from the scene, his mind constricted by indecision. He covered his ears with his puffy hands, trying to shut out the clamor as he sorted through the agonizing alternatives confronting him. Finally he bent over his notepad again, his massive brow furrowed, his lips moving with each awkwardly scrawled letter: "I got . . . to go . . . now."

In the next tower down, Mozetti looked up from a tattered *Collier's* magazine to see combatants and spectators swirl out into the floodlit area near the fence. A rising plume of smoke was silhouetted against the flickering orange glow above the mess hall.

"Ho-leee *shit*!"

Mozetti's tower mounted a .30-caliber machine gun. Dropping his magazine, he swung the weapon around to bear and jacked a cartridge into the breech. Even more prisoners were milling around now in the brightening glow. Two of them were thrashing about on the ground near the fence. One of them appeared to be battering the other with a coffeepot.

Mozetti took a deep breath, murmured, "Shit . . . house . . . mouse," closed his eyes, and aimed a short burst into the cloud of smoke billowing above the fence line.

Aug was with the first steel-helmeted contingent led into the fray by Captain Maxwell. Two water-heavy fire trucks lumbered through the double gates behind them, the *braaap! braaap!* of their klaxons competing with shouts, police whistles, and the rising high-pitched whine of trucks bringing in reinforcements from all over the camp.

"Fix bayonets! Form wedges! Move straight into the bastards!" Captain Cadwallader Aloysius Maxwell had come to fight. Six-gun held high, jaw thrust forward, he plunged in, exhorting his troops into battle.

Aug heard the stuttering of intermittent machine-gun bursts added to the din and, up ahead, the growing roar of the flames. He reached up and snugged down his heavy steel helmet. Sirens keened in the night. Searchlights flickered on around the perimeter, swept back and forth along the fence lines, and stabbed into the shadows between the buildings.

But the enemy, Aug noted as his squad steamrolled through the jostling throng toward the fire, hardly seemed menacing. On the contrary, they appeared to be enjoying themselves immensely.

"Professore!" Aug turned to see Batinelli waving at him from the crowd, grinning and jumping up and down in delight as they swept past.

The unscheduled entertainment in B Company had drawn a charge en masse from throughout the Italian compound.

"Guarda! Guarda! C'e fuoco!"

"Cos' e che brucia?"

Several hundred enthusiasts from A Company arrived to help three hundred seventy B Company men carry sixteen red fire buckets. They were joined almost immediately by would-be bucket-carriers from C, D, and E companies. Some ran back to get buckets from their own barracks; more than a dozen competed to turn the handles of a half-dozen available faucets, while others fought for a better hold on the initial sixteen buckets. Intermittently, individual participants would break free from the pack, dash up to someone else, point at the flames, and yell something, waving their arms wildly.

Except for the lack of music, it occurred to Aug, it was a lot like the Pratalli-Fiallo wedding the previous summer at the picnic grounds.

"Closen up your ranks!" Sergeant Bleeker shrieked. "Move up, Anberger, goddammit!"

Appreciatively, the Italians moved aside to let them through, wherever it was they were going. *"Bene! Bene! Che eccitamento! Fantastico!"* A sight and a night to remember.

In a machine-gun tower down the line from Mozetti's, Cooper was fast asleep on the floor, propped up against the back wall with his shoes off, a beautiful grin widening across his glistening bridgework. Cooper was always falling asleep, in the shower, at the table in the mess hall, even standing in formation in the hot sun.

"Cooper," Blackie Sifko insisted, "could fall asleep chasin' a pig. An' that's a fact."

What he was chasing in his dreams on this particular evening was Una Mae Diller's tantalizing bare bottom, two white feather pillows bobbing just beyond his grasp as she scrambled, laughing, up the steep creek bank behind her daddy's barn. Una Mae wasn't wearing any drawers. Cooper didn't have his britches on. Just as she reached the top of the embankment, Una Mae grabbed for a handhold, missed, and started sliding down the precipitous slope toward him, her jiggling white cheeks looming larger, ever larger in the moonlight.

The clatter of nearby machine-gun fire dissolved the picture like steam above a kettle.

Cooper brought his head up groggily, blinking his eyes. Una Mae's daddy was shooting at him with a *machine gun*? Before he could get all the ingredients sorted out properly, he heard a second burst of fire.

"Somebody's attackin' this fuckin' place!"

He pushed his shoes aside, rolled cautiously to his knees, and, one hand groping behind him, found his steel helmet. The assault would be coming from the desert behind him.

Though untested by enemy fire, Cooper was no coward. He jammed his helmet down around his ears, took a deep breath, and came up fast, swinging the machine gun to the rear.

"Sheee-it!"

There was no window in the back wall.

Turning his head, he saw the fire down at B Company. He folded his arms across the top of his weapon and spit with emphasis. Whatever was going on down there was too far away, too many dumb asses running around in front of the fire to tell who was who. Enviously, he wondered what the men in the other machine-gun towers had found to shoot at.

He traversed his weapon to the left, scanning the darkened barracks buildings spread out in the compound below him. He pulled the bolt lever back and let it slide forward, injecting a cartridge into the breech.

Private Ruggieri walked out of the latrine, absentmindedly buttoning his fly.

Dang-dang-dang! Dang-dang-dang-dang-dang!

"*Dio!*" Ruggieri scurried back into the latrine, his fly still unbuttoned as, just outside the door, clanging steel-jacketed bullets sent a big refuse can leaping crazily into the night, battering it back into the shadows, kicking up tiny geysers of dirt around it.

From a dispute over spaghetti sauce, the ruckus in B Company had escalated into a major event. Everybody had come, including the two off-duty guard companies. But it was Captain Maxwell's party. He ranged behind the wedges of bayonets, waving his long-barreled six-shooter like a saber. He drove his squads into this throng of excited spectators, urging his men forward, then back again, as the crowd of onlookers adjusted obligingly to accommodate him.

Bobbing about in the midst of the throng, seeking a better vantage point, Private Amador Batinelli suddenly spotted Sergeant Bleeker standing alone on the barracks steps. Chortling over this unexpected opportunity, he struggled through the press of bodies to the foot of the steps, drew himself up, and saluted Bleeker smartly.

"Good mor-ning . . . Ser-geant Asshole!"

Bleeker swung wildly at him with his nightstick, lost his balance, and fell down the steps into a mud puddle.

Over the ascending clamor, Aug heard powerful engines gun and accelerate. Behind the blazing mess hall, far too late, the two fire trucks finally began pumping. Heavy streams of water battered the blackened skeleton of the building, set clouds of steam hissing into the air, and doused the pressing crowd with water and chunks of charred wood. One of the high-pressure hoses twisted loose from careless hands and, snapping about like a maddened serpent, smashed through the front window of one of the barracks, whipped out again, and was finally tackled and subdued by a jumble of sodden fire fighters and happy spectators.

Gradually the din subsided.

The flames were doused, the mess hall reduced to a soggy mass of ashes and blackened timbers. The spectators were shooed back to their barracks. Unit by unit, the helmeted troops moved out through the gates, chattering excitedly over this, their first confrontation with "enemy soldiers."

Aug was very pleased with himself. He had a war wound. He had cut his hand when he tripped over a fire hose, fell into the blackened remains of the mess hall, and encountered an exploded can of anchovies. Others proudly exhibited a scratch, a bruise, or a torn uniform they would write home about. Chattering animatedly, they clambered back into the waiting trucks. The party was over.

Captain Maxwell found Second Lieutenant Flowers about to board a jeep.

"I want a detail in the compound the rest of the night." He paused, organizing his battle plan on the spot. "Eight men walking in pairs. With ax handles."

"Ax handles?"

"Ax handles. I don't want any of these dumb bastards losing a weapon in there we'll have to go find. Tell 'em to beat on the head of any no-good son of a bitch they find sneaking around. These guinea bastards have any escape plans up their butts, now's the time they'll try it."

"Yes, sir, Captain. I'll get Sergeant Bleeker on it."

One last look at the now nearly deserted field of battle and the captain turned and strode off into the darkness.

The compound quickly became quiet again. Dark. Asleep.

Outside the fences, the 575th's guard truck slowly circled the perimeter, halting at each sentry post, at each tower, changing the guard, grinding ahead to the next post. Those who had gone on duty six hours earlier climbed down stiffly, tired after their extended shifts. Others climbed up the ladders and vanished inside. Big Sam Claybin had a girlie magazine hidden inside his shirt, Garnett a dollar harmonica.

The searchlight in Tower Five had been left on. The new occupant toyed with it briefly, sweeping its yellow-white beam across the darkened stockade, then switched it off. The guard truck moved on to Tower Six at the northwest corner.

The new sentry got out and looked up at the tower.

"Cooper?"

No answer. *"Cooper!"* Silence. *"Cooper, you sumbitch, you asleep up there?"*

In "The Alley" separating the Germans' stockade from the Italians', two new sentries started their measured pacing toward each other and back again.

In the small barracks behind the guard hut, Cloony sat on the edge of his cot in the dark, staring out a window at the starlit sky. He snapped on his flashlight, bent over his notepad, and wrote, "Wel."

After a moment, he turned the light off again and sat there in the darkness, waiting for the next words to come.

CHAPTER EIGHT

☆ ☆

AUG squeezed his eyes closed even tighter, gritted his teeth, drew his knees up to his chin, and, whimpering in despair, pulled the scratchy woolen blankets up over his ears.

But he could still hear the bugle.

And Bleeker.

"Up! Up! Hit the floor! C'mon, snap shit!" The lights flashed on, and Bleeker came down the aisle, popping his hands together, kicking footlockers, shaking corpses into semiconscious awareness.

"Outa there, Garnett! Move it, Anberger! Up! Up!"

Aug sat up stiffly and swung his feet over the edge of his cot. He groaned. With his eyes still clamped shut, he found his pants, hauled them up as far as his knees, and fell back onto his blankets again. All around him, limp figures in twisted olive-drab underwear were writhing, protesting, to near-vertical postures, like earthworms suddenly exposed to light by the turn of a shovel. Yawning, scratching, mumbling incoherently, they groped blindly for clothing, towels, shaving gear.

From a far corner came the protest: "What's the sense of gettin' up in the middle of the fuckin' night to eat breakfast 'fore a man can see his hand in front of his face?"

And from the opposite corner, the logic: "Cleary's afraid if we can *see* it we won't *eat* it."

Mess Sergeant Cleary was subject to continuing vilification for his choice of cuisine and its preparation.

"Cleary," Blackie maintained, "could spoil a pan of dishwater. An' that's a fact."

Aug tugged on one sock and then the other, and crammed his swollen feet into stiff boots reeking of sweat and dubbin. He picked up a towel, sniffed tentatively at it, and joined the tattered parade down the aisle and out into the chilled darkness to the latrine.

It was not a place to search for refinement.

"The hell kind of blades are these?"

"Marlins. My mother sent 'em to me with some cookies."

"Get a better shave with a fuckin' cookie."

"Sheee-zuss Christ! Flush it! Is that *you* over there, Kibby?"

"He couldna *et* that. Sump'n crawled up his ass an' died."

It was 4:45 A.M., nearly an hour before sunup, just like the morning before and the morning before that. The fact that many of them had been pressed into action the night before, facing flames and imagined perils in the Italian compound, earned them no holiday. That became even more apparent when, fifteen minutes later, they stumbled out of their barracks, stuffing shirttails in, fumbling with buttons and belt buckles, to find the captain standing there, feet spread wide, in the starkly lighted area in front of the orderly room.

"Oooh, shit. Bad news."

It was *always* bad news when the old man showed up for reveille.

Sergeant Bleeker, looking as if he'd been up for hours and couldn't wait to get started again, stepped importantly to his place, facing the company a few paces in front of the captain. Coming to attention himself, he swelled his chest and yelped, "Companeee . . . tensss-*hut*! Reee-*port*!"

"Firs' P'toon present an' accounted for!" It was an accounting based largely on optimism. Sergeant Howard *hoped* they were all there. His head ached too bad this morning to try counting.

"Secon' P'toon presen', cown for!" Sergeant Stoff sounded as if he had a mouthful of beer. His service record referred to a "shortened frenum lingua," after which someone had helpfully penciled in "tongue-tied."

"Third Platoon present an' accounted for!"

Bleeker pivoted about and saluted as he snapped his heels together. Click!

"All present an' accounted for!"

The captain jerked a salute back at him, acknowledging the routine report. "At ease!"

"Oooh, *nooo*!"

"Ho-leee . . ."

"Heeere we *go*."

In the cold hush before dawn, it wasn't necessary for him to raise his voice. "Fall out at oh-seven-hundred with weapons and full field packs." The deep shadows hid his sardonic grin. "We're going to take a little walk."

Muffled groans. Muttered protests.

"A-kin *ass*!"

"How come we're not goin' overseas this time?"

"We go overseas at night, asshole."

"Mother said there'd be days like this."

"Up all night with them fuckin' Eye-ties. I'm *tired*!" In West Virginia-ese, the word came out "tard."

But only a few would escape. Not those who had walked four-hour shifts in the compound with ax handles. Not those with minor injuries suffered in the melee. Not even Kaplowitz and Billy Lawler, whose respective attentions to typewriter and filing cabinet usually kept them safe in the orderly room.

"Old man's got a burr up his ass," Garnett declared.

"That's a fact."

There *were* those who would not participate, of course. First Sergeant Garrison had twenty-four years in, goin' on thirty, and as far as anybody could tell, Garrison didn't do *anything* he didn't want to. The longest hike the elephantine, cigar-chewing top kick ever made was to his 1939 Hudson every afternoon at sixteen hundred, when he drove over to the PX for a pitcher of beer and some hard-boiled eggs with his cronies. Mess Sergeant Cleary wasn't going. He had to plan destruction of the evening meal. PFC Maciel wasn't going. Maciel, the lucky bastard, was charge of quarters in the orderly room until oh-eight-hundred. Second Lieutenants Michaels and Flowers weren't going. Flowers and Second Platoon were still on guard detail, and Michaels hadn't come back from Tucson the previous evening.

First Lieutenant Isaac Bauman wasn't going, either. Lieutenant Bauman, a formerly successful gynecologist from Cleveland, was the company doctor. He presumably was reading medical journals somewhere—anywhere to avoid the captain—or had taken a Greyhound back to Cleveland. Nobody had seen him for two days.

"What's the merit in conducting sick call?" he wrote his wife, Sarah, "when this entire pitiful organization, including its commanding officer, is beyond treatment? What medication can you prescribe for idiocy?"

The most significant trauma he had treated to date, he informed Sarah, was a seared anus, the result of a fart-lighting competition one night—won hands down by Kibby. It was symbolic, he suggested, of his war effort.

He had long since given up on getting promoted. The only way he could make captain, he told Sarah, was if someone first made the captain a major, "and nobody's that stupid."

An hour after mess call, the bugle blew again, and while the rest of Piebald slept in, the 575th limped out of the company area in parade formation.

Aug eased his steel helmet back a little and sighed. His shoulders were already sore. In addition to his heavy rifle, he carried extra ammunition, a trenching tool, a blanket and shelter half, first-aid supplies, spare socks and underwear, mess gear, C rations, and a full canteen.

These were the essentials for a summer stroll through the desert with Captain Cadwallader Aloysius Maxwell.

The captain led his troops across the adjoining parade ground with yard-long strides, Bleeker scurrying beside the column on shorter legs, quickening the cadence count to keep up.

"Hut! . . . Hut! . . . Hut, toop, threep, foor!"

The captain paid no apparent attention to Bleeker's cadence. That was for those who followed. He strode ahead aggressively, head thrust forward, jaw set, as if he were leading an assault up a fortified hill, his colors flying behind him.

"Hut! . . . Hut! . . . Get in step, Kapalitz! Straightnin' up that rifle!"

Skipping along next to Aug, Kaplowitz tried to find the step, while using both hands to adjust the unfamiliar burden on his shoulder. "What's 'straightnin' up' mean?" He giggled, and Aug shook his head in resignation. Throughout the column, isolated helmets bobbed up and down out of rhythm with the rest. They identified a matched set of fallen arches, some enfeebling muscular or skeletal problem, or more likely, merely the owner's inability to set one foot down in front of the other in synchronization with anyone else. There was a lot of that.

Whenever the captain led the way, Aug noticed, the route of march through camp always brought the company past the headquarters building, directly beneath Colonel Ratnekof's window. As they neared the building this morning, the captain glanced back and, taking the cue, Bleeker raised his skreaky voice to a showier cadence count.

"Y'left! . . . Y'left! . . . Y'had a good home but y'left, right, left, right!"

It was a chant the captain remembered from that other war twenty-five years earlier.

"Count cadence," Bleeker shrilled. "Count!" And the platoons dutifully responded in a descending singsong, "One, two, three, four. One, two . . . three-four!"

It was a grand morning for a parade and a stellar performance, not at all dimmed by the teetering steps of the marchers or the disconnected stride of their grim-faced leader, who was again drawing ahead of them. All that was missing was the glitter and thunder of a sixty-piece marching band and a cheering crowd lining the way to a waiting troopship.

Colonel Ratnekof had to be impressed with the determined precision of the ranks, and with the obvious dedication of the company's commanding officer, following an arduous experience the night before in the compound.

Colonel Ratnekof, however, was not in his office. At that hour, no one was.

"Colummm llleft . . . hhharch!" The guide-on pivoted as smartly as he could without a big toe on his right foot, and the rest of the company followed him through the turn, hurrying to dress up their lines as they straightened out again and bore down on the main gate. The sentry there straightened and threw a halfhearted salute as the captain strode by, then modified it to a rigid middle finger for the rest of the company. He drew approximately sixty jabbing middle fingers in return.

"Up yours, asshole."

"Stick this."

On command, two outriders broke free from the column and trotted ahead to halt any traffic approaching on the highway. The captain marched straight across the road without looking left or right and, as the front rank reached the edge of the pavement on the far side, Bleeker sang out, "Route step!"

The company broke cadence immediately. Shifting weapons and snug straps to more comfortable positions, they began plowing ahead through deep sand and shoulder-high clumps of mesquite and greasewood.

"One line!" Bleeker clambered onto a small hummock of sand and rocks and stood there, glowering down the column, waving his arms like a traffic cop. "One line, gol dang it!"

The command was anticipated, but, for Aug, one of life's simpler pleasures was making Bleeker look bad.

As the soldier in front of him slowed to squeeze into single file, Aug blundered into him enthusiastically, then took two steps back. Behind him, one heavily burdened figure bounced clumsily off another, like sacks of potatoes piling up on a conveyor belt. The entire column was instantly thrown into disarray.

"Gollll . . . *dang* it!" Bleeker came down off his mound and flung himself into the tangle, grabbing and shoving, spitting like a cat in a dog fight.

"Move out! Hold it! Back up there!"

Aug promptly stopped, and Garnett happily piled into him from the rear a second time.

"Not *you*, Rooster Neck, you dumb ass!"

Garnett took the opportunity to stick his rifle out and goose PFC Cavender, and Cavender—"*Yiiii!*"—threw his rifle away and leaped into the middle of a greasewood bush, losing his helmet along the way.

"Garnett, you sumbitch! I'm gonna kick your butt!"

Kaplowitz was perhaps the only one in the maelstrom not trying to make things worse, but bumped off balance, he tripped over an exposed tamarisk root, grabbed wildly at a pack in front of him, missed, and tumbled over backward into a shallow depression. He waved his arms and legs helplessly in the air like an upended beetle. Aug stooped to roll him right side up.

"Is my nose bleeding?" Kaplowitz took his fingers away from his nose and inspected them fearfully. His eyeglasses dangled from one ear as he lurched from one knee to the other, trying to regain his feet. "I get nosebleeds real easy."

"You better get up," Aug said, "or Bleeker'll make something else bleed."

"Back in line, Karapitz! Move it out, Rooster Neck! Get your asses in gear!"

Slowly the line sorted itself out, the troops bitching half seriously, elbowing for position. They plunged forward again, slogging clumsily through the loose sand, straining to regain the pace. The column stretched out in uneven segments, starting and stopping, for more than one hundred yards, threading in and out amid the ragged vegetation, finally drawing in upon itself again like an elastic snake.

The sun had been up for more than an hour, and it was already beginning to get hot. Aug lifted his helmet and mopped his streaming brow with a forearm.

His shop teacher in high school, Old Man Morse, had always maintained, "Hiking is a very poor form of transportation," and Aug agreed with him. His boots felt as if they weighed ten pounds apiece.

In front of them, the captain strode resolutely ahead through the prickly underbrush, disdainfully sweeping aside twigs and foliage obstructing his path, stepping over small obstacles, only reluctantly detouring around patches of cactus and heavy stands of growth. If he had a specific objective in mind, it was not apparent to anyone else. He slid down into a dry river wash, churned across the sandy bottom, and clambered up the far side without looking back or slowing his gait, back straight as a rifle barrel, arms swinging loose at his sides, left hand brushing the butt of his old six-gun. He carried an officer's pack, lighter and more compact than the bulky loads weighing the men down. A small stain of wetness spreading just below it was his only acknowledgment of the heat and strenuous pace. His mind was on his only real objective.

This bunch of no-good sonsabitches was already the best-trained unit in camp, and he was going to make them *better* trained. How could Colonel Ratnekof not be aware of that? He had to be aware of it. They were ready to ship out—any dumb bastard could see that. What sense did it make to keep them here, standing guard duty over a pen full of dagos and krauts who had *surrendered*, for crissake, when they could be over there *shooting* some of the sonsabitches?

He ducked under a low-hanging cottonwood limb, skirted a clump of prickly pear cactus, and set his sights on a red-brown crag of lava on the near horizon.

He should have had Lieutenants Flowers and Michaels out here, too, and Bauman, the little Jew bastard. Bauman thought all he had to do was hold sick call every morning and give somebody a pill or stick a needle in his ass. Flowers, the goddam fairy, still had the guard, and Michaels, the bandy-legged little son of a bitch, hadn't come back from whoring around Tucson. He grinned. Michaels was a good-looking little son of a bitch. The little runt probably had his dick stuck in something right now, all the way up to his armpits.

A mile out from the main gate, Garnett's green fatigue uniform, like everyone else's but the captain's, was soaked through, sweat streaming out from under his helmet liner, dripping off his nose and chin. He hitched up his pack to relieve the pain in his shoulders.

"Hey, Hamburger. You know what LSMFT stands for?"

Anberger was already so tired he considered not even responding.

"Lucky Strike . . . means fine tobacco."

"Uh-uh." Garnett tried to spit at a darting lizard, but his mouth was too dry. "Limited Service, more fuckin' training."

Anberger shifted his rifle to the other shoulder, wiped at his face with his sleeve, and kept plodding ahead.

Aug half turned to look behind him. Mozetti had dropped back a few yards, but was still coming. Behind him, Kaplowitz was lurching from one side of the trail to the other, his face flaming red, eyes glazed behind his thick lenses. Aug mopped at his forehead again and struggled on. His chest hurt, his shoulders ached, and his legs felt like cast-iron pipes.

A few yards up the line, Billy Lawler was miserable. Both arms were numbed by the constricting web straps of his pack, he had a blister on one heel, and his jock itch was beginning to heat up. He wasn't wearing any undershorts, and the sweaty crotch of his fatigue uniform rubbed against his inflamed scrotum like sandpaper. Billy was trying to work up enough nerve to step out of line and plead his bad knee.

He didn't have a bad knee. That is to say, he didn't *actually* have a bad knee, but his service record said he did, and that was supposed to keep him out of this kind of shit. That was one of the advantages of working in the orderly room; you could add anything you wanted to to your service record. All you had to do was type it in when nobody was looking. Billy had already awarded himself an expert rifleman's rating.

Billy, Garnett said, "couldn't hit a cow in the ass with a banjo," but he bought himself an expert badge at the PX and wore it, pinned above his breast pocket alongside a good conduct ribbon, whenever he went into town. Everybody knew he hadn't earned the badge.

He had his head down and was trudging along mechanically, one foot, then the other, blindly following on the heels of the man in front of him. The man in front made a quick left around a tall stand of cholla cactus, and Billy walked right into it.

"Owwwww! Fuck! Ohhhh, *shit!*"

He dropped his rifle into the sand and danced up and down on his toes, his hands fluttering above the clusters of bright yellow spines biting deeper into his crotch with every bounce. Sergeant Crawford grabbed him from behind and yelled at him to stand still, while his delighted companions gathered around, offering little help but ample commentary.

"Hey, Billy's growin' flowers on his britches!"

"Jus' grab aholt of 'em, Billy. They'll come loose with yer cock."

"Maybe your cock'll swell up. That ain't all bad."

Crawford forced him to stand still and handed him a small pocket comb. "Slip it under the spines an' lift. That's the only way to get 'em off. They got little barbs on the end of each one."

Delicately, ooohing and wincing with each move, Billy managed to pry the clusters off the front of his pants, tears running down his cheeks to join the sweat dripping from his chin. Sergeant Crawford was the only one who offered sympathy. The others were just glad of the excuse to rest.

Crawford accepted his comb back, grinning as he watched Billy exploring his front for more spines.

"They call that stuff jumpin' jack. You just get close to it and it jumps at you."

"How 'bout jumpin' Billy?" Garnett offered helpfully. "Hey, Billy," he said, brightening, "now you can get yourself an expert *cactus* badge, too."

"Awright!" Bleeker glanced nervously toward the captain, who had stood nearby without comment. "Let's move it out! . . . You're havin' such a good time," Bleeker growled at Garnett, "maybe you'd like to do this double-time."

Reluctantly they worked themselves back into line and resumed the march, Billy keeping his head up now, giving all forms of plant life plenty of passing room. His plans for his bad knee were forgotten. Every few minutes, he dropped one hand to his crotch, certain he could feel cactus poison spreading through his wounded genitalia.

A mile farther on, they came to the layered face of an outcropping of red rock topped by a thin layer of rice grass and, at the far end, the magnificent yellow bloom of a palo verde plant. The captain stopped and growled at Bleeker, "Give 'em a rest before they break into tears."

"Ten minutes! Fall out! Smoke 'em if you got 'em!"

They needed no further encouragement, some collapsing in the sun on the spot or crawling painfully into the narrow strip of shade offered by the outcrop.

Aug sat down heavily in the shade, gratefully leaning back

on his pack, his arms flopped outward, his legs, numb from the hips down, straight out in front of him. Mozetti crashed to earth a few feet away.

"Oooh . . . *piss*!" Mozetti said. "Call the fuckin' ambulance. I can't go another step."

Aug unhooked his canteen to get a drink, and immediately others did the same, but before he could swallow any water, the captain's voice cut across them like sandpaper.

"One swallow!" he barked. "It's about time you learned some water discipline. All you need to do is wet your throat, not *drown* yourself."

"Sheee-it," somebody muttered. "I'm so full of sweat, I'd drown somebody if I fell on him."

"You're so full of shit, you'd smother him."

"There any snakes around here?" somebody asked. "I can't stand snakes."

"I read in the paper," Kaplowitz said, "about some man camping out in Arkansas who woke up with a big rattler coiled up on his chest, sleeping."

"I wake up with a fuckin' rattler on *my* chest," Mozetti said, "I'd be *gone*. That sumbitch'd be sleeping six inches up in the air."

Laughter.

"Wouldn't that be something?" Mozetti said. "Stick your ass in the goddam army—fuckin' *war*—and instead of getting shot by some son of a bitch in Germany or Japan, you end up in fuckin' Arizona and get killed by a goddam snake."

Getting killed in the war.

Aug was patriotic enough, he guessed. He wasn't *un*patriotic. But the way he saw it, there wasn't *anything* worth getting *killed* for.

He remembered his uncle Nick telling him that.

Uncle Nick had been a U.S. marshal and Aug's only hero. When Aug was just a little guy, Uncle Nick had taught him how to whistle through his fingers, how to shoot a BB gun, and how to throw a spiral with a football. Once he brought him a live king snake as a pet, but his father made him turn it loose after he stuck it in his sister's bed one night as a joke.

When Aug was about eight, he got his first bicycle. It was secondhand, but it was a shiny red "Monkey Wards" Hawthorne with balloon tires and a horn, and one day, while riding it, he almost got hit by the vegetable truck right in front of the house. He always rode his bike in the street; everybody knew that. There weren't any sidewalks. But when his father came home and heard about it, he made him lock the bike up in the garage for a week.

Aug would never forget. He was sitting out on the front steps that night, feeling sorry for himself, and Uncle Nick came out, sat down beside him, and draped a big arm across his shoulders.

"Everything gets to looking a little brown sometimes," he said, giving Aug a squeeze. "It happens to everybody. But you're going to find out when you get older that, looking back, there wasn't anything that was really worth getting all upset about. It all works out. And there's *nothing*—remember that"—and he jerked a big thumb out at the street—"there's nothing worth getting killed for."

That was a Saturday night. The next Tuesday morning Uncle Nick walked up to a house in San Francisco to serve some kind of papers, and the guy inside shoved a twelve-gauge shotgun out a little window in the front door and blew Uncle Nick's head clean off his shoulders.

So much for things worth getting killed for.

"Awright! Field strip them cigarettes! Let's go, on your feet! Off yer ass, Anberger. Let's hit it!"

The captain led them across and down the face of a broad slope, the men slipping and sliding behind him on the loose surface, grabbing for handholds in the sparse vegetation, scattering showers of small rocks ahead of them. He managed to reach the bottom of the incline without falling and turned and set his sights again on the majestic bulwark of red lava looming above the desert floor a mile or so ahead.

Halfway back in the column, Aug swallowed with great difficulty, his mouth and throat dry. It was getting hot for damn sure now. There was no breeze down in the draw. He shrugged his shoulders in the web straps. His pack felt like a hot stove.

The captain picked up his pace a little, a move detected immediately by those following.

"The fuck's he doing', chasin' rabbits?"

"He see sump'n up there I don't?"

"You fellers just go ahead without me. I think I'll stop off for a beer."

"Shit, a beer and a piece of ass'd kill me."

The sun climbed steadily in front of them, a relentless white-hot flare sucking the color out of the sky, glaring off the bleached rocks in the dry washes. The heat crowded in behind it. It filled the lungs and nostrils, making it difficult to breathe, much less tramp through the loose sand, rocks, and underbrush pressed down by packs and heavy weapons.

A tiny kangaroo rat hesitated in the pale shadow of a fish-hook cactus and watched the strange procession troop by.

"Keep moving, Krapalitz! Closen-up that gap!"

"Oooh, I *am* getting a nosebleed."

CHAPTER NINE

☆ ☆

THERE was one seeming incongruity in Captain Maxwell's abrasive, apparently single-minded personality. It was commonly—*proudly*—acknowledged in the 575th's barracks that "that ole bastard gets more ass'n any man in this outfit."

Given the fervor of his troops in this arena, the legend might not have been justified, but there was no denying the captain's predisposition toward the opposite gender.

Showered, shaved, and changed into fresh suntans, he strode out of bachelor officers' quarters and climbed into his old Dodge coupe. The bay rum could be smelled ten yards away.

He started the engine and sat there for a few moments, frowning as he depressed the gas pedal and let it up again, listening to the noise rising and falling behind the fire wall.

Clack-clack-clack-clack-clack-clack-clack-clack!

The goddam old wreck had a hundred thousand on it, he figured, and the piston slap, or whatever the hell it was, was getting worse. He grunted. It could have a hundred and *fifty* thousand on it. That crooked son of a bitch in Oakland probably turned the numbers back. He stabbed at the accelerator once more, wincing at the clattering response, then shifted into reverse and backed away from the building. A cloud of pale blue smoke eddied out from under the back bumper as he headed up the deserted street.

The sentry at the main gate was lounging in the open doorway of the guard shack. He condescended to pull himself into some semblance of attention as the captain's car approached.

The man's cartridge belt was stained and his boots poorly polished. His uniform looked as if it had been wadded up in the bottom of a barracks bag. The captain's foot reached for the brake pedal, and he opened his mouth to make some comment, but changed his mind. Screw him. Those sloppy bastards just made the 575th look better. He answered the soldier's careless salute with a perfunctory wave, drove out onto the highway, and turned to the right, toward town.

It had been a long day. The temperature had climbed above 115 degrees. It was past seven o'clock now, the sun just a red afterglow in the west, but it was still over a hundred. He had marched them at least twenty miles, he guessed, circling around to the north behind Pima Peak, crossing the highway again, and coming up on the camp from the back. Three men had been left at the highway for pickup by the medics. Blisters. He snorted. They'd find out what real blisters looked like before they shipped out of here.

That Jew-boy, Kaplowitz, got a nosebleed. A cream puff. Wouldn't say shit if he had a mouthful of it. An improvement in the orderly room, though. At least he could add without counting his fingers. Better than that dumb hillbilly, Lawler. He grinned, remembering Billy dancing around with the cactus in his pecker. Jesus. What they had given him to work with.

Next time he'd get Lieutenant Flowers out there, too. The goddam sissy would probably stop and let 'em rest every two or three miles. What he ought to do is set up an ambush out there and let 'em walk into it. He considered that possibility. Why hadn't he thought of it before? Bury a couple of fifties, camouflaged, and shoot their asses off with blanks. That'd show the no-good sonsabitches. Ambush. That was a hell of a good idea.

Hot as it had been, he'd enjoyed his role in the day's march. Fifty-four years old and he could walk every one of them into the ground. He liked to show the bastards, even though hiking bothered his knee sometimes. He massaged it with one hand, remembering that moonless night on a deserted point of Lake Ontario shoreline.

* * *

A crested roadrunner, head bent low, darted across the highway in front of him and into the brush on the other side. He was looking forward to a relaxing evening and some good rye whiskey. Not that Manny ever *had* any good rye.

Manny Freitas, a Portagee refugee from the apricot orchards south of Oakland, was the proprietor of the El Rancho Café, one of three saloons in Piebald and, by unwritten rule, the one set aside for officers. The enlisted men drank and chased whores, when they could find any, at the Lucky Corral, or the Top Hat, up at the other end of the street. Other than getting drunk or starting a fight, there wasn't a whole hell of a lot else to do in Piebald for entertainment.

The first landmark, coming into town, was the blue and yellow Richfield station on the left side of the highway. Just beyond it, separated by a couple of weed- and junk-infested vacant lots was the El Rancho Café, its name spelled out in flowing red and green neon script. It had a flat roof with a fringe of Spanish tile around it. The two square windows on the near side were tipped up on their corners, like fat diamonds set in the white stucco. Architectural design, Piebald style.

There were only four cars in the graveled parking lot tonight— a couple of faded pickup trucks, a Chevy, and a yellow Olds convertible with a black top. Maxwell waited for a pickup towing a high-sided cotton trailer to pass, then swung into the lot, tires crunching the gravel, and parked next to the convertible.

The lot was illuminated by the El Rancho's glaring neon sign. The R was out. El ancho. Somebody had told him *ancho* was the Spanish word for "wide" or "broad." The Broad. That wasn't bad; he'd had a fair amount of success there. He'd also heard it referred to as El Raunchy. Pretty close, too. He climbed out and checked his reflection in one of the convertible's dusty windows.

On duty or off, the captain prided himself on his uniform— shoes and brass gleaming, razor-sharp creases, tie folded in between the third and fourth shirt buttons. Tonight he was wearing the narrow, folded cloth cap the men in the barracks called a cunt cover. He checked the silver captain's bars on it for smudges.

"A woman's voice in the apartment below . . . a clarinet is

moanin' mellow and low ..." The big Wurlitzer jukebox greeted him as he pushed past the heavy wooden door.

There were only four or five customers at the bar. His eyes went immediately to the woman.

She was a good-looking blonde, bare-shouldered in a vivid red and white striped sundress, and instinctively, he connected her with the yellow Oldsmobile. She was talking to an officer he knew casually, a major attached to Supply.

Up at the far end of the bar, three sunburned ranchers in straw cowboy hats and long-sleeved white shirts were hunched over their beer bottles in quiet conversation.

The blonde and the major turned as the captain came through the door, and the major, in an apparent effort to appear suave, raised one hand in careless acknowledgment. "Evening, Cad."

"Well ... good evening." He fed the major a big smile, clapped him warmly on the shoulder, and as if he hadn't noticed the woman, slid easily onto the stool between them.

The major was visibly distressed. "Uh, Cad, I was talking to—"

"Oh, *excuse* me." Maxwell swiveled around to face the blonde, effectively blocking the major's view. "I didn't mean to interrupt." The hell he didn't. "I'm Cad Maxwell." *Good*-looking woman.

"Hi, I'm Sharon Stevens." He'd bet that was more information than the major had managed to get. She smiled broadly, obviously amused by the joust between the two. "Cad. That's an interesting name. Is that your given name or"—she smiled teasingly—"a descriptive nickname?"

He smiled back at her. "A borrowed name, from the back of a dictionary." Jesus. She really had a set of jugs.

"It's not often," he continued, feeling his way into the game confidently, "we are favored with the presence of a lady in here." It was his favorite line.

She pretended concern. "Is this a men-only saloon?"

"Absolutely not. Many women frequent this establishment"—he should know, he'd made a run at every one of them—"but few enough ladies."

"Why, thank you, kind sir." She went along with the play,

tilting her head to one side and batting her eyelashes theatrically.

She kept turning to look toward the rear of the room. The big jukebox, a glittering display of flashing red and yellow lights, was back there, flanked by doors labeled "Heifers" and "Bulls."

Along the wall opposite the bar was a clutter of chrome-legged tables and chairs and a long wooden shuffleboard table. Affixed to the wall above the table was the matted, dusty head of a long-ago-departed bull moose. It was not likely any of the El Rancho's regular patrons had ever set eyes upon a living moose, and this tattered, glassy-eyed example did little to prepare them for the experience.

Behind the bar, thumbtacked to the wall above the indirectly lighted glass shelves of liquor bottles, was an array of faded black-and-white photographs.

She leaned forward to peer at them. "Someone here, I gather, is a fight fan."

"Our good host, Manny Freitas." Gregory Peck couldn't have delivered the line more urbanely. "Manny, according to Manny"—he gestured toward the proprietor, who was dunking glasses at the far end of the bar—"was a welterweight of great promise 'somewhere east of the Mississippi' during a carefully undefined time period." When he smelled the musk of romance in the wind, the captain's entire personality changed. Few of his peers at camp, certainly no one in the 575th, would have recognized him now.

"What, for heaven's sake, is that?" She pointed at a limp pouch of indeterminate material dangling from a nail amid the yellowing photographs.

He grinned at her crookedly and winked. "Manny's proudest possession. That, he assures us, is . . . Jack Dempsey's jockstrap."

She laughed out loud, just as he had hoped she would, throwing her head back and closing her hand over his on the bar. "That's *marvelous*!"

"*A drifting smoke ring frames a vision of you . . . and I'm so lonesome and blue . . .*" The music was magnified by the room's emptiness.

He edged a little closer on his stool, his knee just touching hers. "Looks like you could use a refill." He signaled to Manny. "What is that, a manhattan?"

"Oh, no. No, thank you." She put her hand over the glass. "I get tipsy. And anyway, we really ought to be going, if we're going. Phoenix is a long way from here."

We? Going to Phoenix? Jesus. This was going to be a lot easier than he'd thought. He wondered suddenly if she could be a high-class whore. He looked at her breasts more boldly this time. Hell, he'd go . . . five bucks maybe.

"My husband and I . . ." She looked toward the rear of the room again and suddenly brightened. "Well, *there* you are. I was afraid I was going to have to send this gentleman in there to look for you." A tall, good-looking young captain in air corps uniform was walking toward them. "Darling, this is . . ." She turned back to the captain, putting a hand on his arm. "I'm awfully sorry. I've forgotten your name."

Ooooooh, *shit*! Her *husband*. The red, white, and blue fighter plane nosed over and went spinning toward earth, trailing fire and a dense cloud of black smoke. Shot down again.

Mechanically he went through the ritual, shaking hands, exchanging the obligatory words, scarcely looking at either of them. Son of a *bitch*! The couple began moving toward the door, still smiling and mouthing polite phrases. Disgusted, he turned back toward the major.

The major was gone. The ranchers at the far end of the bar had disappeared, too.

"*I hear some footsteps that remind me of you . . . and I'm so lonesome and blue . . .*"

Manny, expressionless—was that son of a bitch laughing at him?—stood across the bar from him, massaging a glass with his dirty towel. "You want another one?" He nodded at the captain's glass as he took the woman's away and swiped at the bar with the towel.

The captain looked down the length of the deserted bar and back at Manny. "Yeah. Make it a double." *I'm awfully sorry, but I've forgotten your name.* He caught Manny's eye, jerking a thumb toward the door.

"That blond bitch . . . the one who just left . . . ?"

Manny nodded noncommittally, busy with the ice and the Old Overholt.

"Prick teaser."

Manny slid the double rye toward him without comment, and the captain picked it up and took a long swallow. Goddammit. Things had looked pretty good there for a while. He should have realized that kind of material wouldn't be screwing around a dump like this, unless she was a hooker. Well. He smiled ruefully, raised his glass to Dempsey's jockstrap, and took another big swallow.

Manny moved to the other end of the bar, going through the motions of being busy, avoiding further discussion of the incident. The captain waved irritably at a pesky fly. It wasn't the first time he'd been shot out of the saddle, and it wouldn't be the last. He finished his drink in another gulp and watched Manny walk over to the Wurlitzer jiggling a handful of nickels. If Manny didn't want to talk, he played the jukebox.

"Hey there, mister, where's my sister Annie? Hey there, mister, where's my sister dear? She loved to sing and dance and I thought that just perchance . . ."

It was past midnight when Johnnie Marie came into the bar with a lieutenant from Special Services. Johnnie Marie worked at Mountain Bell with Fae Manning. There were four operators over there, and Johnnie was the youngest and best-looking.

The captain sat alone, hunched over on the same bar stool where he'd begun the evening. A full glass and an empty one stood in front of him on the bar beside a sodden wad of paper money. He turned his head as Johnnie Marie and the lieutenant came in, then swiveled clumsily toward them.

He regarded the lieutenant for a moment—"Tenant"—then leered at Johnnie Marie. He started to say "Young lady" but changed his mind halfway through and decided to say "Young woman." It came out "young layman."

"Siddown." He patted the empty stool next to him. "Buy y'drink?"

Johnnie Marie smiled at him and shook her head. "Thank you, Captain"—she nodded at an empty table under the moose head—"but we're late for the Moose Lodge meeting." She tugged at the lieutenant's arm and stepped to one side as they went past, making certain she was out of arm's reach.

The captain followed them with his eyes. Johnnie Marie was wearing a snug green dress, tight across her bottom. He'd sure like to get into that. He hiccuped loudly and swiveled heavily around toward the front door, alternately opening and squinting his eyes in an effort to improve the focus. The door. All he had to do was negotiate a course through there, make a right turn, make another right turn, climb into his automobile, and drive out to camp, out to the officers' club. Maybe there was something going on out there, though he couldn't imagine what. He hiccuped again. There sure as hell was nothing going on here. Bracing himself against the bar, he managed to get to his feet and, teetering there, cautiously freed one hand and peered intently at his wristwatch.

Too goddam dark in here. Well, who cared what time it was, anyway?

He shoved the clutter of crumpled bills toward the back of the bar, waved one hand vaguely in Manny's direction, then turned unsteadily and lurched toward the entrance. It was a heavy, reinforced door, and he stiff-armed it open with both hands in front of him, banging it back loudly against the recessed entrance, and careened out into the darkness. His momentum carried him across the narrow sidewalk, over the curb, and out into the street a few feet before he could brake to a halt.

He turned about carefully and surveyed the front of the tavern, reorienting himself. A big yellow cat stood half in shadow at the corner adjoining the parking lot, observing him warily. The captain lifted one hand in greeting.

"*Awf'ly* sorry." He hiccuped again and took a half-step back to steady himself. "But I've forgotten your goddam name."

The cat ducked around the corner into the darkness.

The officers' club at the Piebald was a one-story, added-on-to structure that had once served as the camp's dispensary, and it was barely large enough to squeeze in the members whose reluctant contributions sustained it. It endeavored to mask with dim lighting and shuttered windows what its split bamboo and linoleum decor lacked in aesthetic appeal. The bar, by turning back toward the rear wall at both ends, achieved barely enough length to accommodate seven wicker-top stools. A dozen or so persons could crowd chairs around the three tiny tables near the entrance, but on those infrequent occasions when more than fifteen or twenty persons appeared at the same time, many of them were forced to stand.

A small, low platform was wedged into the far corner to the left of the bar. It was built for a combo of Italian prisoners, but their uninhibited music had proved to be so deafening in the cramped quarters that the idea was quickly abandoned. A small table sat on the stage now, holding an olive-drab portable phonograph and a stack of scratchy records scrounged from Special Services.

At first glance, blurred as it was, the captain could see that his expectations of the club had not been excessive. Not counting the Italian polishing glasses behind the bar, there were only five persons in attendance. Two nurses and a couple of doctors from the camp hospital sat together at one of the tables, and an officer whose identity he couldn't make out from the door sat alone at the bar. He grunted in disgust and leaned forward, aiming for an open expanse of the bar, both hands in front of him to ward off the shock landing.

"Hey!" The officer at the bar managed to save his drink by lifting it high. A metal napkin holder and a glass of paper straws crashed to the floor.

"Well, Cad, out celebrating the good news?"

The captain twisted around to regard the other officer. Goddam lieutenant from Headquarters Company. For a moment he'd thought it was that asshole major from the El Rancho.

"Wha' good news?" He began inching toward an unoccupied stool, holding tight to the bar.

"*What* good news?" The lieutenant seemed genuinely surprised. "Hell, I understand you're shipping out."

The captain stopped trying to climb onto the stool. Carefully he turned to look at the lieutenant again.

"You trying to bullshit me? Joke or something?" Through

the alcoholic fog, he became aware of his whole body going rigid, his breathing interrupted.

"I figured you must already know." The lieutenant was obviously pleased to find himself breaking the news. "I was up in Colonel Ratnekof's office. That's where I heard it, about five o'clock. Uh, seventeen hundred."

Shipping out? *Shipping out!* Could this goddam idiot know what he was talking about?

"You bullshitting me?"

"No, goddammit. You. The Five-seven-five. I heard the old man tell his clerk to cut the orders, said he wanted them first thing in the morning. You been gone somewhere?" He chuckled. "I gather you have."

"Been in town a little bit." He looked down at his hands, clenched tight on the edge of the bar. It was happening. It was sumbitch, honest to jumpin' Jesus Christ happening. He turned back to the lieutenant.

"He say where we're going? Europe? The Pacific?"

"You know as much as I do, Captain. All I know is you're going. Hey, lemme buy you a drink."

But the captain turned and—head up, gait remarkably steady—strode away from the bar and out the door. He forgot all about his car parked there, one wheel cocked crazily atop a whitewashed stone. He forgot about the El Rancho and the blonde. He forgot about everything but the news as he walked into the night toward his company.

All those bastards, his fellow officers, laughing about him and the way he trained his company, about him wanting to go overseas, get into the fighting. Well, he'd done it. He'd done it. He was going to take this outfit over, just like he'd told them he would, into combat. Even his own men hadn't believed him, but they were finally going to get into it, just like he'd almost done back in 1918 when Wilson and the frogs and the goddam limeys screwed it all up. He walked faster, past the darkened PX and the theater. Up ahead, across the dark expanse of the parade ground, he could see the perimeter lights of the company area.

CHAPTER TEN

☆ ☆

T 'TAAA ... *t'taaa* ... The rasping, brassy notes of the bugle echoed and re-echoed off the barracks walls as, all over the company area, lights began popping on and the 575th came awake. *Ti-tada, Ti-tada, Ti-tada, T'taaa, T'taaa, T'taaa.*

Call to arms.

Aug came awake slowly, hoping it was only a bad dream, squinting against the glaring overhead light.

The shouted commands of noncoms mingled with the curses of men spilled unceremoniously from their bunks, the clatter of footlocker doors slamming open, the thud of boots on wooden floors, shrill police whistles.

Outside, Sergeant Bleeker was already in position, waiting for them. His steel helmet, cartridge belt, and leggings were perfectly in place, as if he'd had an extra half hour to prepare. "Move it! C'mon! Get 'em out here!"

"What the hell's happenin' now?"

"What's that bugle call?"

"Call to fuckin' arms."

"It ain't mail call, so never mind your letter opener."

"Move it, goddammit! Get your ass in the street! Fall in! Gitcher interval! Anberger, where's your goddam rifle?"

All three platoon sergeants were still stuffing in their shirts, buttoning up, as they herded their sleepy-eyed charges into formation.

"Compan-*eeee* ... tens-*hut*! Reee-*port*!"

"First Platoon present an' accounted for!" Probably.

"Secon' P'toon presen' cown for!"

"Third Platoon present an' accounted for!"

Lieutenant Flowers was officer of the day. As the captain appeared out of the shadows, striding purposefully toward center stage, Bleeker pivoted and saluted Flowers. "Company all present and accounted for!" Lieutenant Flowers turned and saluted the captain, then repeated the report.

"At ease!"

The captain's gaze passed slowly across the company as the men shuffled to more relaxed stances, eyeing him with suspicion.

"This company"—he spoke so quietly that Aug found himself straining to hear from the rear rank—"is on alert. All leaves and furloughs are canceled, all personnel restricted to the company area." He paused, waiting for that news to register, for them to wonder why. "Less than thirty minutes ago, I got the word from headquarters." That was mostly true. That goddam lieutenant was assigned to headquarters, wasn't he? "We're shipping out."

He could hear the company react to the announcement, hear the murmur pass down the line, though he couldn't hear the words.

"Bullshit."

"Is he kidding?"

"This fuckin' outfit honest to God shipping out?"

The captain glanced at his watch. Coming up on oh-two-hundred.

"Some of you may have personal affairs that need taking care of. Get it done. No mail will be permitted. Your families will get an APO card after we sail. If you've got one in the oven, you'd better change your insurance." He grinned, but they couldn't see it in the darkness. "You may have been there when the keel was laid, but you're not going to be here for the launching." He remembered his old top sergeant delivering that line twenty-five years ago.

He glanced at his watch a second time. "When this formation is over, all noncoms report to the orderly room." He glanced at Bleeker. "Dismiss 'em."

"Companeeee . . . tens-*hut*! Fall out!"

Aug's stomach had that same hollowness again, the way it had felt when he found the draft notice in the mailbox. The dark night seemed colder than usual. Were they really *going*? His thoughts went back home, to his mother and to Boner and Angie. It was just past midnight back there. They were all sound asleep. Around him, the company dissected the news as they trooped back into their barracks.

"Bullshit."

"I don't know. It don't sound like bullshit this time."

"*Somebody's* out of his fuckin' head."

"He didn't say *where* we're goin'."

Aug sat down on his bunk. All at once, the chill of the night, the crude way of life, the Spartan barracks, the whole ridiculous, gritty existence that was Piebald didn't look so bad. Playing make-believe soldier, playing war with the captain and Bleeker and the rest, when he stopped to think about it, had actually been fun. But this sounded *serious*. Absentmindedly, he slid his bayonet out of its scabbard and tapped the butt end against his collarbone.

That would *still* hurt.

It was not a thought to drift off to sleep with.

He wasn't the only one to lie awake that night.

At 0800 sharp, the captain was at the door of Colonel Ratnekof's office. The colonel seemed surprised to find him there when he walked in twenty minutes later. The captain was wearing fresh fatigues, web cartridge belt, and leggings. Combat gear. He had considered wearing his steel helmet, but opted instead for the cunt cover.

"Morning, Cad. Come on into my office. Have a seat. You want a cup of coffee?"

"No, thank you, sir." A stiff shot of rye would go better. He had a goddam cannonball in his stomach.

The colonel walked past him into the outer office and returned a moment later with some papers. "Well, I guess this is why you're here."

"Yes, sir."

The captain had to fight back a silly grin. There they were, the *orders*.

"What's it going to be, Colonel—Europe or the Pacific?"

The colonel looked up at him. He seemed suddenly uncomfortable. "Where did you hear about this?"

"Last night, at the officers' club."

The colonel looked down at the paperwork, then back at the captain. "You appear to have some misinformation."

Bile came bubbling up in the captain's stomach. "This lieutenant said . . ." An involuntary gesture with his hands looked like pleading. He put them back at his sides. "He said we were shipping out." He waited for the colonel to respond. "We *are* shipping out?"

"Yes, you're . . . shipping out." The colonel cleared his throat. "You're moving out of here."

"The krauts? Or the Japs." Impatience crept into the captain's voice. Why was the owl-eyed asshole stalling?

The colonel cleared his throat again and shuffled the papers. He started to smile, but stopped. "Well, Cad, I guess if you put it that way . . . it's the Japs."

The captain had been hoping for Europe, but he was careful not to show disappointment. "All the same to us, Colonel. Doesn't make any difference. We're ready for them."

"Cad." The colonel looked out the window, then back at him. Again he tried a smile that didn't work. "You're going to Arido."

"Arido. Where the hell—?"

"It's about seventy-five miles east of here. You're relieving the Five Fourteenth. They're going to Fort Custer for combat training, and you're taking over at . . . the relocation camp."

The captain didn't understand. "The relocation camp?"

The colonel nodded. "For the Japanese-Americans moved off the Coast. You'll still be reporting to me."

They stared at each other.

He couldn't remember the last time he'd wanted to cry. He shuffled his feet, wondering how to end the scene.

I'm awfully sorry, but I've forgotten your name.

May 27, 1943

Dear Son:

How are you? We really enjoyed your last letter. Did you get the cookies your sister sent? Tomorrow we go down to the Red Cross to start folding bandages. A lot of the women in town are doing that now to help out. I bought one of those flags to hang in the window from a man who came to the door, the kind that says we have a boy in the army.

Marjorie Slezak got married Sunday to John, her boyfriend. He's got a deferment because he's going to school. We were invited but your father said he wasn't going on account of him getting the deferment. I said it's not John's fault but you know your father. I guess the big news is that Norman (I can't say the name you call him) has joined up in the marines. He left for camp on Wednesday. I pray both of you will be safe until this awful war is over.

That's about all for now. We miss you. Your father says your captain sounds like a good man. I hope so. Be a good boy and write soon.

Love,
Mother

CHAPTER ELEVEN

☆ ☆

THE hawk nervously shrugged its rust-colored shoulders and lifted its wings, as if debating leaving its perch on the dead saguaro. Its talons made dry, crackling noises as it stepped around uneasily on the rotted-out hulk. It was a Harris hawk, identified by the broad band of white at the base of its tail.

It swiveled its head around in short, angry jerks, glaring at the convoy of trucks blustering across the desert floor and churning up a long, billowing plume of dust below the rocky slope.

The column was moving fast despite the unpredictable terrain, the sudden dips and turns hidden by brush and cactus on either side, the precipitous drops into dry washes that gouged pale scars across the rutted dirt road.

The thick dust billowed up from beneath the wheels, nearly obscuring the vehicles in the rear two-thirds of the convoy. It came up over the tailgates like an impenetrable yellow shroud, stuffing itself in beneath the tarpaulins, enveloping the choking and spitting passengers.

"Gah *damn!*" Blackie Sifko blew ineffectively at the dust eddying around him. He dabbed at his red-rimmed eyes with his little finger. "Like tryin' to blow a fly out'n a flour barrel."

"I hear you talkin'," someone responded, "but I can't find you."

"Lorrr-*dee!*" complained another sufferer. "I could sure use me a beer."

"Pass your canteen back; I'll fill it up for you."

"I'll give you something to fill up."

Aug was scrunched into a rear corner, as far from the churning dust as he could get, but he could taste it, smell it, feel it gritting between his teeth. On the bench seat across from him, Mozetti had his field jacket pulled up over his nose, his steel helmet tilted down over his face. Next to him, Kaplowitz was similarly wrapped up. He hadn't emitted a giggle in the past half hour.

Aug brushed a dusty sleeve across his red-rimmed eyes while contemplating the events of the past three months, the bizarre chronology that had begun when he opened the mailbox and found the draft notice there. For him it was a rare moment of self-analysis.

He was surprised to have felt some initial disappointment on learning they were not actually going overseas. With Boner in the marines now—wouldn't you know Boner would get into the marines?—he for the first time had felt a little sheepish about his rear-echelon role in the war. He had always been in a position to tease Boner, to poke friendly fun at him—big, dumb Boner—and he had the disquieting feeling their roles had suddenly been reversed.

His fantasy of wearing a marine dress uniform, driving up to Mary Jane Mendenhall's house in the red Buick—dark blue jacket, gold buttons, and spotless white hat—seemed less and less attainable as each day went by. The marines weren't rescuing anybody from the army. Maybe he could just resign: *I certainly have enjoyed knowing you, Captain, but I've got to be running on home to join the marines. If you have the time, tell Sergeant Bleeker I said good-bye. And that I'm the one who short-sheeted his bunk.*

Going home—a parade up Washington Avenue led by the high school band and maybe a fire truck. He and Mary Jane in the Buick, smiling and waving. She was throwing flowers. The people on the sidewalk were supposed to be throwing the flowers, Old Lady Pereira with her orange cat, Miss Longnecker, the high school principal, Old Man Griffith with his apple and carton of milk, and his father.

Pop!

The image of his father throwing flowers was too much of a burden for any fantasy. If he showed up for the parade at all, his father would likely find something else to throw.

He squirmed his butt left and right, seeking a more comfortable position on the hard slats of the bench seat.

The shipping-out scare had made one thing plain: if this sorry outfit *should* somehow manage to find itself "going over," however unlikely that possibility seemed, he would have to find a way to avoid being included. Once he was overseas, whatever that involved, he was in the army *forever*. Good-bye white hat and gold buttons, and Mary Jane Mendenhall, too. He cupped his hands over his face, drew in a cautious breath, and exhaled. He shook his head. He was just kidding himself.

He extended one heavy boot to nudge Mozetti. "Hey, Moz. How do you get out of the army?"

Mozetti pushed his helmet up just far enough to fix Aug with a distrustful look.

"That's a joke? I don't know. How *do* you get outa the army?"

"Not a joke. I'm serious."

Next to Aug, Billy Lawler waggled his head dolefully. "There ain't no *way* to get out. No, sir. Less'n they give you a Section Eight." He gave the subject some additional thought. "Or you get shot dead."

Additional counsel issued from within the opaque cloud.

"You could shoot yerself in the ass. Two assholes is def'nitely goin'-home stuff."

"Shit, they'd be sendin' this whole fuckin' truck home, then. I count *fourteen* assholes."

"Up yours."

Aug squeezed his eyes shut tighter and went through his diminishing list of options.

Up at the front of the column, the captain's thoughts were on a directly opposing dilemma. How the goddam hell was he going to turn this latest setback around? If that goddam Colonel Ratnekof thought he was sending him out into the sticks to get rid of him, the no-good son of a bitch, he was mistaken.

"Kick this thing in the ass, Bruener."

"Yes, sir."

The jeep was already bounding crazily over the dips and bumps at a mad pace. PFC Bruener gripped the wheel desperately, wrestling the squat little vehicle through the road's sudden-appearing changes in direction, its rear wheels sliding in the loose dirt and sand. Bruener's eyelids drooped at half-mast, a congenital malady—modified catacleisis—which required him to tilt his head back so he could see where he was going. If it had been left to him, he would have been going a whole lot slower, but every time he took his foot off the accelerator the captain darted a malevolent look at him.

"Stick your *foot* in it, goddammit!"

"Yes, sir."

The captain rode—left hand on top of the windshield, right foot outside braced against a front fender—as he might have sat a bucking bronco. He was wearing his steel helmet.

On the unyielding little bench seat behind him, Lieutenants Flowers and Bauman were bouncing about, hip to hip, struggling to remain inside the vehicle. Daisy was sitting as straight as possible, eyes wide, feet braced, obviously trying his best to emulate the captain's erect posture. Lieutenant Bauman was hunched forward, both hands clenched on the back of the driver's seat. His eyes were shut tight, and his lips moved silently as if he were reciting Sh'ma. Or cursing under his breath.

In a big six-by-six truck behind them, Lieutenant Michaels rode the cushioned front seat with only a modicum of dust and discomfort. A half-smile played about his lips as he watched the plunging jeep and its occupants.

The column charged through a stand of mesquite and organpipe cactus and around a long, sweeping curve, dipped down into yet another wash, and bounded over the crest on the far side to find their objective finally laid out before them.

"There it is," the captain growled, half to himself.

"Yes, *sir*," Daisy chirped from the rear seat. "It looks very . . ." He stopped there, unable to compare the desolate scene to anything with which he was familiar.

Bruener tilted his head back for a better view.

There was very little to see—a cluster of a dozen or so long whitewashed single-story frame buildings with faded red tar-paper roofs awash in a sea of brush and cactus. From a quarter-mile away, the buildings seemed scarcely higher than the dry yellow-brown growth engulfing them. Beyond them, a high embankment of loose dirt, apparently a dike of some sort, stretched away to some rocky outcroppings on the horizon.

As they drew closer, they came upon a small sun-baked drill field on the left. Here the 514th, the company they were relieving, was lounging in loose approximation of platoon formation, surrounded by barracks bags, small arms, and wooden footlockers. They straggled to their feet as the trucks charged into view and slid to a halt in the loose sand at the edge of the narrow road.

"You'll be *sorrreeeee!*" came the mocking chorus from the soon-to-depart.

"I can't see *nothin'* yet, an' I'm *awready* sorry."

"You guys go on ahead," Aug offered. "I'm gonna show that other outfit there how to get back to Piebald."

"Them bastards already figured out how to get back. How do *we* get back?"

They climbed down from the trucks, dragging their rifles and heavy barracks bags behind them.

"Compared to this place, by God, Piebald looks *good.*"

Blackie turned slowly, surveying the parched desert and Spartan accommodations, his new home. He leaned forward and spit. "Gah *damn!*"

A hundred yards up the road stood an unpainted and unoccupied sentry shack. The captain's eyes narrowed, his lips stretching tight across his teeth as he regarded it.

A pudgy red-faced officer walked up to the captain's jeep and stuck out his hand.

"Maxwell? Cap'm Bruce. Welcome to Arido." His drawl suggested a southwestern origin.

The captain tossed an abrupt salute at him, then awkwardly shook his hand. He jerked his head in the direction of the guard shack up the road.

"Where's your sentry, Captain?"

Bruce looked up the road as if the question hadn't ever occurred to him, then smiled and tilted a thumb toward the ragtag assembly on the drill field.

"Out on the parade groun', I guess. Hell, we just pulled 'em *all* in this mornin' so's they'd have time to get packed up."

The captain's head jutted forward. "You don't have sentries on *any* of your posts? Since this morning? How many guard posts *are* there?"

Bruce stopped to consider. "Lessee." He ticked them off on his fingers. "Six. No, seven. Eight, countin' the main gate up there."

"Sergeant Bleeker!"

"Yes, sir!"

"Put a guard detail together. On the double! Eight men and a corporal of the guard. Rifles and full cartridge belts." He turned back to Captain Bruce, who seemed surprised by his counterpart's concern.

"Hey," Bruce said, "no hurry." He chuckled. "Besides, your sergeant'll never *find* the posts unless somebody goes along to show him. Most of 'em are three, four miles apart out there"— he chuckled again—"and some of the shacks have been torn down to make bonfires."

The captain's head tilted forward another notch.

"Lot of people think the desert's hot all the time," Bruce said, "but it gets *cold* out here at night durin' the winter."

The captain brushed the weather report aside. "What's the routine here? You run jeep patrols in between posts? Do you have any wire up? If your sentries are three, four miles apart, how the hell do you stop the goddam Japs from just *leaving*?"

Bruce grinned and shook his head. "Hell, we don't have any *barbed* wire up, 'cept'n a little west of Camp Two to keep the cows out. These people could leave any time they wanted to, I guess. Not officially, of course; they'd need a pass for that." He made a sweep of the prickly landscape with one arm. "But where the hell would they go? The sentries ain't there to keep these people from duckin' *out*. It's mostly to keep other people from sneakin' *in* . . . to steal watermelons and stuff."

The captain's stare might have withered a more perceptive

man. He turned to look up the road toward the vacant sentry post, then back to Bruce.

"Where's the compound?"

Bruce winked and raised an admonishing index finger.

"It's not a *compound*, Captain, and not a *prison* camp, either. Washington—the War Relocation Agency—is *very* sensitive about that. It's a relocation settlement."

He gestured up the road. "Camp One's up that way beyond the water tower—about five thousand people in there, I'd guess. Camp Two's laid out toward that butte—maybe another six thousand over there. I don't have an exact count; that ain't any of our problem."

He glanced back toward the parade ground, then at his wristwatch. "Tell you what. Would you like a tour? Let me get my people started loadin' up. Then I'll show your guard detail where the sentry posts are and give you a look at the place at the same time."

He turned toward his company. The captain glared up the road at the empty sentry post, then twisted around, his eyes scanning the soldiers milling about. "Sergeant Bleeker!"

"Yes, sir!"

"What the goddam hell is this, a cattle stampede? Get these men in company formation!"

"Yes, sir!"

The captain jerked a thumb at the sentry shack. "And by oh-nine-hundred tomorrow I want a coat of *paint* on that shack. Place looks like a goddam YMCA camp!"

"Yes, sir."

Bleeker's police whistle stabbed the still desert air.

"Compa-*neeee*! Fall *in*!"

"First Platoon, fall in on Savidge! Savidge! Get your ass over here!"

"Getcher head outa your ass, Garnett! Getcher interval!"

"Anberger! Where's your goddam rifle?"

When Captain Bruce returned a few minutes later, Sergeant Bleeker had the guard detail—Aug was not surprised to be included—already loaded into a weapons carrier. Lined up behind the captain's vehicle was a second jeep mounting a .30-caliber machine gun. Bruce seemed about to comment on the machine gun, but closed his mouth and climbed onto the little seat behind the captain with Lieutenant Flowers. Lieutenant Bauman had already disappeared.

Bruce waved Bruener up the road toward the guard shack. "Most of the traffic comin' through the main gate here is government," he said. "WRA people." He repeated the full name, "War Relo*cation* Agency," as if it amused him. "The *internees* driving vegetable trucks into town mostly use gate four, over on the other side."

The captain twisted around in his seat. "You've got *Japs* driving back and forth between here and town?"

Bruce studied him for a moment before replying. "They ship *tons* of produce out of here, Captain. All kinds. For the war effort," he added. "They drive it into Mesa Verde, to the railhead, and load it into boxcars."

"You send 'em in under escort, I assume."

"You mean under *guard*?" Bruce chuckled. "Hell, no. They know how to get there and back; it ain't but ten miles. We got an MP patrol in town; you will, too, I guess, and we usually have 'em stand by at the loadin' dock." He chuckled again. "Just in case any of the local heroes get drunk and decide to attack 'Japan' from the Bent Horn Saloon. We've never had any trouble, though. A few shoutin' matches."

The nearest sentry post sat on a small rise. A few hundred yards beyond it, some features of the relocation camp became evident. Through the morning haze, Aug could make out a small city of drab, elongated single-story buildings devoid of any landscaping. Those nearest appeared to be warehouses. Parked outside one, apparently a motor pool, was part of a fleet of trucks. As Bruce had said, there was no *barbed* wire in view. There was a smooth-wire fence a few yards beyond the sentry shack—to delineate a boundary—and only a few indistinct figures moving about on the dusty, dreary streets.

When Bleeker had the first sentry posted, the captain raised an arm and waved the contingent forward, toward the camp, but Bruce countermanded him with a tap on his shoulder.

"We'd be better off goin' around, Captain. The WRA don't

cotton to our showin' ourselves in there any more than necessary. Out of sight, out of mind."

"The *WRA* isn't in charge of this *post*," the captain snapped.

"No argument there," Bruce said, "but they're in charge of this relo*cation* camp; you better believe it. An' paradin' through there with that machine gun you got would just about turn them government types inside out."

The captain's eyes narrowed to slits, and his lips again stretched tight across his teeth. But with a jerk of his head he signaled Bruener to comply. The three vehicles backed and hauled around and started off again in the direction Captain Bruce indicated.

Some of the sentry posts on the perimeter, all of them unattended, seemed even farther apart than Bruce had said. Rather than providing strategic overviews of the camp, they had been placed to monitor the narrow dirt roads leading over the desert toward the site from several compass points.

Posting and briefing the sentries consumed nearly an hour. Aug was the only one yet to be assigned when Captain Bruce directed Bruener up a narrow, rock-strewn road to a rocky ledge overlooking much of the sprawling complex called Camp Two. He crawled out of the jeep and stood beside the captain, pointing out features of interest below.

It was noontime, and Aug could see a lot of people slowly moving about, singly and in groups, on the dusty roads between the buildings. All of them were walking. There were no vehicles in sight.

"Over there," Bruce said, "that square-lookin' building, that's the WRA headquarters; next to it the hospital and, over yonder, the commissary. What the internees can't get there, they order through the Sears catalog. The school—grammar school and high school combined—is over in Camp One. Most of the teachers are conchies—conscientious objectors."

The captain snorted but made no comment.

"This mess of buildin's runnin' from here all the way over to the far side are all barracks. *Four families* crowded into each one, if you can believe that, nothin' but thin partitions in between." Lieutenant Flowers climbed out of the jeep and reached back for a pair of binoculars to take a closer look.

"There's a mess hall on each block," Captain Bruce continued, "and two latrines—one for the men, one for the women. The women's is jus' like the men's. No trough on the wall, of course, but no privacy, jus' the row of stools. They got washtubs and such in there for doin' their laundry." Bruce waggled his head slowly. "I personally don't see how they can stand it, steppin' all over each other like that, after ownin' their own homes an' all, wherever they come from. Furniture made outa orange crates, when they can find 'em, an' you wanta have"—he made a vague gesture—"you know what I mean, *relations* with your wife, you gotta hang a blanket up."

He waggled his head again. "But the *biggest* complaint—you hear it all the time—is the *dust*."

The captain grunted, his expression grim.

"I mean, when the wind comes whoopin' through here"—Bruce waved his arm to demonstrate—"all the dirt and sand jus' picks up an' moves over yonder, and it don't go *aroun'* those buildin's; it goes right *through* 'em. They ain't nothin' but tar-paper shacks with wood floors full of knotholes, an' most of the knotholes fallen out."

Another grunt.

Aug saw a man in a dark suit pedaling down one of the streets on an olive-drab bicycle. Captain Bruce pointed him out.

"Looka there. There goes ole Father Yamazaki. He's a good fellow," Bruce chuckled, "for a 'Piscopalian. He tells everybody he's in charge of M an' M—morale and morals. He's got his hands full there, I'd guess, all the younguns with hot pants sneakin' off across the dike at night, into the brush."

The long dike, thrown up from an irrigation canal, formed the southern border of the camp.

Lieutenant Flowers lowered his binoculars and pointed. "Some of those roofs down there . . . they've got big holes in them. It almost looks like they've been bombed."

Bruce nodded, hands on his hips. "Matter of fact, Lieutenant, that's jus' what it is. There's a twin-engine trainin' field jus' west of here"—he pointed—"an' it seems like every other graduatin' class celebrates by stagin' a night raid, bombin' these poor people with melons, fire extinguishers, water bags, an' all kinds of crap. The WRA raises hell every time it happens, but shoot, it don't do any good. Next graduatin' class, it'll be the same thing all over again. Those roofs are just tar paper over plywood. A watermelon goes through there like a two-ton safe. It's a damn wonder nobody's been hurt."

The captain's face was impassive. "Good for the no-good sonsabitches."

Bruce tilted his khaki hat forward and rubbed the back of his neck vigorously. "You know, Captain, these here people are all American citizens. Most of 'em, anyway. 'Cept'n for the old folks, the issei—they call the ones who were born in *this* country nisei. You got engineers down there, music teachers, architects, druggists, all of 'em workin'—those who can *find* work here—for nineteen dollars a month. You got farmers, merchants—"

"Goddam enemy aliens is what they are," the captain interrupted. "If we hadn't shipped 'em out here, the sonsabitches'd be blowing up bridges, sabotaging factories, and poisoning the water supply. Instead of watermelons, they ought to drop a few blockbusters in there."

Bruce studied the toe of one boot for a moment and then shook his head. "Some of them kids you see walkin' aroun' down there, just a few months back, were high school cheerleaders an' football heroes. All I can say is, Maxwell, but for the grace of God that might be you an' me down there, packed into one of them—"

The captain interrupted him again. "If you wouldn't have any objection, Captain, why don't you hitch a ride back in the weapons carrier? I want to check the perimeter over on the other side."

Bruce looked at him without expression, nodding his head. "All right, Captain, I'll do that. And . . . you take care." He shook hands politely, turned for one last look at the camp below, and walked back to the weapons carrier.

When he had gone, the captain pointed to the far side of the camp. "See that irrigation canal over there, Bruener? Get us over there."

Bruener tipped his head back to survey the scene from beneath his sagging eyelids. "There's no perimeter road past here, Cap'm. We'll have to go back all the way around."

"The hell we will," the captain growled. He pointed straight ahead. "We're going right through the middle of those sonsabitches."

CHAPTER TWELVE

☆ ☆

AUG'S hands were beginning to blister, and the machine-gun pit was still only knee deep, not half deep enough. He straightened up and slowly bent over backward, easing the pain between his shoulder blades. He dropped his shovel and reached for his canteen. Dobbins, working next to him in the circular trench, continued to chip away with his shovel for a few minutes, then threw it aside and sat down heavily on the edge of the shallow excavation.

"Whooo-*eee!*"

It was hot.

On the far side of the pit, bull-necked Private Lemoyne Ryker continued to dig steadily—*chunk! . . . chunk!*—slamming his heavy pick into the hard-baked ground without pause. Sweat drenched the sleeves and back of his fatigue blouse, glistened on his cheeks and forehead, and dripped from the tip of his crooked nose. Ryker wore a perpetual sullen expression on his face, flushed now with his exertions and some smoldering fire that seemed to burn within. He had taken no notice of his two companions, with word or action, since the three of them had stepped down into the pit shortly after breakfast.

Ryker was a loner.

And he was regarded in the company as a mean son of a bitch.

According to the word Kaplowitz had passed along from the orderly room, Ryker had been accused of beating a fellow coal miner to death with a shovel.

"And he's in the *army*? How come he's not in jail?"

"That's what Sergeant Garrison wanted to know. Lieutenant

Michaels said he was never officially charged, just accused. The mine fired him apparently, and right after that, he was drafted."

Aug knew how *that* worked.

When, a few minutes later, without even a look toward either one of them, Ryker climbed out of the pit to go to the latrine, Dobbins turned his head slowly and watched him go.

"Now, I'd call that man ornery," Dobbins said. "You hear about him and Donaldson the other night in town?"

Ryker and baby-faced Donaldson? Aug shook his head and took another swig of warm water. "What about 'em?"

"Ryker's in the Bent Horn, sittin' up at the bar all by hisself, drunker'n a skunk, an' in comes Donaldson, all liquored up on a couple of cherry Cokes or somethin'. An' he sashays over to Ryker, taps him on the shoulder, and says, 'You know what? I got three dogs at home, an' I call every one of 'em Ryker.' "

Aug brought his canteen down. "What'd Ryker do?"

"He didn't do nothin'. He put his head back and laughed like all get out. Buys Donaldson a drink." Dobbins shook his head in amazement. "Been me, he'd've beat me to death with the nearest spittoon."

"That's funny," Aug said. He turned and watched Ryker walking away with a rocking gait, his feet wide apart like a wrestler. He had a thick neck and sloping, chunky shoulders and held his arms out from his sides as if he were wearing a gunbelt. "That's a *mean* son of a gun."

"I wouldn't wanta meet him in no dark alley."

Dobbins had a khaki handkerchief knotted around his neck. He pulled it partway up over his sunburned face and blotted the sweat dripping off his forehead.

"Doggies! It's hotter'n a two-dollar pistol out here."

In a unit where skeletal malformations were commonplace, Dobbins was celebrated for the magnificence of his knock-knees. In platoon formation, he was the only one who stood at attention with his heels ten inches apart. Short of orthopedic reconstruction, there was no way to remedy the stance; it was the best he could do.

"Man could run a wheelbarrow through there," Blackie observed, "if he was a mind to."

Among those in the unit who hailed from the backwoods of

Kentucky, Dobbins was a standout, in that he was perceived to have some "learnin'." Before he was drafted, he admitted, he had taught briefly in a one-room schoolhouse.

Aug liked Dobbins. As a group, the boys from Kentucky and West By-God Virginia were not altogether enamored of strangers in any form. Aug and the other late arrivals had immediately been labeled "them fuckin' Californians," and there had been one or two physical confrontations—cultural conflicts—before things settled down to separate tables in the mess hall.

Aug had won grudging acceptance from the majority shortly after his arrival, thanks to a "judo lesson" with Lieutenant Michaels.

The lieutenant had called for someone to step forward and put a headlock on him, and when nobody volunteered, Michaels had pointed at Aug and called him out. Aug, grinning self-consciously, aware he was about to be knocked on his tail, loosely applied the hold around the lieutenant's neck.

While Michaels was explaining the step-by-step procedure for breaking a headlock, Aug was tightening his grip, burying his thumbs, setting his hip, digging in his heels. And when it came time for Michaels to make his move, there was no way Jarold (NMI) Rustyanek, Private, Army of the United States, was going to be pried loose. Not with a tire iron.

Down they went into the dirt, the lieutenant becoming concerned all of a sudden about being able to breathe.

"Yi!" Rebel yells burst from the throats of the boys from Potter Crick and Bald Knob. They did enjoy a good rough-and-tumble, particularly when it was an officer getting thumped. Any officer.

"Hoooo-haw!" Dalt Cooper snatched his cap off and slapped it against his leg, stomping the dirt with his runners. "Git 'im," he said, the suggestion being, of course, that Aug git Lieutenant Michaels.

Straining, gasping, they thrashed about on the ground for almost a full minute before Aug, half afraid to—afraid not to—relaxed his grip and let the lieutenant roll free.

"Judo," Michaels explained croakily as he staggered to his feet, "requires moves made before the other guy can prepare his defenses." Aug, trying not to grin foolishly, was having difficulty finding an alternate expression. When the class was dismissed, Michaels called him aside behind the mess hall.

The lieutenant stood there in front of Aug for a moment, his head down as he brushed dirt from his once-spotless uniform, then took a step closer and jabbed him in the chest with an index finger. "You ever try that on me again, you wise bastard, I'll kick you right in the balls. You understand?"

"Yes, sir." Under the circumstances, Aug thought that was sufficient response. Michaels looked as if he might kick him in the balls anyway.

He was not at all surprised to see his name first on the list for KP the following morning.

He might have been surprised, however, to hear Michaels leading the laughter at the officers' club bar that evening, retelling "the judo lesson" story. "Wise little son of a bitch."

The incident immediately lifted Aug to semi-hero status in the barracks. If the company was slow to confer membership privileges upon the rest of the Californians, Dobbins made Aug one of the early exceptions.

"You got to understan'," he told Aug, "a lot of these ole boys jumped a foot the first time they heard a toilet flush. I've rubbed *my* ass with plenty of corncobs. You an' them other fellers was brung up in a house with more'n one faucet, an' *all* of them on the inside."

Aug nodded, only half listening. It was too hot today for Dobby's homespun philosophy. He bent to retrieve his shovel, and Dobbins sighed heavily, wiped the back of his neck, and reached for his own.

The machine-gun pit was to be four feet deep and eight feet across with a pillar of dirt left in the center to mount the weapon. The pit and several like it were Captain Maxwell's first *adjustments* to the routine at Arido. On the morning following the company's arrival he had added four sentry posts to the perimeter and ordered deep trenches dug across all of the exits from the camp. The ditches were spanned by narrow, hastily constructed plank bridges, restricting traffic in and out to a slow crawl in single file.

The senior WRA official had immediately, heatedly, and with

the weight of Washington, D.C., behind his position, ordered the trenches hastily filled *in*.

"Your assignment here, *Captain*," the official pointed out without warmth, "is to maintain the *perimeter* of this facility. The *perimeter*," he repeated with added emphasis, "*outside* the camp. The camp itself, its occupants, and its entire operation are none of your concern. Should we ever need your assistance *inside* the boundaries, we will so inform you."

No-good Jap-loving civilian son of a bitch. The captain's response was immediate: "Sergeant Bleeker!"

"Yes, sir!"

"Get a pick and shovel detail together. I want machine-gun pits here, here, and here—both sides of the road—covering every gate."

He jabbed at the rough map again. "And make goddam sure they're *just* outside the gates. Like"—he grinned—"right up against them. Any slant-eyed son of a bitch tries to come out of there without a pass, put a thirty-caliber string of pearls up his ass."

Bleeker hesitated, mouth open. "You want we should *fire* on them?"

The captain made a noise deep in his throat and glowered at the sergeant. "Well . . . hell, no. We wouldn't want to get anybody upset by firing on the goddam *enemy*. But just make sure *nobody*—including those WRA assholes—gets in or out of there without the proper *paperwork*." He pointed a finger. "And make sure the sentry takes plenty of time to read every word of it."

He'd show those no-good sonsabitches who was running things *outside* this place.

Dobbins's and Ryker's assignment to the task had been the luck of the draw. Aug's was only the continuation of Sergeant Bleeker's ongoing remedial program.

Aug had countered by reporting for sick call.

There were a dozen or more men in line outside Lieutenant Bauman's makeshift dispensary that morning, a not unusual turnout. Attendance was always largely a diversionary tactic. The medications most frequently prescribed—APC pills or blue ointment—were as routine as the complaints—hangovers or crabs—and were dispensed by Lieutenant Bauman without comment or ceremony. "What kind of pills am I going to hand out," he wrote Sarah, "when the only help for most of this unit, including its commanding officer, would be lobotomies."

Sarah wrote back that he sounded depressed and that she had mailed him a kosher salami.

Aug hadn't given his ailment a whole lot of thought, and when it was his turn at the doctor's little wooden desk, he was not well prepared.

"What's *your* problem, Rustyanek?"

Aug's mind went blank. He cleared his throat in an exploratory manner, hoping for some respiratory difficulty to reveal itself. Then, on the wall behind the desk, he noticed a large multicolored illustration of the male urinary tract.

"I need to go into the hospital. I've got"—sudden inspiration—"I need to be circumcised."

Lieutenant Bauman's watery eyes, magnified twice over by his thick-lensed glasses, regarded Aug with marked distrust. He was not unaware of Aug's reputation.

"And what brought you to that conclusion? Are you having difficulty urinating?"

Aug shifted his feet. "No. Well . . . some, I guess."

Lieutenant Bauman sighed and put his medical journal down. "All right. Haul it out. Let's look at the damn thing."

Aug complied.

"Peel it back."

The doctor observed the maneuver with his head half turned, then waved a disdainful hand. "You don't need to be circumcised."

Aug was somewhat offended. "Well, I *might* need to be." He shifted his weight to his other leg. "Maybe not right now."

Lieutenant Bauman had declined to endorse preventive surgery.

Aug took another swallow of flat-tasting water from his canteen and wiped his mouth with the back of his hand.

"Dobby, how'd you ever get a job as a schoolteacher if you never went to college?"

Dobbins chuckled. "Shoot. I jus' barely finished high school."

"Then how'd you get hired as a teacher?" Aug believed about half of what Dobbins told him. He knew for sure—Kaplowitz looked up his service record—the man had a college education.

Dobby was just trying to blend into the scenery with his fellow hillbillies, the way he talked and all.

Dobbins shrugged and picked up his own canteen. "They *needed* somebody. They ain't ord'narily that many schoolteachers hangin' aroun' Bethel Crick. The *real* teachers had both went off t'war." He tilted his head back and took a long pull from the canteen. "Didn't take me longer'n one sneeze to figure out teachin' was better'n diggin' coal."

Aug looked at Dobbins sideways. "You replaced *two* teachers?"

"No, just the one."

"You said the real teachers *both* went off to war."

"Hell's fire," Dobby said, "maybe there was only the one. I didn't count 'em."

He leaned over and grabbed his shovel again, conjured up another deep sigh, and poked at the rocky soil.

"What we orta do," he said, "is get us some black powder and *blast* us a hole here."

Aug looked up. "Where would you get the black powder?"

It was black powder that had propelled the infamous beer can through the lab window at Piebald, but there was no ceremonial cannon to be fired out here in the desert.

Dobbins shook his head. "I didn't mean honest to God *do* it, Rooster. I jus' meant it'd be a whole lot *easier* that way."

Aug yawned and rested both hands on the end of the shovel handle. "Where *would* you get some, I wonder, if you had to?"

"My pap used to buy it by the keg. Loaded his own am'nition."

"Fat chance of finding a keg out here."

Dobbins stopped jabbing his shovel at the dirt and sat down again to consider the problem. "You could unscrew a bunch of cartridges and take the powder out of 'em. Might not be *black* powder, but it'd be powder."

Aug gave that some thought. "Your old man knew something about guns?"

"My pap knew *everything* about guns." Dobbins wiped his streaming face again and nodded. "He was a caution, I'll tell you. We had us a fat-ass ole sheriff back home used to carry an automatic jus' like the one Bleeker's got. An' one day Pap gets holt of it somehow, takes it apart, an' files the *sear* off jus' a teeny bit. That little dinky part"—he crooked an index finger to demonstrate—"is the only thing that stops it from lettin' everything go all at once like a machine gun." He slapped his knee and waggled his head back and forth, chuckling.

"The next time that ole sheriff gets his gun out to shoot at a squirrel, he pulls the trigger an'—*bam-bam-bam-bam-bam!*—that ole automatic goes straight up in the air and back over his shoulder." Dobbins laughed aloud. "He blew out the front window of Marble's Barbershop, put two holes in the cash register, busted one of the mirrors and a couple of bottles of Tiger Balm hair tonic. Killed 'em dead. Wonder he didn't kill no*body*." Dobbins laughed again. "That Pap, he was always funnin' somebody."

"It was just like the one Bleeker has? His pistol?"

"Same thing. Jus' exactly."

Aug scratched the point of the pick back and forth a couple of times in the bottom of the trench.

"How many cartridges would you have to unscrew to end up with"—he separated his thumb and index finger by two or three inches—"maybe that much powder?"

Dobbins considered the question carefully. "It'd take a mess of 'em. What are you figurin' to do, make you a bomb?"

Aug sat down on the edge of the ditch again. "I did that once, in high school . . . made a bomb."

Dobbins reached up and scratched the back of his head. "A bunch of us used to toss dynamite into the river sometimes," he said, "kill us a mess of fish."

"I tossed this one into the toilet in the teachers' room."

Dobbins smiled and waggled his head.

"You keep horsin' aroun', Rooster, you're gonna get your ass thrown in the stockade. You're probably gonna get tossed in there anyway, you keep pesterin' ole Bleeker like you do. You're worse'n my pap. I swear to God."

Aug recognized a compliment when he heard one. He got to his feet again and halfheartedly pushed his shovel at the rocky earth.

"Uh-oh," Dobbins muttered. "Here comes Conniptions."

Aug promptly dropped his shovel and sat down again.

Sergeant Bleeker swaggered up and stood with his hands on his hips, surveying the progress of the excavation. "You been diggin' at all?"

"Some," Dobbins said.

"Where's Ryker at?"

"Doin' his business over to the latrine," Dobbins said without looking up.

Drawing no notice from Aug, Bleeker kicked a couple of rocks down into the pit. "I hope you get this finished up by tonight, Rooster Neck, 'cause I got some real good news for you."

Aug looked at Bleeker without expression. "Don't tell me . . . you've got syphilis."

Bleeker reddened and clenched his fists. With obvious difficulty, he brought his temper under control and grinned. "The good news is that mosta the company's gettin' passes into town tomorrow. Go in an' raise a little hell."

Aug unscrewed the cap of his canteen, knowing the punch line was yet to come.

"Yeah," Bleeker said. "But *you* don't have to go, Rooster Neck. You get to stay here and whitewash all the rocks aroun' the barracks, the latrine, an' the flagpole."

Aug took a long drink, giving Bleeker no sign of having heard him.

"Won't that be nice?" Bleeker asked.

Aug set his canteen aside, stood, and reached for his shovel again without comment.

"An' when you finish with that," Bleeker said, "you got guard duty t'morrow night."

Aug's face remained expressionless.

"Ain't that good news? What'sa matter?" Bleeker asked, his voice rising. "You're always full of jokes. You got no jokes to make?"

But Aug kept picking away at the dirt, whistling a little tune, and Bleeker kicked some more rocks down into the pit and turned and stomped away.

"I don't think that feller likes you," Dobbins said.

"You'd kind of get that impression," Aug agreed.

August 14, 1943

Dear Son:

It was nice to get your letter. Your friend Angie is always asking about you but says you don't write her. She says she thinks you're mad at her, but she won't say why. She's almost ready to be a nurse now. Another year to go, I think. Maybe you'll see each other. You have nurses and things like that in the army, don't you?

I'm glad you didn't really have to go overseas. I saw Norman's mother at the post office (she never calls him by that name you use) and she said he wrote to tell her he was shipping out somewhere but couldn't tell where. I just pray to God you both will be safe, wherever you're sent, until this awful war is over.

Your father says one of the tires on Mr. Sushiwara's Buick is flat. But he's not going to fix it, he says.

Be a good boy and do like your captain tells you. You don't want to get into trouble.

Love,
Mother

P.S. Did you ever get the cookies Marian baked?

CHAPTER ☆ THIRTEEN ☆

MAIN Street petered out just beyond the abandoned Seaside gas station, and the captain slowed and turned off of the pavement into what might loosely have been called Mesa Verde's residential district.

It was early evening. Lights were on inside the houses, and the venetian blinds were open. He saw a family at the supper table, father and mother and two youngsters, one of the boys wearing a bright green football jersey. Next door, a skinny, bald man in jeans and a torn undershirt was drinking from a beer bottle as he leaned against the wall, talking on the telephone.

As a child drifting through the prairie states with his father and mother, the captain had seen a lot of towns like Mesa Verde.

Preacher Maxwell would drive his creaking old wagon slowly down Main Street to its far end, double back on Second Street and again on Third, if there was one, appraising the townspeople's receptiveness to The Good Word and, more important, their willingness to pay for it. The captain often fancied he could still smell the sour, mildewed tent and taste the gritty dust that came up over the tailgate, and feel the continued lurching and lifting, the unending jarring transferred from rough road to bruised posterior through the thick, unyielding folds of canvas.

And he could still hear the taunts of the impudent boys gathered on the street corners, jeering and sometimes flinging a dirt clod or an apple core at the embarrassed youngster perched awkwardly in back of the wagon.

His father would select a suitably located vacant lot and

round up a couple of stalwarts to set up the tent, grudgingly paying them two bits apiece if he couldn't convince them it was God's work. It wasn't a very large tent. There was a patched flap of canvas hanging to the ground at the rear, dividing off a small space where the family slept and took its meals.

He remembered his father as a cold and humorless man given to extended, stonelike silences, shutting out everything around him for days at a time. But stick his thumb in that Bible, give him a handful of slack-jawed believers to look out upon, and he was transformed on the instant into a foot-stomping, sweat-popping harbinger of everlasting righteous retribution.

"That preacher man," folks said, "could talk a hog into havin' kittens."

Mesa Verde looked like all the other little towns in the Southwest. In the summer it got up close to 130 degrees and the wind blew and the sand got into everything and some days the only thing moving on the streets was tumbleweed. On Saturday nights the Indians came in off the reservation in their rickety scrawny-horse wagons. They parked the squaws and the kids under the water tower at the railroad yard, and somehow, in a two-saloon town that wouldn't serve Indians, they managed to get drunk and pass out in the gutter. The sheriff or his deputy just rolled them over against a building where they wouldn't get run over and "let 'em lay."

All of the boxy paint-peeled frame houses on the dusty back streets had big swamp coolers up on their roofs. Here and there a front yard was graced by a drooping pepper tree or, more frequently, a lopsided house trailer or the remains of a rusting, dismembered automobile. None of the homes had lawns out front, although, here and there, he could see a few had been attempted.

Halfway down the block, he had to steer left to avoid a big depression in the street. There was a yellow fire hydrant at the curb that looked like it had sprung a leak and undermined the roadway before they got it fixed. The underground pipes were still exposed.

He made a couple of right turns and got back onto Main Street. Drugstore, grocery, barbershop, shabby Mexican restaurant. There were two churches, an Eagles lodge, two bars, and a boarded-up movie house. It looked like it had caught fire. The bullet-riddled sign at the city limits claimed a population of 1,154, but if there really were that many farmers, alfalfa growers, and would-be ranchers here, most of them, he thought, must already be at home or still in the fields. There was nobody out on the sidewalks.

He parked outside the Staghorn, so designated by the red-painted rack of horns hanging askew over its front door and the blinking red neon sign above it on the flat roof. Nearly all of the vehicles at the curb were pickup trucks. He pushed through the door into the smoke and noise.

"You're trompin' on my heart, like you have right from the start, and it wasn't just no grade school Valentine ..."

The big multicolored Wurlitzer against the back wall was going full blast, a spirited shuffleboard game was in progress to one side, and a half-dozen determined-looking couples were rocking back and forth on the tiny dance floor among the chrome-legged tables. It smelled like every bar he'd ever been in: cigarettes, beer, and bodies.

"Now you're sorry as can be, an' the one you want is me, but this old boy belongs to someone else ..."

He stood just inside the door and surveyed the noisy early-evening crowd with some surprise. There must have been fifty people in there. For a cow town on a Tuesday night, the place was jumping. Expertly he surveyed the room, looking for targets of opportunity.

" 'Scuse us, Off'cer."

A potbellied rancher, his mottled face glowing red beneath his straw hat, teetered past in high-heeled boots, towing a tall, dark-haired woman behind him. As she went by, laughing, she swayed against the captain and, as if reaching out to steady herself, touched him below the belt. *Low* below the belt.

"Sorry." Her eyes found his momentarily, and the lazy smile disputed the feigned apology. *Hello.* The heavy front door swung shut behind them as they went out onto the sidewalk.

He turned and pushed the door open and watched them weave, arm in arm, along the cracked sidewalk. As they rounded the corner into the darkened parking lot, he heard the woman give a startled yelp and laugh loudly again.

She didn't look all that bad. More than that stewed cow-chip kicker could handle.

"Hey! Cap'm!"

He turned to see who was calling.

"Stop that peekin' out th' door an' come here an' dance with me!"

From the edge of the crowded floor, a short, stocky woman leaned forward, feet wide apart, looking up at him with a sly grin. She had a beer bottle by the neck in one hand and, in order to remain near upright, gripped the back of a chair with the other. Her tremendous bosom threatened to spill out of her scoop-necked cotton blouse onto the floor.

For an instant, he thought it was Fae Manning, one of the Mountain Bell telephone operators back in Piebald. Fae had a front like that. As a gesture of admiration one night, he'd poured a full glass of green crème de menthe down the canyon, and Fae, taking offense, had picked up a pretzel bowl and thrown it at him. She missed and the heavy crockery dish shattered against Manny's precious jukebox, knocking out a big chunk of colored glass down near the floor.

He smiled at the woman as generously as he was able and raised one hand, palm out in refusal. He wasn't ready to commit himself for the evening. Not yet, anyway. The woman, refusing to be dismissed that easily, released the chair and, concentrating mightily, lurched forward to grab the back of the next nearest one.

"C'mon, Cap'm, you ole son of a bitch! Come dance with me!"

A skinny, bespectacled rancher in boots and jeans stood up at the table next to her, grinning.

"You wanta dance, Sally? Shit, I'll dance with ya."

He clamped one arm around her ample waist, lifted high the hand with the beer bottle, and stamping his left foot with vigor, whirled her away like a rotund Statue of Liberty. Foam spiraled out of her beer bottle onto everyone around them as she threw her head back and shrieked with laughter. The captain grinned in spite of himself.

The heavy door bumped him as it was pushed open behind him and, stepping out of the way, he turned and saw the tall, dark-haired woman standing there alone, grinning at him.

"You don't get around much, Captain." She punched him lightly in the chest. "That's where you were the last time I saw you."

He smiled, bowed from the waist in his most courtly manner, and waved her in with an exaggerated flourish.

"Come in, come in," he said. "It's not often, I'd guess, they are favored with the presence of a lady in here."

Aug turned his head and covered his nose and mouth with a sleeve as the weapons carrier slid in next to the unlighted sentry shack, the truck's headlights yellowed and dimmed by a billowing cloud of dust.

One of the men hunched over in the back of the truck called out, "Hey, Rooster Neck, we winnin' the goddam war out here?"

"Ole Hitler see *this* sorry place," someone else responded, "he'd say, 'Fuck it; *you* keep it.' "

Hodge, Aug's replacement, swung his legs over the side of the clumsy vehicle and dropped heavily to the dirt, holding his rifle high as if he were fording a stream.

Aug crawled up into the open bed of the truck and slumped down on a bench seat next to Lovell Jimmerson. Jimmerson had one eyeball that stayed rolled up under its lid, nearly out of sight.

"From his off side," Blackie insisted, "he looks like Orphan Annie."

Jimmerson had just come off number four, a couple of miles up the road from Aug's post. A stubby freckle-faced youngster from West Virginia, he wanted to be a telegrapher for the railroad when the war was over, and he was trying his best to master the Morse code. When they went on sentry duty at four that afternoon, he had passed Aug a wrinkled sheet of paper with the alphabet penciled out in dots and dashes, so Aug could send practice messages to him with his flashlight in the darkness.

He looked at Aug reproachfully. "I don't see no fuckin' mule aroun' here."

Aug turned toward him. "What are you talking about?"

"You flashed 'dah-dah, dit-dit-dah, dit-*dah*-dit-dit, dit,'" White-Eye said. "'Mule.' Said you killed a *mule . . . didn't* you?"

Aug laughed and clapped him on the shoulder as the truck lurched toward the next post. "You need a little work yet, Jimmerson. What I said was, I'd just killed a stupid *mole*—m-o-l-e. Smacked it with my rifle butt." In the dark Aug couldn't see the blank expression on Jimmerson's face, but he could imagine it. Aug shook his head and laughed again. "Killed a mule."

All the way back to camp, Jimmerson had his head down, his lips moving, as he tapped out the code with his rifle butt on the floor of the weapons carrier. "Dah, dah, *dah-dah-dah*, dit-*dah*-dit-dit, dit."

"You'll have that one down pat," Aug assured him, "if a train ever runs over a mule."

Jimmerson nodded in agreement. "Dah-dah, dah-dah-dah, dit-dit-*dah*-dit . . . No, goddammit!" He snapped his fingers in frustration. "Dit-*dah*-dit-dit . . ."

The truck drew up to the guard barracks, and the men clambered out and clumped inside. They could sleep or play cards now, write letters home, or do whatever they wanted to until it was time to go out again, just before midnight. Four hours on, four off, until the new guard detail took over the next afternoon at 1600. Aug yawned and looked at his wristwatch. It was only eight-thirty. Too early to go to sleep.

The captain sneaked a look at his watch. She was already working on her second double shot of Old Taylor.

"And what keeps an attractive young woman like yourself busy in a town like this?"

"You mean, in a dump like Mesa Verde." She laughed again and took a swallow from her drink. When she laughed or flashed her wide grin, he could see a gold inlay back in there. "I work at my husband's dry cleaners."

She quickly raised an index finger. "Now, don't look so down in the drawers, sweetness. He's not in town." She made a noncommittal gesture. "Who knows where the hell he is, this frigging war? We were only married a month." She waggled her head slowly. "He told the draft board, 'How come *I* gotta go; I'm *married*,' and they said *being* married was one thing; *getting* married to keep out of the draft was another." She shrugged and took another swallow. "True love. But he didn't make his move early enough."

He lifted his glass for a sip and let his eyes slide down over her. She was about thirty, he guessed, maybe a couple of years older. She had blue-gray eyes and dark, softly waved hair, one lock tumbling across her forehead. Kind of a large nose with a bump on the bridge. Not a bad-looking body, though. She was wearing a blue high-necked dress. He wondered if the bumps were hers or foam rubber.

"How about *you*, Captain? Where are you stationed? If that's not a military secret." She touched her mouth with one finger—"Loose lips sink ships"—and gave him that mocking half-smile again.

He nodded in the general direction of Arido. "I've got an outfit out in the desert. *Temporary* assignment." He sat up a little straighter and flexed his shoulders. "Combat training. We're on our way over pretty soon, next couple of months, probably."

She raised her eyebrows. "What kind of training is *that*, out in the *desert*? The war's already *over* in North Africa, isn't it?"

He grimaced and turned his head. *Smart-alecky woman.* "I'd rather not talk about it." He made a show of looking around for unfriendly ears. "Not in here."

He took another swallow. At least she lived here in town; he wouldn't have to spring for a room. He'd noticed a run-down cluster of tourist cabins out on the edge of town. He rolled his wrist over as casually as he could and stole another look at his watch.

Aug picked up his flashlight and stepped out of the door of the guard barracks.

He flicked the flashlight on and looked at his wristwatch. It was almost ten-thirty; they would be going out again in an hour and a half, so it wouldn't do any good to lie down. He wouldn't be able to sleep until he came off shift again at four o'clock. He'd get maybe an hour before first call at five-thirty. It didn't matter that the bugle call wasn't meant for them; it still woke them up. Then one more shift, eight till noon, and they would be done.

Behind him, from the gloom somewhere down the double row of cots, a liquid snore rattled and bubbled, stopped, and began again. Garnett wasn't really asleep yet, he was just warming up, getting the feel of it. Aug yawned and stretched. He was bored.

A ring of bright lights on tall utility poles circled the cluster of buildings, throwing long, dark shadows across the company area. To the west he could see a few scattered lights of Camp One and, beyond, over against the butte, the faint yellow glow in the sky that was Camp Two.

A cool breeze drifted softly through the encampment. There was absolute silence, which seemed almost a disturbance in itself. Until now he couldn't remember ever having been anywhere where there was *no* noise. *Nothing.* He couldn't remember ever noticing the silence before, either. Not even the yip of a coyote disturbed the sleeping desert. There were a couple of bitch dogs in camp, and sometimes, when they were in heat, the coyotes would be out there all night, just beyond the reach of the lights, yapping and shrilling their raucous demands.

He went down the steps and along the graveled pathway to the latrine.

A head-high partition inside separated the sinks and showers from a row of seven stools. The seat of the stool nearest the door was painted bright red, reserved for anyone known to be infected with venereal disease. Gonorrhea—"the clap"—was not an uncommon enlisted man's affliction, and there were frequent surprise "short arm inspections" to discover any new infectees.

> Step up smartly and do not salute,
> Unbutton yours pants and pull out your root.
> Stand at attention and give it a squeeze,
> If nothing comes out you can stand at ease.

"Shoot. You ain't been in the army," Blackie insisted, "till you had the clap an' been in the guardhouse at least once't."

Private Gregory was standing in front of the long, low metal trough that served as a urinal. Gregory's uniform, even when he first put it on, always looked as if he'd slept in it out in the rain. He had just come off post number one, a hundred yards up the road.

"I'm *hungry*," he said, finishing and stepping back after a final shake. "You reckon anybody's over in the mess hall?"

"I didn't see any lights in there."

Gregory was the company's number one chow hound. He was *always* hungry. "That sumbitch could smell a ham samwich," Blackie claimed, "in a tent fulla tear gas."

"They orta set out somethin' for you when you come off guard," Gregory grumbled, buttoning his fly. "I ain't et nothin', I'll bet, for more'n four hours." For Gregory, four hours without food was equivalent to a religious fast. He went out the door, still grumbling, working on his fly.

Aug followed him out into the darkness a few moments later. He stood in the doorway, surveying the shadowed company area. The only building showing lights inside was the orderly room.

He walked across the hard-packed assembly area, past the flagpole, and went up the stairs. Corporal Stitch had charge of quarters tonight. Stitch was a nice guy—maybe he could bum a cup of coffee from him. Stitch had the flattest feet Aug had ever seen. Like undersized ironing boards.

"I seem t'have neglected to ask your name," the captain said, raising his eyebrows and making a conscious effort to focus on her face. He had slid his chair around next to hers, and one hand rested easily on her thigh.

She wrinkled her nose. "Lucille. I hate that name."

He shrugged. "Nice name."

Lucille. That night in Detroit, after he'd escaped on the old booze boat.

She had an upstairs room in the back above a Chinese restaurant on Dix Avenue. The whole building had smelled like chop suey and soy sauce. And mildew.

"You look kinda cute without your clothes on," she'd told him. "What happened to your knee?"

"I fell on my ass chasing a trolley. How'd you get that scar?"

"Goddam sailor sliced me with a broken bottle." She lifted her left breast and fingered the raised purple half-circle beneath it. "Son of a bitch almost cut it off."

Later, when she padded barefoot down the hall to the bathroom, he slid his money and the long-barreled six-shooter under the lumpy mattress.

The new Lucille smiled at him and put her hand over his. "You want to dance?"

"Can't." He tapped his knee. "Took some shrapnel in it in France. Stiffens up on me sometimes."

She looked away and sipped at her drink.

"Thanksgiving's coming in two weeks," she said. "You and your men going to have a big hoo-rah out there in the desert? Turkey and pumpkin pie and everything?"

He made an indifferent gesture with his glass. He hadn't given any thought to it at all, wasn't even aware the holiday was approaching.

"I'd think you'd be throwing *some* kind of a wingding for your men," she said, swirling the ice in her glass. "Home away from home and all that. You being the post commander."

He sat up a little straighter. She was right. He *was* a post commander. Sort of.

"I was givin' some thought to throwin' a little party, maybe." His lips were beginning to feel numb. "Nothin' much. Break up the routine."

Lucille poked at the ice in her glass with her little finger. "I haven't been all alone on Thanksgiving since I was a little girl."

He raised his glass, spilling some rye down his chin.

"I was thinkin' 'bout . . . maybe lettin' them bring their girl-friends. Or wives or somebody."

"That would be nice," she said. "I suppose you've already asked someone."

Lieutenant Michaels came into the orderly room about eleven o'clock.

"Sit down, sit down." He motioned Aug and Stitch back to their seats, pulled out the chair from behind First Sergeant Garrison's desk, and sat down himself. Leaning back in the chair, he swung both feet up onto the desk blotter. "What's going on tonight, Stitch?"

"Nothin', Lieutenant. All quiet."

Michaels gave Aug a sidelong glance, a half-smile twitching his lips, and drew his .45 automatic out of its holster. He pulled the slide back and let it return, injecting a cartridge into the chamber.

"You ever shoot one of these, Rustyanek?" Michaels was one of the few in the company who called Aug by his true name.

"Yeah. Some. A friend of mine back home had one."

Boner did have one like that. That part was true.

"Can you hit anything with it?" Michaels sighted along the barrel, squinting one eye.

"Not much."

"You got a dollar on you, Stitch? Bet you a dollar I can shoot the knothole out of that bookcase, first try."

Stitch's face was a mixture of alarm and delight. "In here?"

Boom!

The report inside the confines of the tiny room was deafening. Aug's ears rang like a gong.

There was a large hole an inch to the right of the knothole.

Boom!

A second hole appeared on the opposite side of the knothole.

"Piss," Michaels said. He swung his feet off the desk and got up out of the chair. He peered at the splintered bookcase. "I got it bracketed; next round I'd have been right on." He holstered the pistol and walked to the front of the orderly room and looked out the window.

He glanced at his watch. "What are the lights doing on in Third Platoon barracks?"

"They got a poker game going," Stitch said. "I figured with the captain in town . . ."

The half-smile came back. "Lights out is lights out, Corporal. I guess I'll have to go over there and put 'em out myself."

He went out the door and down the steps and after a few

moments of quiet they heard *Boom! ... Boom! ... Boom! ... Boom!* When they went to the window and looked toward Third Platoon barracks, the ceiling lights were out. All four of them.

A few moments later they heard Michaels leave the motor pool in his jeep to make the rounds of the sentry posts.

It was a warm night.

The park Lucille had mentioned was nothing more than a little grassy area in the traffic circle a block from the saloon. It was dominated by a flagpole and a concrete monument honoring Mesa Verde veterans of World War I and was surrounded by an iron picket fence.

Lucille was drunk. They were both drunk.

She kicked off her shoes at the fence, leaned forward to kiss him wetly on the lips, and held up her arms. "Liff me over . . . lie on the grass and neck."

He grunted. Necking wasn't what he had in mind, but, grimacing, he stooped to pick her up, one hand beneath her knees. She was bare-legged. The factories were making parachutes now instead of hosiery, and women were painting their legs with tan makeup. He straightened with difficulty and—shifting her weight, struggling to regain his balance—stumbled toward the fence and tried to lift her over the sharp spikes.

"Look out! Don't . . . Oh! *Owwww!* Son of a *bitch*!"

Aug stood on the steps of the orderly room, looking down the graveled pathway toward the officers' quarters. Michaels had the guard; the captain was in town. The building's other occupants were apparently absent. There were no lights showing.

He had never seen the inside of the officers' quarters, and he had often wondered if it was much different—fancier, maybe—than his own severe accommodations. Idly, he went down the steps and strolled along the graveled pathway toward the darkened building. As he reached the steep wooden stairway leading up to the front door, he clicked his flashlight off. He turned and looked behind him. There were lights in the orderly room, as there would be all night, but no one in view in the shadowed campground.

He turned again and looked up at the dark windows in front of him. The building seemed to hunch its shoulders and glower back at him. *Officers' territory. Out of bounds for enlisted men.*

As he started up the steps one of the boards screeched loudly beneath his boot, as if warning him.

Rooster Neck, you're gonna get your ass run right up the flagpole! Inside, his flashlight revealed a small sitting room, a few chairs, and a low table with magazines on it, with narrow doors leading off at either side.

He had no trouble identifying the captain's room. His holstered six-shooter hung from a nail over his cot. His blankets and spotless white sheets were stretched drum-tight beneath the thick pillow. At the end of the bed stood an olive-drab metal footlocker with brass trim, the captain's name and rank stenciled on the lid. His boots and shoes, reflecting the beam from Aug's flashlight, were lined up in precise parade formation beneath a neat row of crisply pressed uniforms on wire hangers.

A steel helmet with painted-on captain's bars sat on a wooden shelf above the uniforms.

Inspiration surfaced—inspiration of the sort Constable Vervais, Miss Bunker the librarian, Miss Longnecker and Mr. Griffith, Joe Marble the undertaker, and Old Man Bilmeister might recall painfully.

He took the helmet down and, humming happily to himself, loosened the chin strap. He had seen a metal butt can in the little sitting room, and carrying the helmet by its strap like an Easter basket, he went out and got it. It was half full, rank with crushed cigarettes, wet cigar butts, and ashes.

He emptied it into the helmet.

Then he went back into the captain's room and, turning the beam of the flashlight up, located a metal electrical conduit running along the exposed ceiling joists. There was a piece of metal strapping, loose at one end, hammered in next to the bare light bulb. He hung the helmet upside down from the strapping, cut the light fixture's long pull-string loose, and reattached it to the webbing inside the helmet.

At the sink in the adjoining bathroom, he filled the butt can with water, went back into the captain's room, and climbed up onto the bed. The warm glow from the flashlight, left on the floor, gave him ample light to see what he was doing. Careful not to slop any onto the floor or blankets, he reached up and poured the water in with the butts and ashes, filling the steel helmet to the brim.

He unscrewed the light bulb.

Wiping his hands, he climbed down and surveyed his work.

Wouldn't old Boner get a kick out of this? He'd have to write him.

He took the pull-string between thumb and finger and gently tested the balance of the helmet. It wouldn't take much of a tug. Just somebody reaching up to turn on the light.

Aug was already back on post number five when the captain's jeep came rocketing down the final hundred yards toward camp on the wrong side of the road. The left front wheel caught some loose sand and the jeep veered sharply, plowed through a clump of greasewood and ocotillo, ricocheted off a stump, and bounced back up to the road again with the captain still clamped on to the steering wheel.

The little vehicle slewed to a halt in front of the motor pool, and he fell out of it.

No-good son-of-a-bitchin' woman. Goddam pissy-assed *drunk*. He raised himself to one elbow and grinned. But a good-looking one. Busted her ass on that picket fence.

His cap fell off as he rolled over in the dirt and managed to find the ground with his hands and both knees. He reached one long arm out for the jeep, got a tentative handhold, and, after one false start, made it to his feet. He teetered there, head down, feet wide apart, a fragile triumph over the dictates of gravity.

He chuckled. She's got two or three *extra* holes in her ass now.

He leaned forward, made a quick adjustment for wind direction, and lurched into the darkness toward his quarters. Someone had left a large anvil sitting out on the floor of the motor pool; he missed it by inches. Similar good fortune steered him out the far side of the building and across the open ground to the front steps of the officers' quarters.

Negotiating the stairway in an erect posture, however, was too much to ask of himself at this late hour. "I'm a goddam *post commander*." He slowly lowered himself to his hands and knees and crawled up the splintery steps, across the porch, and through the door. If any of the other occupants of the building were in residence, they gave no sign.

Oughta wake up Michaels. That son of a bitch got no respect for nobody. He chuckled. But I like that li'l bastard. Oughta wake up Flowers, the goddam fairy. Him and his blue eyes, wavy hair. Gets too much sleep. He snorted and grinned again. "Get his ass started on Thanksgiving fes . . . tivities."

Lu-*cille*. Would you like to come to the party? "*Love* to." Sergeant Cleary would have to requisition some goddam turkeys somewhere. Bring in some booze. Have a li'l party.

Finding no merit in climbing to his feet for the brief remainder of the journey, he crawled on into his room in the dark.

"Turn on the goddam light," he mumbled. He had no particular reason to. It was just the customary practice upon entering a dark room. With one hand out in front of him, he found the edge of his cot and, using that as an anchor, struggled to his feet.

He made two blind swings for the pull string, but failed to make contact. The second swing turned him halfway around, and he lost his balance again and fell heavily onto his cot.

"Hell with it." One leg was already partway up on the bed, and he swung the other one up next to it. What did he need a goddam light for? Nothin' to see.

CHAPTER FOURTEEN

☆ ☆

Eᴅɪᴛᴏʀɪᴀʟ, *San Francisco Call-Bulletin*

On this day of giving thanks, on the churned-up south shore of the Volturno River, barely 20 miles north of Naples, exhausted infantrymen of the American Fifth Army lie in the foul-smelling mud wondering how they are going to fight their way across the rain-swollen stream and into the town beyond. It has been raining without letup for what seems like a month. Over on the east coast, the Eighth Army isn't doing much better. Italy is a pockmarked, varicose-veined leg, and the entire offensive line is hung up below the craggy calf muscle like a tight-fitting garter.

On this Thanksgiving Day, halfway around the world in the Pacific, the Second Marines are hunkered down in the sand and broken coral on a tiny fragment of purgatory called Tarawa. Inching from one shallow depression, from one burned-out bunker to another, they blast away desperately at shadows among the jumbled crisscross of coconut palms flattened by the offshore bombardment. And they are fired upon by a fanatic enemy. The marines landed on this low-lying atoll just two days ago and more than 7,000 sons of the emperor already lie dead around them.

On this day of thanks, the 575th was getting ready for a party.

It was a surprise party. The captain had dropped it on them

without preamble two nights earlier, following the flag-lowering ceremony. He described it as "a goddam Thanksgiving blowout your mother would be proud of."

Triggering greater reaction was his announcement that a bus would be requisitioned from the motor pool at Piebald so they could transport guests to the event. "Your old ladies, if they're close by," was the way he put it, one corner of his mouth twisting into a grin, "or a piece of ass from town if you can find one."

Aug and Mozetti exchanged glances. Thanksgiving and "a piece of ass from town" seemed somewhat incongruous. Beyond that, in-depth carnal pleasures were still largely fantasy for both of them.

Aug's only real experience with sex had been that one time, graduation night, at the whorehouse in Napa with Boner and Bert Rooney, and he was still trying to forget that. Mozetti had a few graphically descriptive tales of catch-as-catch-can action on a burlap sack in the vineyards back home, and he had returned from overnight passes in Mesa Verde with some equally lurid accounts. But Aug suspected his sawed-off Italian friend was no more experienced than he, because one prerequisite of an overnight pass was a condom—Lieutenant Bauman distributed Silvertex rubbers that were only slightly thinner than inner tubes—and Mozetti's supply appeared to be steadily *growing*.

Overall, the company's response to the captain's Thanksgiving announcement was the customary skepticism.

"Thanksgiving party? The fuck's he talkin' about?"

"Prob'ly cold cuts with stuffing."

"Turkey shit on a shingle, more like it."

"Whatever it is, I ain't eatin' it if Cleary's cookin' it."

"Fuckin' Cleary could mess up cold cereal."

The object of the men's scorn had been ordered to spare neither energy nor culinary imagination in preparation of a sumptuous Thanksgiving repast. When it was pointed out in the orderly room, however, that the mess sergeant's idea of gourmet cooking was keeping the ice cream and the potatoes and gravy in separate heaps, a detailed menu was composed and delivered to Cleary personally by Lieutenant Flowers.

This, of course, wounded Sergeant Cleary.

"Fuck's *this* shit?" he snorted, displaying the offending document to PFC Houghton, whose scaly complexion seemed even more florid that day than usual.

"Cream a t'mata soup," Cleary read. "Big fuckin' deal. Olives, pickles, celery." He stopped and pointed a stubby finger. "Turkey? What'd they *figger* I was gonna serve 'em, jackass balls?"

He read on. "Sweet p'tatas, cream corn, 'sparagus. Nobody in this fuckin' outfit ever *seen* a piece of 'sparagus. Cro . . . croy"—he tried to wrap his lips around the strange word—"what the fuck's croy-sants?"

Houghton peered over the sergeant's shoulder while absently scratching himself. His face lit up. "Them little curled-up rolls." He sketched one in midair with a peeling index finger. "Like the half-moon on a privy."

Cleary flipped the menu into a sinkful of greasy dishwater.

"The fuck *they* know about cookin' a meal?"

Even more indicative of a special occasion was the dispatch of a jeep to the Mexican border. "Reconnaissance" was typed on the trip ticket; beneath that, someone had penciled in "Procurement." Whatever the designation, the aim of the mission was precisely defined: the acquisition of two ten-gallon jugs of Mexican rum.

"Send somebody," the captain growled at First Sergeant Garrison, "who can find his goddam way home." He turned away, then back again. "Without drinking it all before he gets back here."

Garrison chose Sergeant Crawford and, inspiration having then apparently fled, Billy Lawler. They were given a rousing send-off at the motor pool and, that evening, an even more enthusiastic reception upon their return. Billy Lawler did his best to look important, sitting there in the back of the jeep with his skinny arms around the two big basket-encased jugs, but the role was difficult with the tufts of hair sticking out from under his cap.

"Ole Billy," Blackie chuckled, "was sittin' there grinnin' like a possum in a slop bucket."

There was some discussion about posting a twenty-four-hour guard over the two jugs, but in the end it was deemed adequate to lock them away in Sergeant Cleary's pantry.

* * *

On the afternoon of the appointed day, the borrowed thirty-passenger bus drew in from town with only four partygoers aboard—Cooper and Blackie and the young ladies of their choice, P-38 and Big Hoover. Actually, neither of the guests was very young. Neither of them was a lady, either. There were only two whores in Mesa Verde, and Blackie and Cooper had corralled both of them. Cooper was asleep, of course, stretched out across the back seat. His date sat by herself, blowing a desultory stream of cigarette smoke out the window as she viewed the encampment without enthusiasm. Tall, with frizzy red hair and a spotty complexion, she had acquired the name P-38 because she had long, scrawny legs like the twin booms of the Lockheed fighter. With a cockpit in between.

Big Hoover, who stood a full head taller than Blackie and outweighed him by thirty pounds, had earned her nickname as the result of one considerable talent.

"That woman could suck a pig through a fire hose," Blackie insisted. "An' that's a fact."

Only two others, Bruener and Garnett, had managed dinner dates. Bruener, his head tilted back so he could see where he was going, drove up in a dented '37 Nash convertible with Lillian, the wife of Henry Nez, the Navajo bartender at the Bent Horn Saloon.

"Ole Henry, he don't give a hoot." Bruener shrugged. "He said, she wanted to, go ahead."

Lillian suffered constantly from black bile melancholia. She was crying. Already tanked, she was chewing sunflower seeds and, between sobs, spitting out the hulls. The white cable-knit sweater covering her considerable bosom was liberally peppered with debris.

Garnett arrived an hour later, grinning, horn blaring, in a big powder blue Cadillac hearse. He had four giggling teenage girls in there with him. One of them, the driver, was the daughter of the town undertaker. Many of the observers on hand expressed pleasure that Garnett had thought to bring along some extras, but Lieutenant Flowers drew him aside and waggled a stern finger at him.

"I think this most unwise," he said, turning his head and

looking sideways at Garnett as if he were reprimanding an unruly child, "bringing those teenagers out here."

Garnett raised his shoulders and turned his palms up. "Sheee-it, Lieutenant, *I'm* a fuckin' teenager."

Shortly before the dinner hour, the captain pulled up in his old Dodge coupe with Lucille sitting erect beside him. She was wearing a little black hat with a veil across her forehead and, although it was unusually warm for November, her best white wool dress and her treasured black and white rabbit stole.

"Dressed up like a black an' white pony," Anberger observed.

"Don't look like no pony to me," Jimmerson countered. "Leastwise, *I* wouldn't mind havin' a ride."

The captain's brass was gleaming, his best dress uniform sharply creased. He helped Lucille out of the car with a flourish—she was carrying a small inflatable rubber cushion—and, taking her by the elbow, stalked through the appreciative knot of onlookers without glancing right or left. Lucille smiled brightly at those around her. She appeared interested in inspecting the company area, but the captain firmly turned her instead toward the officers' quarters.

Anberger nodded. "Ice cream's maybe comin' before supper."

Jimmerson agreed. "Dit-dit-*dah*-dit, dit-dit-*dah*, dah-dit-*dah*." His spelling suffered when he got excited.

Aug, Kaplowitz, and Mozetti sat on the front porch of the orderly room and watched the captain urge Lucille up the front steps of his quarters.

"You don't suppose that old . . ." Aug said.

"You're fuckin'-A right," Mozetti assured him.

Kaplowitz giggled.

Aug shook his head in disbelief. "Where's his wife? Sergeant Crawford says they've got a little girl. Can you imagine that wrinkled-up old man with a baby girl?"

"He's probably taught her to chew tobacco."

"As a matter of fact, can you imagine the woman who'd marry him?"

* * *

It was not a marriage made in heaven. It was spawned at Sweet's Ballroom in Oakland, a big, dimly lighted drinking and dancing hangout during the last gasp of the big band era.

It was a good place to find unescorted women, and the captain had taken to dropping in there two or three nights a week, sipping judiciously on a beer for an hour or more. Still subsisting on meager commissions from the bail bond office, beer was all he could afford

Jean was funneled into the place one night as a prank by two free-swinging nurses at the county's Fairmount Hospital, where she worked in the administrator's office. She had taken the clerical job as a temporary measure after her college major, classical music, failed to provide sustenance. Strong-willed, if naive, a determined virgin whose defenses had never been seriously tested, she neither smoked nor drank and barely tolerated those practices by others.

She was "hardly the type to frequent a public dance hall," a point she made firmly as she was propelled through the door into the disharmony of band music, loud voices, and clinking glassware. Her companions vanished quickly into the jostling crowd on the dance floor, leaving her alone at a tiny table, nervously jiggling the ice in a glass of Coca-Cola.

She was not unattractive. Several men asked her to dance, but she refused, barely murmuring a response and avoiding their eyes. Finally a young sailor approached, grinning impishly, and rather than continue to sit there, exposed to the eddying throng, she accepted, taking her purse with her.

They were moving stiffly about at arm's length when another seaman, drunk, made a particularly graphic proposal to her from the sidelines. Instantly, a fight started, and as the two sailors slugged away at each other in a smear of blood and broken teeth on the polished floor, a tall, angular man with a crooked grin appeared suddenly at her elbow.

"The cavalry has arrived," he said, and smoothly guided her away.

Shaken, disgusted, she wanted to leave immediately, but he persuaded her to wait until the disturbance subsided, until she could find her friends. She let him lead her to a table in a corner but refused his offer of a drink, and he waved the cocktail waitress away without ordering anything for himself.

"It's not often," he told her, "they are favored with the presence of a lady in here."

It was apparent he was a gentleman. She heard herself agreeing that it was indeed a coincidence that he, too, had come into this horrid place for the first time this evening and that, like her, he ordinarily spent his free time reading and listening to good music.

Gradually she began to relax. He had a disarmingly easy manner, and he had been to so many places and done such interesting things—his years as a security officer on the New Orleans docks, in law enforcement in San Joaquin Valley, and as a federal undercover agent pursuing bootleggers on the Canadian border. And there was the undeniable glamour of his war wound, the shrapnel he'd taken in his knee in France, at Château-Thierry during the Second Battle of the Marne.

His limp caused him some discomfort now and then, but—he shrugged—it was nothing.

She blinked once when he mentioned having graduated from "the Academy"—didn't army officers graduate from "the Point?"—but let it go. He said he had been forced to accept a nothing job temporarily, "associated with law enforcement." She understood. Jobs were not plentiful. They both ordered Coca-Cola.

Later she insisted on leaving with the two nurses, but she gave him her telephone number.

They were as unlike as Montgomery Ward and Neiman-Marcus, as Haydn and honky-tonk.

A woman weds when one day she meets someone she wants to marry, a man when suddenly, for no definable reason, he decides he's ready to get married. A red-nosed judge at the Oakland City Hall performed the perfunctory noontime ceremony.

The new Mrs. Maxwell paid the three dollars.

When the moment of gastronomic truth finally arrived, PFC Raber's rendition of mess call on his bugle suggested he had already dipped into the Mexican rum. Even when he was sober, Raber was no expert with his horn.

"What the hell was that? Laundry call?"

"Turn aroun' an' blow it with yer mouth, Raber!"

"That sumbitch couldn't blow flies off'n a cow patty."

But the mess hall was resplendent.

From somewhere, Sergeant Cleary's staff had acquired red and white checkered paper tablecloths. A pumpkin surrounded by clusters of varicolored fruits, nuts, and dried vegetables sat in the center of each table, with silverware and paper napkins defining each place. Orange and black crepe paper streamers dipped gracefully between the exposed rafters and, at the far end of the room, white candles stood at either end of a table set for the officers. A skeptic might have noted that both candles were partly melted, listed slightly to one side, and sat in empty tuna fish cans from which the labels had been peeled. But they were candles nonetheless.

"*Lookit* this place. If that don't beat all get out."

"Fuckin' food looks almost good enough t'eat."

"Cleary musta had it sent in."

Stainless-steel containers were heaped with glistening appetizers, vegetables, mashed potatoes, dressing, and hot gravy. A huge mound of sliced turkey awaited with ample choices of white or dark meat. Mess Sergeant Cleary, his face flushed with a mixture of pride and half the contents of a fifth of Four Roses, stood by the steaming platter carving generous slabs from a big golden-brown gobbler and forking them onto the metal trays passing before him.

Blackie, following Big Hoover down the line, stopped and pointed at the carcass. "That *air* a turkey, ain't it, Cleary? There don't seem to be as many buzzards outside t'day."

Cleary pointed his big carving knife at Blackie and opened his mouth, but before he could think of a proper response, Blackie and Big Hoover were headed for a table, laughing.

"Smart-mouth son of a bitch." Cleary reached under the counter for his Four Roses and took another pull at the dark bottle.

By the time the captain, Lucille, and Lieutenants Michaels and Flowers entered the mess hall—no one had seen Lieutenant Bauman for three days—the banquet was in high gear. Early starters were back in line for seconds, an unprecedented occurrence in

Sergeant Cleary's memory. And it was already apparent the two ten-gallon jugs of Mexican rum were not going to be sufficient, even when diluted half-and-half with canned pineapple juice.

Wearing white towels around their necks in honor of the occasion, KPs circulated among the tables with wide-mouth metal pitchers, pouring the potent mixture into white porcelain coffee mugs thrust toward them.

Big Hoover's voice could be heard over the din, telling dirty jokes and pounding the tabletop with her fist as she brayed hoarsely at her own punch lines. Impulsively, she grabbed Blackie around the shoulders and gave him a bone-popping hug. Blackie laughed and crossed his eyes. P-38, smoking a fat, black cigar and downing the contents of every mug she could reach, was laughing, too. She was wearing a low-cut peasant blouse, and Dobbins kept trying to toss olives down the crevasse every time she leaned across the table to snag another mug.

P-38 aimed a bright red fingernail at him. "You get olive juice on this blouse, you skinny little fart, and I'll give you a pair of knock-nuts to go with those knees." The whole table stomped their feet and laughed; no question, this party was on its way to becoming a good one.

Two tables over, Billy Lawler was trying to convince one of Garnett's teenagers that she should take a stroll with him across the dike into the desert, but all four girls were sticking together like grits, sipping at their rum drinks and shrieking with laughter every time one of them dribbled some down her chin.

At the table behind them, Bruener's date was still crying. She had both elbows on the table, clenched fists supporting her tousled head, her cigarette vibrating up and down between her lips with every shuddering sob. She was very drunk. Bruener was trying to cheer her up, but nothing appeared to work, not even copping a feel.

From the officers' table, Lucille looked out onto the scene happily. She had taken off her rabbit stole and the little black hat with the veil. She and the captain had had several stiff belts of Old Overholt in his quarters before coming to dinner. That was when the stole had come off, and she had had to stay alert to keep the rest on. The rye combined with the rum and pineapple juice was beginning to spread a warm glow through her body. She caught Lieutenant Flowers's eye and smiled at him, but he reddened and ducked his head after a furtive glance toward the captain. Lieutenant Michaels winked openly at her and grinned.

She nudged the captain, who was making quick work of the big pitcher of rum and pineapple juice on their table.

"Aren't you supposed to make a speech?" she asked him. "Propose a toast or something?"

He stopped with his cup halfway to his mouth and looked at her blankly, and then out at the roisterous crowd.

While everyone else in the company was either standing guard or eating turkey and getting drunk, Aug sat behind a wooden desk in the orderly room as acting charge of quarters. His only assigned responsibility was answering the telephone, which had proved to be no burden at all. Kaplowitz had assured him there was little reason for it to ring unless someone wished to speak with Captain Maxwell, and on this warm holiday afternoon no one had yet invested a nickel for the thrill of that experience.

During the day, looking after things from the orderly room was ordinarily the responsibility of First Sergeant Garrison, but the top kick had eschewed the party and gone into town. Aug was well aware the assignment was not a reward. He had grown accustomed to being handed whatever sorry job was available.

The morning after the inverted-helmet incident in the captain's quarters, Aug had braced himself for whatever retribution was sure to follow; he was certain to be the primary suspect. First Sergeant Garrison had adopted Miss Longnecker's policy toward the investigation of anything strange occurring in the company; bust Rooster Neck's ass first. The likelihood that anyone else would have the temerity to get into the captain's stuff would seem inconceivable to Garrison.

But there had been no mention of it at all in the orderly room, according to Kaplowitz. Later they learned that the captain had not been doused with polluted water and cigarette butts, because Fong Wing, the little Chinese from Manteca assigned as "officers' dog robber," had discovered the booby trap early next morning while the captain still snored. Without questioning its purpose or origin, he had merely defused and removed it and gone about his duties with mop, dust rag, and shoe polish.

Aug ended up on KP the next day, but that was far from unusual. He always seemed to be on KP, latrine detail, or guard duty.

He got up from the desk and stretched. He'd be lucky if there was a turkey sandwich left by the time the rest of them finished. Idly he walked over to the first sergeant's desk and thumbed through the paperwork in the In-Out box. Nothing of interest. He slid the top drawer open. The duty roster for the next day lay there. His name was first in line for guard detail.

Just beyond the desk, a closed door guarded the captain's office. Aug opened it and looked in. The room was almost bare, a yellow wooden desk and two matching straight-backed chairs. On the wall above an olive-drab pencil sharpener was a large sepia-toned panoramic photograph of a unit of World War I doughboys in puttees and tin hats. Aug went closer and inspected it. They all looked happy. And very young. He guessed it was the captain's old command, but he couldn't recognize him among the blurred and faded faces.

Behind the desk was another door.

He opened it. It was the captain's private toilet.

It was an old-fashioned toilet, the kind flushed by pulling a chain attached to an overhead water tank. Aug stood there awhile and studied it, contemplating its possibilities.

The telephone rang loudly.

He stepped out of the captain's office and looked accusingly at the bulky black instrument. It rang again. Kaplowitz had as much as *promised* him it wouldn't ring. Nobody had told him what to say if it did.

He picked up the receiver.

"Hello."

Obviously, something more than that was called for. "Five Seventy-fifth."

"Who is this?" It was a man's voice. He sounded a little irritated.

"It's Aug. Rustyanek. Private Rustyanek, the orderly room."

"Let me speak to Captain Maxwell."

"He's not here . . . exactly."

"What the hell is that supposed to mean?"

"He's here. But he's down at the party."

There was momentary silence on the other end of the line.

"This is Colonel Ratnekof. Are you the charge of quarters?"

"During the party, I guess."

The colonel's voice suddenly sounded tired. "I don't suppose you could shed any light on a requisition I have here for an eighty-one-millimeter mortar. No, I'm sure you couldn't."

"Mortar?" Aug bit his lip to suppress a laugh. "You mean for like . . . between bricks?"

More silence on the other end.

Colonel Ratnekof began speaking in flat, measured tones, as if to make certain his message was getting across.

"You go wherever this *party* is, Private, and tell Captain Maxwell to call me back . . . *immediately*. Is that clear?"

"I'll tell him, Colonel, but from here it sounds like everybody's gassed to the ass." That ought to help things along.

"That's very interesting," the colonel replied. "You go and tell him. Right now. Tell him I'm waiting here by the phone."

And he hung up.

Aug rolled his eyes and grinned. Oh, boy. The captain's nuts were in hot water again. He could sympathize with the colonel's position; what the heck would the company do with a mortar? He started for the door, then stopped. Wait a minute. He couldn't just walk away from his post, could he? Leave the desks and chairs, all the paperwork, and the captain's private bathroom unguarded? No, sir. Not according to the General Orders. Not until he was properly relieved. Suppose the colonel called back, or President Roosevelt or somebody?

Humming a happy tune, he sat down at his desk again and picked up a tattered copy of the *Saturday Evening Post*. The captain would get the colonel's message just as soon as possible. A soldier couldn't go running off and leave his post.

The colonel would understand.

The captain stood unsteadily and banged the edge of his plate with a fork to get the group's attention. There was no noticeable drop in the decibel count. He raised his voice as if he were speaking to them in formation.

"My li'l ladyfriend here"—he grinned crookedly and laid a proprietary hand on Lucille's shoulder—"tells me I'm s'posed to say somethin' . . . p'pose a toast."

At a table in the rear, a three-way tug-of-war over a rum pitcher was threatening to explode into violence. Cooper lay nearby, facedown on the floor next to the wall, asleep or passed out, no one had bothered to check. Bruener's date was under the table now, her head down on her arms, sobbing loudly. Across the room, Big Hoover was on her feet, pantomiming yet another obscene narrative for an enthusiastic audience.

"S'good to have a li'l party now an' then," the captain said. "Get ever'body t'gether." He reached for his cup and took a generous swig. A loud hiccup straightened him up and moved him back a half-step. He frowned and, losing his train of thought momentarily, veered toward familiar ground. "We're goin' over there . . . overseas . . . pretty goddam soon now." No one in earshot seemed startled by that announcement. "An' . . . an' . . ." His voice trailed off. "S'good to have a li'l party now an' then, get ever'body t'gether."

"You already said that," Lucille commented.

He turned toward her, as if surprised to find her sitting there, then turned back to his inattentive audience.

"An' in the meantime, any . . . those li'l slant-eyed bastards other side of that fence"—he waved a long arm in the general direction of the camps—"try comin' out of there, shoot their goddam yellow asses off!"

Command or boastful commentary, it was a memorable Thanksgiving toast.

Lucille raised her eyebrows. She was getting smashed. "Shoot *who*? What kind of desert training is that? We haven't been invaded, have we?"

The captain put one hand on the table to steady himself and looked at her as if seeing her for the first time. He swallowed and hiccuped again loudly. "Goddam right . . . invaded. No-good sonsabitches."

Preparing to sit down, he swung one foot back to maintain his balance and kicked his chair out from under himself. He grabbed the checkered tablecloth on the way down, taking everything to the floor with him—pumpkin centerpiece, plates, cups, and silverware. Lucille did her best, but the pitcher of rum landed bottom side up—"Look *out*!"—in her lap. "Son of a *bitch*!"

The telephone rang once more.
"Private Rustyanek, orderly room."
"Did you tell your captain I wanted to talk with him, soldier?"
"I'm waiting for someone to relieve me, so I can leave my post."
A lengthy silence on the other end of the line.
"All right." More silence. "When you see your commanding officer again, Private, you tell him I've thrown his requisition for a mortar into the wastebasket and I don't want to see another one. *Ever.* You got that?"
"Yes, sir."
And the colonel hung up.

At the far end of the mess hall, Anberger was on his hands and knees under the table, trying to establish communication with Bruener's date. Lillian had finally stopped crying, but she was still lying on the floor facedown, snuffling into the sleeves of her sweater.
"Gawd a'mighty, woman," Anberger said, "what'sa matter with you? Ain't you havin' a good time?"
Lillian rolled over and sat up, bumping her head on the table, and threw her arms around his neck.
"I wanna have your bay-beee," she wailed.
This announcement brought several heads under the table in a hurry.
"Sheee-it, woman." Anberger grinned red-faced at his inverted audience. "I ain't *got* no baby. But if'n I did, you could sure enough have it."
"You dumb peckerhead," Bruener offered from the sidelines, "she wants her an' you t'*make* one!"
Lillian got both arms farther around his neck and squeezed even tighter, the tears coursing down her cheeks again as she nodded assent. "Yesss! I want to *make* one! Right now!"

Anberger was having a hard time breathing, but he managed to twist his head around far enough to get his mouth free. "You mean . . . ?" The thought struck him funny, and he laughed. *"Here?"*

"Hale, *yes!*" someone caroled.

"Do it!"

"Hooooo *haw!*" Rebel yells echoed through the mess hall.

"Unreel thet thing, boy, an' get on with it!"

The thought did have a certain appeal, but Anberger was too embarrassed to give it a try. Not right there under the table.

A resolute Lieutenant Flowers managed to break up the party and disperse the troops—the captain had his head down on his arms—shortly after someone suggested shoving the tables against the wall and dancing. Daisy leaped into action as Mess Sergeant Cleary, wind-up Victrola in hand, stood up and proudly volunteered his RCA recording of "Whatsername an' Her All-Cunt Orchestra!"

Herded forcefully through the door, the celebrants repaired to the makeshift recreation hall, two buildings down, for beer and song and a crap game.

As the din gradually subsided, Lillian stopped crying, crawled out from under the table, and left with Bruener. Garnett and three of his teenagers joined Blackie, P-38, and Big Hoover for the ride back to town on the bus. Cooper remained asleep in the mess hall.

The captain was too drunk to drive. Lucille rode home, holding a wilted calla lily on her chest, stretched out with Lieutenant Michaels in the rear of the powder blue Cadillac hearse.

December 12, 1943

Dear Son:

It was nice to hear you had a good Thanksgiving. I'm sorry to hear your captain got "skunked"? Tell him he should wash all over in tomato juice. That's what Emmel Hodges used to do when one of his dogs got sprayed.

We went to your grandmother Karel's for dinner. We had chicken because all the turkeys are being saved for the boys in the war. Your Uncle Bernard and Uncle Yuro were there. Uncle Bernard's tire store in Redwood City closed after he couldn't get any tires to sell. We came home early because him and your father got into an argument about gas stamps.

I saw Mrs. Mendenhall at the grocery Tuesday. She said Mary Jane her daughter was going to marry the Lunas' oldest boy Charlie. He was in town last week and he looks real nice in his navy pilot uniform. They have built a watchtower in the patio over at the American Legion Hall and your sister and I are going to volunteer to watch out for enemy planes. Your father says no enemy pilots would fly over here unless they got lost.

Norman's mother said she hasn't heard anything from him in a while. I pray every night you both will be safe until this awful war is over.

Be a good boy.

Love,
Mother

CHAPTER
FIFTEEN

☆ CHAPTER FIFTEEN ☆

THE big weapons carrier was no more than an outsize pickup truck with boards laid across the bed for seats, and Aug was sitting on the bench farthest back. The jolting up and down over the rough road was giving him a hard-on.

The same thing had happened on the school bus that time, when they were taking the field trip to the aquarium in San Francisco. He leaned forward and put his arms across his knees so no one would notice. It wasn't a sexual hard-on; it was just a hard-on. He got sexual hard-ons at night thinking about Mary Jane Mendenhall's sweater. She had never let him touch her there, not really grab one. He had managed to brush the back of his hand across her a couple of times, like when he was yawning or reaching for something up on the dashboard.

He supposed, now that she and Charlie Luna were engaged, he'd have to pick out a new pair to get a hard-on about. Maybe Angie's. He'd thought about Angie a couple of times. Maybe he'd just go on thinking about Mary Jane's. He wondered how Charlie Luna would like that if he knew.

He didn't feel all that bad about Mary Jane, not like he had when he first read his mother's letter. If he'd joined the marines, like he was going to do, she'd probably like his uniform as well as Charlie's, maybe even better, counting the Buick. Mary Jane had never really liked *him*. The big part about going out with her had been making Willis Bilmeister mad.

When Aug got home, he was still going to have to do something about Willis. And his old man.

"Hey, lookit there. A couple o' *real* soldiers."

Ordinarily, when PFC Maciel said "Lookit there," it was hard to tell right away which way to look, because one of his eyes looked in one direction and the other one another way. But there wasn't much else to look at out here, and they all saw right away what Maciel meant. There was a maroon Ford coupe parked at post number three, and two soldiers were standing beside it talking to Anberger.

The minute you saw the way they stood and the way their uniforms fit, you knew what Maciel meant about "real" soldiers. One of them was missing his left arm; his sleeve was pinned up just under the bright yellow sergeant stripes. Their shoes glistened like candy apples in the late-afternoon sun; they had fresh haircuts, and both of them had ribbons and badges all over their chests, like they'd just come from a parade.

And they were both Japanese—Japanese-Americans.

Bruener eased the weapons carrier to a stop, not skidding in broadside in a cloud of dust, the way he did most of the time, and Big Sam Claybin spit over the side and climbed down to take over from Anberger.

Anberger looked up at Sergeant Crawford and jerked his head toward the two soldiers.

"They wanta go in and visit their folks."

Crawford stood up in the open-top vehicle and leaned on the top of the windshield. "You got passes?"

The two soldiers walked over to that side of the weapons carrier.

"We don't have passes, Sarge. We just want to go in and see our families." The one missing his lower arm swung his pinned-up sleeve forward. "We're both out on medical discharges. We were with the Four Forty-second in Italy."

Aug looked at the blue and silver Infantry Combat badges over the double rows of ribbons on their chests. The only medals he could recognize were the Purple Hearts. His hand crept involuntarily to the empty area over his own left shirt pocket. These *were* the real soldiers. *The rest of us are just playing at it.*

Sergeant Crawford, he could tell, had somewhat the same thoughts.

"Shit, fella." Crawford tilted his hat forward and rubbed the back of his head. "We ain't supposed to let nobody go through that gate less'n he's got hisself a pass."

Neither one of the soldiers said anything.

"Fuck," Crawford said. He turned to Bruener, who tilted his head back and took another look at all the ribbons.

Crawford waved his hand in dismissal.

"Go on in. Shit, you got a right. Anybody says anything, jus' don't give 'em *my* name."

"Thank you, Sarge." The way they said it, real quiet, with no expressions on their faces, Aug couldn't tell whether they meant 'You're a nice guy, Sergeant,' or 'What an asshole.' They turned toward their automobile.

"Second thought," Crawford called after them, "anybody says anything, tell 'em I okayed it *personally*."

The soldier with only one arm raised his remaining hand in acknowledgment and got into the car on the driver's side. Nobody in the weapons carrier said anything as the two drove through the gate and down the road toward Camp One.

Anberger climbed up into the weapons carrier, and Bruener jerked it into low gear and started down the perimeter road toward post number four.

Ryker had number four today. As they approached, Aug could see him pacing impatiently back and forth with his Thompson submachine gun slung over his shoulder. The captain had set up the company with one Thompson for every squad, and Ryker always carried the submachine gun instead of a rifle.

Aug could see somebody sitting on the ground, leaning up against the gatepost. There was a black leather briefcase lying on the ground next to him. He didn't look very old. Whoever it was lifted his head. He looked a lot like Jimmy Sushiwara . . .

"Jimmy?" Aug crawled down out of the weapons carrier and went to him.

"Jimmy!"

Jimmy's eyes were glazed over, as if he was having his old trouble, not knowing anyone, but he smiled weakly—"Aug"— and tried to get his legs under himself and get up.

"We're takin' the son of a bitch in," Ryker said, his face sullen.

Ryker got up into the vehicle and took a seat, and Aug pulled Jimmy to his feet. He wanted to ask Ryker what Jimmy had done, why they would be taking him in, but right now he was just happy to see him.

"Come on, get in the truck, Jimmy. We'll take a little ride and talk. I didn't know you were here. Where are your mother and father?" Aug looked up at the others in the vehicle who seemed frozen in place, their eyes wide. "Hey, I know him. I used to work for his parents." He put his hands under Jimmy's arms, lifted him up over the high side of the weapons carrier.

His hands came away slippery with blood.

Aug turned Jimmy halfway around. The back of his white shirt was dark red, almost black, saturated with blood. Blood was pumping out of two ragged bullet holes high up between his shoulder blades.

Aug spun around to Ryker, who was sitting on one of the bench seats, the butt of his submachine gun resting between his boots.

"Did you *shoot* him, for crissake?"

Ryker stared back at him without emotion.

"You *shot* him!"

"Fuckin'-A right I shot the little shit. I *told* him to stop. He jus' kept walkin'."

"*Jimmy!*" Aug scrambled up beside him. "We've got to get him to the hospital!" Oh, sweet Jesus! There was a hospital in Camp One. "Hang *on*, Jimmy. We're going to get you to a doctor!"

But he knew they weren't going to get him to any doctor in time, not with the gouts of bright red blood vomiting out of those bullet holes, spilling over his belt onto the floor beneath the bench seats in a widening viscous puddle.

"Go!" Crawford yelled. Bruener floored the accelerator, and the heavy weapons carrier slewed to one side, bouncing, reaching for the road, its rear wheels spinning. Aug clutched Jimmy to his chest, braced against the side of the vehicle, not caring about the blood drenching his uniform.

They weren't going to get Jimmy *anywhere* in time.

Nobody saw the man and woman running toward them across the big melon field, stopping, growing smaller in the distance now, two tiny figures standing side by side, watching the clumsy olive-drab vehicle speeding up the road away from them.

Deposition of J. (NMI) Rustyanek, Pvt., taken 12-19-43 by C. M. Michaels, 2nd Lt., 575th MPEG

"And what did you do then?"

"I turned around to Ryker and asked him if he'd shot Jimmy."

I asked Private Ryker if he had shot the subject.

"And what did Ryker say?"

"He said, 'Fuckin'-A right I shot the little shit.' "

Private Ryker replied in the affirmative.

"And what happened then?"

"We took off for the camp hospital. But by the time we got there, it was too late. It was too late to do anything for him."

We transported the subject to the hospital in Camp One, where he was pronounced dead on arrival.

CHAPTER ☆ SIXTEEN ☆

THE wind rode over the crest of the jagged butte like a giant wave and swept down the rocky slope toward the tiny cemetery, hurling sand, dirt, and debris before it. The mourners huddled at the graveside were forced to turn and shield their faces as they and the plain wooden casket in front of them vanished, reappeared briefly, and were once again obliterated from view in the swirling dust and grit.

The minister wiped at his eyes once more and raised his voice over the eddying wind. "And we must take refuge in the knowledge that, however mystifying are His ways, there is the certainty . . ."

Aug stood tucked out of sight, a few paces behind the others. He was embarrassed by his uniform. He had already drawn a number of hostile looks. He stood well back at first, hoping not to be noticed, then inched closer, lest he appear to be some sort of official observer. He was aware he was an outsider, not one of them, whatever his reason for being there. He was part of the reason, however unwilling, for the rest of them being there, for the narrow little coffin standing at the edge of the open grave.

"However brief was Jimmy's stay among us, we must all of us be thankful for the privilege of his love and company . . ."

Aug had struggled over the decision to be turned out parade sharp or . . . not parade sharp. He particularly didn't want to look like a soldier this afternoon. He would have given anything to hide among the group in civilian clothing. Most of those at the graveside were Japanese-Americans, but two grim-faced officials, presumably from the WRA, stood to one side with their heads bowed, their hair tousled by the wind.

"When there is the tendency to ask, 'Why, Lord, why have you chosen me to bear this burden?' we must lift our heads and our hearts and, instead, accept as divine wisdom . . ."

Through a gap in the group of mourners, Aug could see Mr. and Mrs. Sushiwara standing together, staring without comprehension at Jimmy's casket. Some intricate paper flowers and a spray of wild poppies and lupine lay on top of it. The Sushiwaras looked much the same as they had at the hospital. He hadn't known what to say to them then, and he didn't know what he could say to them now. What *had* been . . . had no bearing at all on what was now, and he wondered if there ever again would be anything for them to say to each other.

Ryker had been taken to the stockade at Piebald, but Aug knew whatever happened to Ryker would be of little interest to Jimmy's parents. Someone said he would be court-martialed, found guilty, fined a dollar—so he couldn't be prosecuted again—and given a carton of cigarettes. For doing his duty.

A tremendous gust of wind assailed the funeral party. Behind them, at the entrance to the graveyard, a rustic archway artfully woven from stalks of withered ocotillo swayed and bent before the onslaught, but held fast.

Inside the forlorn gateway, artistic hands had fashioned stone pathways among the low mounds of dirt and rock, landscaped modestly with native desert plants. Each grave was well defined from its neighbors, identified with a neat cairn of multicolored desert stones. The cemetery was less than a hundred yards across, surprisingly small, Aug thought, for a community of more than ten thousand persons.

He wondered if maybe it was small because these people were determined not to die here.

The wind came down again and he turned his back and raised one arm to his face. When he opened his eyes again, he saw what looked like a white handkerchief blow through the archway. It tumbled over and over, was lifted up and over the brush outside by an eddy, and was gone.

"Father, we ask that you take Jimmy in your arms and bless him, and keep him safe until the day we are all reunited with your love and compassion."

CHAPTER
☆ SEVENTEEN ☆

"WHAT the goddam hell are you using for brains, Maxwell? *Flypaper?*" Colonel Ratnekof was so mad he was spitting into the phone. "That dumb bastard Ryker is in the stockade awaiting court-martial, and if I had my way I swear to God you'd be in there with him!"

The captain's response was hardly conciliatory. "The man was doing exactly what he was supposed to do, Colonel, what he was trained to do. He pointed his piece at that Jap and said 'Halt,' and the slant-eyed little son of a bitch just kept going. What the hell was Ryker *supposed* to do, say 'Halt, *please*'?"

"If he had half the sense God gave a sack of turnips, he'd have done *anything* but shoot him. In case it hasn't occurred to you, that kid was an American citizen. A *kid*. He was *twelve years old*, for crissake!"

"Twelve years old," the captain retorted, "is old enough to shoot back. He didn't stop and—"

"Horseshit! My ass is getting reamed out all the way to Washington! And what the goddam hell was Ryker doing on sentry duty with a Thompson submachine gun?"

"It was his weapon of choice. I don't remember seeing anything in the General Orders that says—"

"You listen to me, *Captain*; just close your goddam mouth and listen! I don't give a rat's ass *what* you think—you and that bunch of misfits playing war games out there. You've gotten your ass in a sling this time. There's a goddam *congressional com-*

mittee heading out there to look into this—Congressman V. D. Petrovich—and I hope he hangs you up by the *balls*!"

The receiver went down with a slam!

The captain took the receiver from his ear and glared at it for a moment, one fist clenching and unclenching on the desktop. "No-good paper-pushing son of a bitch. What the goddam hell did they give us weapons for?"

" 'Your ass in a sling . . . congressional committee . . . Congressman V. D. Petrovich.' " He grunted. V. D. Good initials for a syphilitic, no-balls politician.

He turned his head and focused on the faded sepia-toned photograph on the wall, his old combat engineers outfit. That was a good war. Or it could have been. There he was, standing right in the middle of the company with his two lieutenants. If only those fat-assed krauts hadn't thrown up their hands and quit. His lips drew tight across his teeth. It had been like that all his life. He was always drawing bad cards, always having to attack uphill.

". . . bunch of misfits playing war games out there."

His eyes narrowed.

Congressional committee coming . . . war games—maybe that wasn't such a stupid idea. If he couldn't get those brass-plated assholes at headquarters to listen, maybe he could convince Congress.

He stuck his head out the door of his office. Sergeant Garrison was draped over his desk in his usual manner, overflowing his swivel chair like a wet sack of oatmeal.

"Sergeant!" he snapped.

Garrison turned his head from the paperwork he was scanning. "Yes, sir." It was a barely audible mumble, as if he were talking in his sleep.

"Get Bleeker and all the platoon sergeants in here."

"Sergeant Crawford's on guard duty. You want him in, too?"

"*All* of 'em. On the double."

Garrison took in a deep breath and let it out—like the hiss of air escaping from an inner tube—and rolled his wet cigar to the other side of his mouth. "Now what?" he muttered under his breath. He clamped his pudgy hands on the arms of his chair and heaved himself up.

The captain went back to his desk, pulled a pad of yellow paper out of the top drawer, and began drawing lines on it.

The sentry post at the main gate had been moved one hundred yards down the road to a point directly opposite the 575th's company area. Aug was on duty there when the gray Plymouth sedan with government plates came out of the brush and drove up to the guard shack. He brought his rifle to port arms and stepped out into the road. More WRA officials, he supposed. It was fun harassing the WRA.

The driver was a balding, stoop-shouldered man with a large purple birthmark under his left ear. There were two persons in the back seat—a bespectacled, effeminate-looking youth in a too-tight tan gabardine suit, and a fat, middle-aged woman wearing a voluminous mustard-yellow dress. A cone-shaped hat of matching color sat square on the top of her head.

Stenciled on the car door in black ink were the words "U.S. Government, For Official Use Only."

"We're here to visit the camp," the driver said. The tired, nonchalant way he said it suggested he and his companions were used to doing whatever they wished to. The driver started easing forward again.

Aug clunked the butt of his rifle against the side of the car and it stopped.

"Do you have a pass? What's the reason for your visit?"

The driver's mouth dropped half open. People just didn't question him like that. He twisted around toward the back seat. The fat woman said, "We're here to look into conditions, soldier; we're from Washington," and the young man in the too-tight suit added haughtily, as if he were introducing royalty, "This is Congresswoman Petrovich."

Aug wasn't certain if he was supposed to salute or shake hands. She was the first congresswoman he had ever seen. As a matter of fact, until that moment he hadn't known there *was* such a thing.

He raised an index finger, said, "Hold on a minute," and

turned toward the guardhouse. "Corporal of the Guard!" he shouted. "Post number one!"

Nothing happened immediately, and he was about to shout a second time when Corporal Binks stepped out the door of the guardhouse, buttoning his fly. He looked puzzled. He had been a corporal for only a few days, and he apparently wasn't sure how he was supposed to respond to the summons. Aug didn't know what the correct words were, either, so he just waggled one hand and yelled, "Come here!" Binks started down the steps, still working on his fly.

"Winky" Binks had a nervous tic that caused his right eye to wink spasmodically during moments of stress. "Lethargic encephalitis," it said on his service record.

"This is Congress . . ." Aug looked back to the car for help.

"Congresswoman Petrovich." She and the young man recited her name in unison. "Velma D. Petrovich," she added.

"They're here to investigate conditions."

Corporal Binks looked at her and winked. "Do y'all have a pass, ma'am?"

"We don't *need* a pass, young man." Binks winked at her again and she looked back at him wide-eyed, not certain of his intent. She turned to her assistant, her face reddening. Congresswoman Petrovich hadn't been winked at in a long time. Not that it was altogether unpleasant.

"Y'all wait right here, if you will, ma'am. All right?" He winked. Twice this time, as if to say, "You know what I mean, Velma," although his actual thought was "What the fuck do I do now?"

The congressional committee climbed out of the car and stood gazing about at the bleak surroundings as Corporal Binks hurried away toward the orderly room.

Captain Maxwell strode down the gravel pathway toward the sentry post with Winky close behind. So these three sorry-looking bastards were Ratnekof's congressional committee. This might be a whole lot easier than he had supposed. The bald-headed dummy with the grape juice stain on his neck had to be Petrovich. The four-eyed pansy next to him was some sort of assistant, he supposed, and the ugly broad with the dunce cap on her head was . . . the congressman's wife? That dress looked like a pyramidal tent.

He pasted a wide smile on his face and extended his hand. "Congressman Petrovich? Captain Maxwell. Welcome to Arido. We're happy to have you here."

The man with the birthmark gave him a damp handshake. "My name's Clemens." He ducked his head toward the woman. "*That's* Congresswoman Petrovich."

Her mouth was clamped down at the corners like a bear trap. "Velma D. Petrovich." She didn't extend her hand.

That dumb son of a bitch Ratnekof. But his recovery was almost immediate.

"*Stupid* of me. Of course. I've been reading a lot about you, Congresswoman." Congress*woman* Petrovich? Jesus, they should never have given them the vote. If she asked what he'd read about her, he was dead. "It's not often," he said, bowing to her slightly, "we're favored with the presence of a lady out here." Jumping Jesus Christ, she was ugly.

Congresswoman Petrovich drew herself up to her full five feet eight and, trailed by her two staff members, allowed herself to be steered away from the car toward the company area. "We're here to investigate conditions at the camp," she said, "and in particular, this shooting." She indicated the disdainful young man hovering behind her. "This is Glen Putnam, my chief assistant."

"Certainly," the captain said, ignoring Putnam completely, "an unfortunate accident. You'll have our complete coopera-tion"—*if the subject comes up again at all*—"and while you're here, we've arranged some maneuvers for you; we're hoping you can join us for supper. We'll be staging an interesting nighttime exercise, one attacker force assaulting the company area and one unit defending."

She stopped. "Isn't that a little peculiar, Captain? That sort of game in the middle of a war?"

"I can assure you"—*fat-assed bitch*—"we're not playing games. Excuse me, but that's a *very* attractive dress you're wear-ing. These are exercises we stage *regularly* out here to keep this unit in constant readiness to ship out. When you get back to Washington, you might want to *ask* someone, as a matter of fact, why combat troops are being wasted out here in the middle of the desert instead of being sent overseas to do what they're trained to do. Where they're needed."

"I'm sure what you're doing here is vital also, Captain."

"I'm sure it is, for some less-qualified unit." He gave her his most gracious smile. "But as you are well aware, the people in these camps are all American citizens. Why would we need *combat* troops here?"

Congresswoman Petrovich looked thoughtful and smoothed down her voluminous yellow dress.

As they reached the center of the company area, the flat report of small-arms fire was heard coming from beyond the buildings on the far side. The captain took her arm and guided her in that direction.

"Daily target practice," he explained. "Every man in this outfit has to requalify continually with pistol, carbine, rifle, submachine gun, grenades—with every infantry weapon in the army's arsenal, plus the shotgun." He looked away to cover a smile. He'd told Garrison to have one of the platoon sergeants set up some targets back there and fake an official qualification course.

"Would you care to take a look?"

The noise of the M1 rifles grew louder—*Boom!*—as they rounded the far corner of the mess hall. *Boom! Boom!*

He stopped short.

The staged exercise was not exactly as he had pictured it, nor was it as according-to-the-book as he had ordered. A half-dozen riflemen were standing in a ragged line, firing randomly at a dozen beer bottles perched on limbs and rocks amid the brush and cactus. They were plainly enjoying themselves, pushing and shoving, needling one another between shots. Like a Sunday turkey shoot back home.

Boom!

"Got one!"

"Got one, my ass! I don't see none of 'em missin'!"

Tongue-tied Sergeant Stoff lounged nearby on an upturned milk box. Suddenly aware of the captain and his guests—all Garrison had said was "Make some noise"; he hadn't said anything about anybody coming back here to look—he leaped to his feet and stiffened to attention.

"Theeth fire!"

Boom!

"Got *that* one, by God!"

"*Theeeth fire!*"

Boom! Boom!

"Bruener, you couldn't hit yer ass in the dark, usin' both hands!"

"*Theeeth fire*, goddammit!"

Startled, the marksmen lowered their weapons and, upon viewing their obviously distressed commanding officer, hastened to assume whichever stance—attention, port arms, or parade rest—seemed advisable to each.

Behind them, eleven of their twelve targets glittered in the late-afternoon sunlight, unscathed.

Congressional Assistant Putnam smirked. "Your men don't appear to be very effective against beer bottles, Captain."

The captain turned to him. "Small target at that distance. Have you ever fired on the range, Mr. Putnam? Sergeant," he said, gesturing at Stoff, "let this man have a try with your side arm."

Putnam's composure faded. "Thank you, but I really don't . . ." He looked to his employer for support, but her expression suggested she found the idea interesting.

The captain took the sergeant's heavy .45-caliber automatic, pulled the slide back, and let it snap forward again, injecting a cartridge into the firing chamber. He set the safety and thrust the weapon at the distraught young man.

Once more Putnam looked to Congresswoman Petrovich for salvation. His lower lip was trembling. "I really don't think I—"

"Nonsense," the captain said. "Nothing to it." He grabbed Putnam's limp right hand and slapped the pistol into it. "Just click that little lever down with your thumb, pick out your target, and start shooting."

After one last imploring look at Congresswoman Petrovich,

Putnam turned hopelessly toward the waiting targets and raised the heavy pistol. His right hand began shaking violently. Squeezing both eyes shut, he bit his lower lip and jerked at the trigger.

Bam! Bam! Bam!

The first copper-jacketed slug plowed into the sand thirty feet in front of him, and the convulsive kick of the weapon pulled the trigger again, sending a second bullet straight up in the air and a third back somewhere over his shoulder as the onlookers scattered.

"Look *out!*"

"Ho-leee!"

"Shoot that sumbitch 'fore he shoots us!"

Silence.

Somewhere out in the brush a solitary songbird trilled.

The pistol dropped from nerveless fingers, and Putnam stood there for a moment, head and shoulders drooping, before turning, palms up, to face the jury. Congresswoman Petrovich started to point, stopped, opened her mouth to say something, then turned her head, blushing.

Her chief congressional assistant had peed all over himself.

The captain opened his mouth to comment on this occurrence when he noticed something that caused his jaws to part still farther: Congresswoman Petrovich's cone-shaped mustard-yellow hat, which still sat upright square on the top of her head, had just acquired a neat, round hole in its center.

He grabbed her elbow and spun her around. "Well, that's enough of that; let's walk over this way. That's a barrel cactus you see there; that's the back end of the mess hall, and this"— he pointed grandly—"is the ice house."

He pulled the heavy door toward him and was about to open it wide for inspection when he spied what appeared to be someone wrapped in a blanket up on the vegetable shelf, sound asleep. He swung the door back, narrowly missing the congresswoman's head—"It's just an ice house"—and steered her in another direction.

Cooper was lying stark naked on his bunk, deep in another inspiring dream, half a continent away. His breathing—more like tormented gasps escaping through his parted lips—was increasing rapidly in both volume and interval. Una Mae Diller's chest was heaving up and down like a big cream-colored balloon deflating and inflating again—like *two* big cream-colored balloons deflating and inflating. Her curvaceous top was draped with the skimpy lace runner off the preacher's piano. Una Mae wasn't wearing any drawers. Cooper didn't have his britches on. He was reaching for one of the two little rosebuds peeking out from behind the lace when someone yelled.

"Tens-*hutt!*"

His fingers closed on emptiness; Una Mae faded into the lilac mist and was gone.

He sat up straight, blinking his eyes. What the hell was the army doin' in the parsonage?

But he wasn't back home in the parsonage, he was lying on his bunk in Third Platoon's barracks, and the captain was coming down the far end of the aisle behind someone. Cooper leaped up and snapped to attention at the foot of his bunk, heedless of his nakedness.

And of his sizable erection.

Cooper was a big boy for his age and, under the circumstances, *anyone* would have had difficulty getting past him in the narrow aisle.

Congresswoman Petrovich, Garnett reported later, "couldn't decide whether to climb over that thing or crawl under it. An' that woman stood there a good spell, makin' up her mind."

"An' that's a fact," Blackie added.

The captain shielded his penlight with his hand as he and Congresswoman Petrovich stood at the rear of his jeep in the darkness, peering at his map.

"This rough terrain here means that Blue Group, the attacking force, has to come this way, through this narrow pass a half-mile back in that direction." He marked the spot on the map with his pencil. "Orange Group, the defensive force, has concealed two men right there above the pass to signal the main body when the attackers start through. Three light flashes aimed ninety-seven degrees by compass. That sets up the ambush in this wash, a mile north of where we're standing."

"If everybody knows where the attack is coming from, how are they going to surprise anyone?"

The captain smiled and nudged her arm with his elbow. "Very good. But they *won't* be coming that way. Sergeant Bleeker and a couple of men will move through the pass in his jeep at twenty-one thirty"—he looked at his watch—"about half an hour from now, and proceed toward the objective to make everyone think this is it and draw their fire, while the *main* body of Blue Group marches west around these ridges and flanks the defenders from right here." He showed her.

"They're not going to be *shooting* at each other?"

"Certainly not. Blank cartridges."

She shrugged and yawned. "If it makes sense to the rest of them, it makes sense to me." They'd had a few belts of the captain's Old Overholt after the evening meal, and she was beginning to feel drowsy. It was a balmy evening. There was no moon, nothing but the stars to faintly outline the craggy ridges around them. She reached up to push at her hairdo, wondering again what had happened to her hat. It had just disappeared. Maybe Putnam had it. Poor Putnam, with his wet pants. He'd been too embarrassed to go into the mess hall to eat, so he and Clemens had gone back to town.

"We'll wait a few minutes," the captain said, "then go on beyond the point of ambush and watch everything develop from there." He turned to her in the dark. "You might want to tell your colleagues about this when you get back to Washington. These men are all disciplined night fighters."

He moved back a step and blew his nose. Jesus Jumping Christ! She was wearing perfume so potent it almost made his eyes water.

"That thing *stinks*, Rooster. Phhhew! Throw that thing away." Blackie turned his head and held his nose with his thumb and little finger. "They gonna *smell* this ambush a mile up the road."

Aug grinned. He had a plan for this bloated, very dead, very smelly Gila monster he'd found floating belly up when the platoon waded across the irrigation canal. The big lizard's rotting orange- and black-beaded carcass was puffed and swollen grotesquely out of shape, the malodorous putrescence within threatening to blossom forth at the slightest mishandling.

It *did* stink! Aug tried breathing through his mouth.

The platoon was hunkered down in a long, shallow depression masked with brush, overlooking a dry wash that cut diagonally across the road leading from the pass. It was excellent cover and concealment. It would be impossible for Blue Group to see them, even after they were right up on them.

"The rest of you fire off your old blank cartridges," Aug said. "Some poor bastard's going to *know* he's been ambushed when this thing smacks him in the chops."

Blackie had to agree with that. "That's a fact."

The captain brought his wristwatch up close to check the luminous hands in the dark. "All right," he said, "let's get down there and watch the fireworks." Congresswoman Petrovich climbed into the jeep with some difficulty and tugged her skirt decorously over her knees. She grabbed the top of the windshield with her other hand as he eased the jeep into gear. The road was little more than two faint ruts in the sand, and with his headlights turned off, the captain had to duck his head out and around the water-spotted windshield to see where they were going.

Eight hundred yards behind the captain's departure point, on a narrow step fifty feet above the narrow pass, Bruener and Kibby were lying on their bellies, side by side under a canvas shelter half. A mile and a half out, dead ahead of them if they had the compass aimed correctly, Orange Group awaited their signal. Kibby shifted about, trying to find a more comfortable position on the rocky ledge.

"I wish I'd brought me a mattress."

Bruener pulled the shelter half up over their heads. "Hold the edges down," he said. "I wanta practice aimin' this thing once more." With the edges snugged down, he could turn on the flashlight and check the compass bearing without the light revealing their position.

His head cocked back so he could see out from under his eyelids, he turned on the olive-drab flashlight and rotated the compass until the cross hair in the lid lined up at precisely 97 degrees. All he had to do was lay the flashlight down just so and . . .

Kibby chose that moment to pass gas.

"Kibby, you son of a bitch! Sheeze!"

Desperate for air—never mind the beam of his flashlight—Bruener grabbed the edge of the shelter half and flapped it up and down, up and down, up and down.

"Three flashes! That's it! They're coming."

Aug heard the platoon settling in on either side of him, clicking off safety catches, locating their triggers, squirming into more comfortable firing positions, as if they were indeed about to open up on a real enemy. Instead of finding a prone position for himself, however, he got to his knees, twisted half around, and dragged the foul-smelling Gila monster to a spot where he could easily grab it by the tail and let it fly.

"Pfffew! What's that smell?"

"I thought Kibby was up in the pass."

"Goddam wind must be comin' this way."

Someone giggled in the darkness.

"We're gonna scare the livin' shit outa them fellers."

"I hope ole Bleeker messes his britches."

"Quiet!" Sergeant Crawford whispered. "They're comin'."

It seemed too soon, Aug thought. Far too soon, if Bruener and Kibby had flashed the signal when the attackers first started through the pass. But he could already hear the muted sound of a jeep approaching cautiously along the narrow road.

"Hold your fire until I give the word," Crawford whispered. "Then everybody hit 'em all at once."

It didn't sound like a whole column coming. It sounded like just one vehicle.

They waited, grinning, scarcely breathing.

The whine of the jeep's engine stuttered as the driver shifted into a lower gear, and the squat black shape of the lead vehicle came up over the rise without its lights on and dipped down into the dry wash in front of them.

"Fire!" Crawford caroled joyfully, and the night split open with rebel war whoops, red-orange stabs of light, and the cacophony of exploding blank cartridges.

In its own trajectory above the smoke and sparks, the obscene carcass of the grinning Gila monster tumbled over and over through the night sky, already minus its thick tail, spewing green slime from within its ruptured guts.

And fell to explode with an awful *splat* against the upper buttress of a mustard-yellow dress.

High up on the slope below the mesa, the coyotes danced about, yipping nervously, ears up, nostrils testing the breeze. Unable to contain themselves any longer, they raised their muzzles to the sky and answered the shrill screams echoing and reechoing across the shadowed desert below.

The congresswoman had another dress, of course, back at the tourist cabins in Mesa Verde, but she couldn't drive back there with that pus and slime smeared all over the front of her. She could barely speak coherently. Some very fast talking, the urging of a hot shower, then a full water tumbler of Old Overholt—a second third, and fourth, in a desperate, try-anything effort to salvage *something* from the disaster—had led inevitably to this brand-new crisis.

Congresswoman Velma D. Petrovich took another swallow of rye and giggled as the sheet fell away, revealing huge white breasts crisscrossed with a network of blue veins. The captain quickly turned his head. Like two barracks bags half full of water. If he was going to work up any enthusiasm for this assignment, it wouldn't be with *that* image in mind. He sat down heavily on the edge of the cot and pulled his socks off.

Her ruined dress was draped over the chair. While she was sobbing in the shower he'd made a couple of passes at it with hot water and some scouring powder from the mess hall, but she'd never get that crap off, not even if she used sandpaper. She might as well burn it.

A playful moan . . . and a flabby arm fell across his bare thigh, pudgy fingers reaching, exploring.

He glanced down at his flaccid pecker. Not a prayer. He hated these goddam *courtesy bangs*. He sighed, stood up and turned off the light, lifted the blanket, and rolled into bed next to her. What the hell, give it a try.

She giggled again. "Let me finish my drinkie. Don't be so impatient." V. D. Petrovich was sloshed.

Maybe if he filled up her glass again, she'd just pass out. When she woke up in the morning, he could tell her how good it was. How the goddam hell did he get himself into this mess? He closed his eyes and dutifully groped for a breast.

Like hugging a goddam water buffalo.

January 11, 1944

Dear Son:

Some awful news. Norman's mother called yesterday on the telephone and said he was wounded on some island. He was shot in the arm by some Jap, and he might lose one of his hands. She said he was coming to the Oak Knoll Navy Hospital in Oakland. I always thought he was in the marines not the navy.

That's all I can write now I'm so upset. I just pray to God you will be safe until this awful war is over.

Love,
Mother

P.S. Somebody went by Mr. Bilmeister's movie house after it was closed last night and shot two holes through the window of the box office.

CHAPTER
☆ EIGHTEEN ☆

WHEN the orders came, they came to Arido without fanfare, an innocuous single sheet of white flimsy in the daily mail pouch from Piebald.

The company was drawn up in platoon formation for the evening flag-lowering ceremony. Aug and Mozetti were leaning against the flagpole, the halyard loose in their hands. Raber was slouched on the far side of the pole, idly humming to himself, spitting on the tarnished bell of his bugle, polishing it with the cuff of one sleeve.

The door of the orderly room opened, and the captain came down the stairs and stalked toward them—*crunch, crunch, crunch, crunch*—over the gravel path. He had a piece of white paper in one hand.

And a smile on his face.

At least it looked like a smile, Aug thought. Sometimes it was hard to tell, the way he stretched his lips tight across his teeth. Sometimes he was pissed off about something.

"At ease!"

Sergeant Bleeker snapped his polished boots together to call the company to attention, then stopped, teetering on his heels, and looked back at the captain. The men were *already* standing at ease.

The captain, as if unaware they were even there, lifted the paper and without preamble began to read aloud: " 'To: Commanding Officer, 575th MPEG, WRA Encampment, Arido.' " He lowered the paper a few inches, his eyes sweeping over them, and resumed: " 'Subject . . . Reassignment Personnel.' "

A stir went through the platoons, the men shifting their feet in the dust, darting questioning looks at their neighbors.

" 'Company will be *relieved* . . . 10/February/44 . . . for transfer back to prisoner-of-war camp at Piebald . . .' "

A low-pitched murmur grew and faded, and swelled again, like the hum of honeybees at the hive.

"Hot shit"—out of the side of the mouth.

"Gettin' outa this fuckin' place"—without moving the lips.

" '. . . for immediate *medical reassessment* of all personnel . . . relative to *reassignment* . . .' " He let it hang there a moment. " 'To *combat* theater of operations.' " He lowered the orders to chest level and repeated the magic word as if to himself. "Combat."

There was unbelieving silence. Then the bees rose again in a black swarm, buzzing angrily, the rumble spreading unchecked from one platoon, one squad, one man to another.

"Whadde say?"

"Combat!"

"*Us?*"

"What's he readin', the fuckin' funny papers?"

The captain stood there, his face expressionless, and let the stunned reaction run its course.

"*Bull*shit. He's always sayin' that."

"This time it ain't *him* sayin' it."

"Ho-lee . . ."

The captain dropped the paper to his side, bent his head, and, hands locked behind him, rocked back on his heels, collecting his thoughts. He raised his head and regarded his troops. He spoke now in a calm, normal tone of voice.

"We've been waiting for the chance for a long time. Training for it. We're ready." He brought the piece of paper up and looked at it again, as if to reassure himself. "And we're going."

He took a couple of steps to his right, stopped, and regarded the company again. A second thought. "How many of you," he asked, "have good conduct medals?"

Good conduct medals?

Aug turned to look at Mozetti and then at the ranks. A few hands went up tentatively, the respondents not altogether certain the distinction was good or bad.

The captain nodded. About what he'd expected.

"When this formation is over, the rest of you report to the supply room and draw 'em."

The bees swirled into the air once more.

"Good *conduct* medals?"

"What the hell for?"

"Shit, how 'bout a fuckin' medal of honor?"

The captain looked at Sergeant Bleeker. "All noncoms in the orderly room. Ten minutes. Dismiss 'em." He spun on his heel and strode away.

Bleeker returned his salute and turned to the company. "Compan-*eee*! Tennns-*hut*! . . . *Dis*missed!"

"Hey, Bleeker," Raber asked, pointing upward with his bugle, "how 'bout the fuckin' flag?"

Bleeker twisted around to look up at the pole, as if hoping the forgotten item had taken care of itself. He did a quick about-face, one hand raised, but the men had already dispersed, some of them already up the steps and back into their barracks. He spun back to the trio at the pole, frowning, as if the oversight were their fault.

Mozetti grinned at him. "What *about* the old flag, Sarge?"

Bleeker glanced upward again and then back at Aug and Mozetti.

"I don't give a shit. Haul it down."

And he turned and walked away.

Raber shrugged, tucked his bugle under his arm, and drifted away in the opposite direction.

Aug and Mozetti stared at each other questioning. *Going overseas?* "Naaah," Aug said. "Never happen." He started hauling the flag down, hand over hand on the halyard. "It'll be just like before. We'll end up going somewhere else. Or nowhere."

"Shit, we're already nowhere."

Mozetti caught the tail of the flag as it flew within reach and began gathering it in. "Besides, the orders said 'medical reassessment.' First, we get another physical."

Angie and her heart pills, and then the bogus X ray. It had been only a few months ago. It seemed like years.

Together Aug and Mozetti stretched the flag out full length, folded it in half lengthwise, in half again, and Mozetti began crimping it into a tight triangle, working it toward Aug and the field of forty-eight stars.

Tah-dee, tah-dee, tah-tah!

Mess call.

Aug tucked the bulky triangle beneath his arm. "I'll take it in. See you at chow."

"Don't sweat it, Aug," Mozetti said. "We didn't pass the first physical; we won't pass this one either. My fucking arm isn't any longer now than it was."

And mine isn't any straighter, Aug thought, starting toward the orderly room.

When Aug walked into the orderly room, he could hear the captain addressing the noncoms in his office. The door was closed.

Kaplowitz was at his desk in the far corner, typing a report. He looked up and giggled. "It looks like somebody else is going to be yelling 'You'll be *sorrreee*' at us," he said.

Aug tucked the flag away on a shelf and sat down on the edge of Kaplowitz's desk. "Yeah." He fiddled with a stack of paperwork, shaping and reshaping it. "This new physical . . . what're the chances? How bad off do you think you'd have to be to flunk it? You know, not be shipped over."

Kaplowitz pulled the sheet of paper out of his typewriter and scanned it, watery eyes squinting behind his bottle-thick lenses. "All depends. Sergeant Garrison said we've taken some heavy losses in Europe." He giggled again. "We must have, if they're contemplating the likes of us over there."

"What about my elbow?" Aug extended his crooked right arm, the one he'd broken as a kid.

Kaplowitz shrugged. "Depends on how bad they need you, I guess, and for what. That *might* keep you at home . . . and it might not. Your expert rifleman's badge might sway them."

"I only qualified as marksman."

"I know, but I put 'expert' on your service record." Kaplo-witz giggled. "I gave myself one, too." Kaplowitz couldn't hit a barn from ten feet away with a shotgun.

Aug fiddled some more with the pile of paperwork. "I guess you could put anything you wanted to on somebody's service record." He looked toward the door to the captain's office. "Or change something on there, if you wanted."

For a city boy, Kaplowitz had learned the army way in a hurry. He gave Aug a sly look. "Do I hear someone offering me his dessert for a week? What do you want changed? I can do anything but promote you to sergeant. I might even be able to do that. Do you want me to give you the clap?"

Aug's face was serious. "How about a bad eye? Like twenty/eighty in one of them?"

"That's easy. Billy Lawler gave himself a rupture. What about your arm?"

"Don't even mention it. Don't write anything about it at all. Just give me a bad eye. Is twenty/eighty weak enough to be put into Limited Service?"

"Weak enough for me. My *good* one is twenty/forty. But they both *correct* to twenty/thirty or something."

"Yeah, but I don't wear glasses. Could you make mine so it *doesn't* correct? On my service record?"

Kaplowitz went over to the file cabinet in the corner, slid the top drawer open, and riffled through some papers. He extracted one.

" 'Twenty/eighty . . . uncorrected.' " He turned and pointed his finger at Aug. "But all your desserts are *mine*, Rustyanek. For a whole week."

He sat down at his desk and threaded a brand-new service record form into his typewriter. "Which eye?" He pointed at the form. "Which one is the bad one?"

Aug glanced at the captain's door again. "I don't know. Make it the left one."

Twenty/eighty. It was bad enough to put someone into Limited Service. Nobody could argue with that.

* * *

The post hospital at Piebald smelled like hospitals everywhere. Not *clean*, Aug thought. *Clean* smelled like . . . like nothing, like fresh air. Hospitals smelled like pills, medicine.

They were all naked from the waist up, standing in two lines. It was much like the setup in San Francisco. Two army doctors were going through the culls, squeezing, prodding, poking, looking this time for candidates—if not perfect, at least good enough for whatever lay ahead. Compared to the pre-induction physical, this was only a cursory examination, the doctors' only apparent attention given to the ailments listed on the service records, the shortcomings that had consigned each man to Limited Service.

Jimmerson's upturned eyeball, Blackie's missing fingers, Garnett's glass eye, Bruener's half-mast eyelids—all brought instant elimination. With embarrassed grins and feigned indifference, they swaggered back down the line, back to where they'd left their clothing, rejects twice over.

Aug swallowed and, conscious of the sweat on his palm, shifted his new service record to his other hand.

At the head of the line, Raber stepped up to the little white table. The doctor took his paperwork and glanced at it.

"Undescended testicle. Drop your trousers and spread your feet." He reached out to confirm the diagnosis. "Is that what put you into Limited Service?"

"I got consumption," Raber said.

The doctor returned to the service record. "I don't see anything here about that. What do you mean, consumption? You mean tuberculosis?"

Raber looked less sure of himself. "Consumption." He offered a weak cough. "Sometimes I can't hardly breathe . . . at all."

The doctor rolled his eyes. "Can't breathe at all. *That* would be a *real* problem. What's your duty assignment? What do you do?"

"Company bugler."

The doctor laughed. "You can't breathe at all and you're the company *bugler*? Nice try, fella." He took a fountain pen from his pocket and wrote something on Raber's record. "Let me be the first to congratulate you, Private; you're in the infantry." Raber slouched away, muttering something under his breath.

The infantry? An icy balloon swelled beneath Aug's breastbone and he inhaled sharply. If you passed this physical, you were going into the *infantry*?

Cooper was next up.

"False teeth? They put you in Limited Service for false teeth?"

Cooper shrugged and scratched his bald pate.

The doctor scribbled something with his pen. "If you get into combat, don't try to bite the enemy. Shoot the bastards." Infantryman Cooper nodded and moved on.

Cloony was just ahead of Aug. Grinning foolishly, he shuffled forward and extended his service record. The doctor looked closely at him, glanced at his paperwork and back at Cloony.

"Where you from, son?"

"Oxnard," Cloony said. "That's on the way to Ventura."

"I've been through there," the doctor said. "They've got good surf fishing in Ventura."

Cloony didn't know how to respond to that. He just grinned and shrugged.

The doctor gently took Cloony's massive lower jaw in his fingers and turned his head slowly left and right, observing the overhanging brow, the structure of his skull.

"You like being in the army, son?"

Cloony shrugged again and chuckled. He spread his big hands apart. "I guess."

"Well"—the doctor patted him on the shoulder—"you're doing all right here, right where you are. You just go on back to your outfit. Okay?"

"Sure," Cloony said. The doctor pointed at Aug and beckoned.

"What's your problem?" He took Aug's service record and looked at it.

"I've got a bad eye."

"How bad? Twenty/eighty, hmmm?"

"No, I don't *think* so. Not *that* bad."

The doctor looked up at him, surprised. "That's what it says here, twenty/eighty in your left eye." He pointed to a chart on the wall behind him and said, "Put this card over your right eye and try to read the letters with the green line under them."

Aug read them.

"Can you read the letters under that?"

"Uh . . . no. Not very well."

"The line you read was for twenty/twenty vision. Put the card over your *left* eye and read it."

"Which line?"

"The one with the green."

Aug read it.

The doctor took a shiny instrument out of his pocket, flicked a switch with his thumb, and said, "Look straight ahead." He bent forward and, peering through the eyepiece of the instrument, directed a beam of light into Aug's left eye and then the other. He returned the instrument to his pocket and picked up Aug's service record again.

"Where did you take your pre-induction physical?"

"In San Francisco."

"Who did it, a veterinarian? I can't see anything wrong with either eye. Do *you* think you're physically fit?"

"Yes, sir. I'm in *great* shape."

"That's good enough for me." The doctor wrote something on the bottom of Aug's paperwork, tossed it onto the pile with the other reclassified records, and waved him away. He beckoned to the next man in line.

Aug took a deep breath, let it out slowly, and walked back down the line.

"Hey, Rooster," Dobbins called, "everything go okay?"

"Everything went *real* good," Aug said. He winked at Dobbins and marched out the door into the morning sunshine.

CHAPTER
☆ NINETEEN ☆

T HERE were three companies crowded into the tiny depot at Warlock. The 575th had been there since 0800. The other two had been there nearly an hour longer after arriving as a unit that morning from another camp farther north. The platoons were strung out in loose formation below the station platform, the men lounging about against their overstuffed barracks bags, smoking, playing cards, complaining easily among themselves. No one—no one down there in the dirt anyway—seemed to know why they didn't just climb aboard the waiting train.

"We gotta wait till they load the beer on."

"Beer, shit. More likely we gotta paint the fuckin' thing first."

Barely ten o'clock and it was already hot. Aug sat by himself in the meager shade, leaning back against one of the platform uprights. He was looking at the little white-striped red ribbon he and the others had drawn from the supply room a few weeks earlier, turning it over and over in his fingers. The good conduct medal. If the captain's outfit was going anywhere, it was going looking good.

Boner wounded. Jimmy dead. The Sushiwaras devastated. The two Japanese-American soldiers with decorations all over their chests, having to ask permission to visit their families. With a flick of his thumb, he snapped the ribbon back into the shadows behind him.

Down at the far end of the platform, he could see the captain, several other officers, and some noncoms huddled in conference, probably devising no one knew what sort of schemes for the cross-country ride to Wisconsin. Whatever the plans were, Aug knew, they wouldn't make any sense. According to the word someone had passed along "right off the red stool," the captain would be in command of the whole train, all three companies.

"Sumbitch'll have us doin' push-ups all the way to Camp McCoy."

"Prob'ly give us target practice, shootin' at the fuckin' buffalo."

"Dumb-shit fuckin' Indians killed all the buffalo."

"The American bison," Private Crowder corrected, "was not indigenous to the arid Southwest and—"

"No shit."

"Up yours, Crowder."

The caucus below the end of the platform broke up, and as the officers tarried for further consultation, the noncoms hurried back to their respective units and called them into formation.

"Fall in! Line up, goddammit! Take your interval! Dress right! . . . Dress! Anberger, where's your goddam rifle?"

The 575th, someone said, having arrived last, would board last.

"Fuckers'll get all the good seats," Billy Lawler grumbled. He spit at a column of red ants and hit his pants leg instead. Billy's fictitious rupture hadn't kept him out of the shipment; Kaplowitz's bad eyes had. Mozetti was going; he was down the line with First Platoon.

None of the noncoms were going—Garrison, Bleeker, Crawford. The word was, the infantry wanted only the grunts.

Anberger craned his neck to peer at the train. "Don't look to me like they *is* any good seats."

His assessment was correct. The cushioned seats had been ripped out of the olive-drab cars, the floors laid bare, and a jungle gym of heavy pipes bolted in place, floor to ceiling. This was the framework for tiers of canvas-bottomed bunks stacked three high and three across, leaving narrow aisles next to the windows on either side. The sole function of the train was to transport troops, and there were no amenities. At one end of each car was a cramped latrine. One stool and one tiny washbasin for forty-eight men.

Up ahead, competing with the evil smells emitted by the engine, was the mess car. Sergeant Cleary was in charge, and "the Chief," PFC Houghton, was in there with him, still scratching and grinning. Cleary was going only as far as the mess car went.

"They orta send Cleary over and let him feed them Germans some of his eggs."

"They got rules against that kinda thing. No torturin' prisoners."

"Cleary's meat loaf could end the fuckin' war in one meal."

Finally it was their turn. Single file, the remnants of the 575th swung their heavy barracks bags up through the narrow doorway and awkwardly climbed the steel steps.

"You fellers go on ahead. I think I'll just drop off at home."

"Shit, I can't go home yet; I promised Emmie Jane I'd come back with a pisspot full of medals."

"Show her the one you got for the clap."

"He can't show her that one; she ain't give it to him yet."

Aug paused before climbing the steps to look back up the platform. The captain was still in conference with a big blond major and a lieutenant. The captain was doing most of the talking. The other officers and noncoms had dispersed.

Inside, the travel accommodations were not greeted with enthusiasm.

"What the hell are them things, chicken roosts? Where we s'posed to sleep?"

"You're lookin' at 'em, Mother Hen. Jus' don't lay any eggs on me."

"You sleep with your mouth open, I'll lay somethin' on you."

Aug picked a middle-high outside bunk next to a window. He was still stowing his gear away and dragging his blankets out of a barracks bag when the car bucked forward and stopped, bucked once again, and started rolling. Good-bye, Piebald; good-bye, Arizona; good-bye, pretty soon, the whole country maybe, and hello, somewhere else. He poked his head out the window for a final look.

The captain was standing alone on the platform, watching the train draw away from him.

The door at one end of the car opened, and the big blond major and the lieutenant started through.

"Sir? Major?"

The major grabbed one of the bunk rails to steady himself.

"The captain—Captain Maxwell. Isn't he coming?"

The major laughed and looked at the lieutenant to share the joke. "No, he's not. The old bastard busts his butt trying to make silk purses out of sows' ears, and when somebody finally decides, by God, he's done it, they leave him back there to start all over again with another sorry outfit. Kick in the ass. But that's the way the cards fall."

Aug put his head out again, banging his ear against the edge of the window in his haste. Leaving him back there to start all over? No handshakes, no "good luck," no anything?

The station was fast receding into the distance. He started to wave good-bye, but he was afraid it would look like a mocking gesture.

The stupid wind, for God's sake, was starting to make his eyes water.

The engine's whistle sounded for a crossing up ahead. *Whoooooo, whoooooo, whoo, whooooooooooo!*

Dank white clouds of steam blew past the window, smelling strongly of coal. The train swept around a long, looping bend, and when Aug looked back again, he could no longer see the station.

Or the gaunt figure standing alone on the splintered wooden platform.

But who's going to look out for us over there?
I'm awfully sorry, but I've forgotten your name.

After The Ball Was Over

"IT should be right over here somewhere. I remember the wind coming down off that slope, kicking sand and crap all over us." Aug pivoted awkwardly on the uneven ground and looked around. "There were graves all around here . . . headstones. Not headstones, little markers made of desert rocks. Rock pathways. Pretty." He pointed. "There was a low stone wall over there and a gate, sort of, made out of cactus or something."

He tried to kick some sagebrush aside, to look for some physical evidence of Jimmy's grave, but he stumbled, lost his balance, and, hopping about, almost fell. Like a one-legged man at an ass-kickin' contest. That's one thing he couldn't do any more, he guessed, stand on one leg and kick with the other.

Boner stood in the middle of where the graveyard had been and turned slowly, looking around. "Nothing here now. But it's been five years, I guess, or more. They must have dug everybody up and buried them somewhere else. I wonder where the Sushiwaras went."

Aug shrugged. "No idea. I guess a lot of them never went back."

They walked over to Boner's paint-blistered surplus jeep and climbed in, Aug sitting with his heavy plastic leg stuck outside, braced against the narrow fender. He remembered the captain riding that way, with one hand on top of the windshield.

He pointed. "See that butte over there? There's supposed to be a monument up there somewhere."

There was no longer any road to follow, just the rubbled

desert floor, littered here and there with scraps of black tar-paper roofing, an occasional rotted timber, and the bleached remains of concrete slabs and crumbled footings. Boner controlled the bucking steering wheel with just one hand, the one that went with the stiff elbow, his right hand relaxed in his lap.

"How's Angie doing?" Aug asked.

"All right, still getting sick every morning. She says this is it, though. Two's enough. She said to tell you she still can't see you as a teacher, by the way, and, if you change your mind, she's got these pills."

Aug laughed. Angie. "Sometimes I agree with her. But . . . come June."

"Yeah," Boner said.

The monument, or what was left of it, had been built on the little outcropping overlooking Camp Two, where the captain had first been taken by Captain Bruce to view the relocation site. Boner stopped the jeep, and they got out and moved slowly around the ruins, wincing at the vandalism that had reduced the memorial to four gutted stone walls. The roof was gone. There was no evidence there had ever been a roof.

On one wall of the defaced monument, there was a clearly defined discolored rectangle. Boner chipped at it with a piece of broken glass. "Probably a plaque of some kind," he said.

"The names of those who died here maybe."

"I wonder if Jimmy's name was on it."

"I guess."

They sat down side by side on the edge of the little plateau and gazed out over the rough landscape where five years of flash floods, wind, and drifting sand had obliterated most of what had been a city of more than ten thousand persons. Now there was just greasewood and mesquite and cactus blending into the scattered green carpet extending beyond it to the horizon.

"We never got in here much," Aug said. "The WRA wanted us out of sight, so the people wouldn't feel like they were being held here. You know, like prisoners. Which they were, anyway, I guess. There weren't any barbed-wire fences or guard towers, though. Not like at some of the camps."

Boner didn't say anything. He picked up a little piece of red volcanic rock and chucked it down the slope.

"I remember sitting on a hill like this," Aug said, "one night outside this little town in Germany, looking toward the town and wondering if some German kid was sitting down there looking up where I was. I didn't know him and he didn't know me, but because of somebody else we didn't know, we were both out there, miles from home, waiting for daylight so we could try to kill each other."

One hand strayed to the plastic leg and he tapped on it absently with the tips of his fingers.

They sat there for a while longer, not saying anything, each lost in his own thoughts. Then they stood and moved past the monument again. The inside of it was covered with graffiti. Across one entire wall someone had sprayed the word "bullshit."

Boner nodded. "That's what it was, Aug. All of it."

The wind came up as they turned and started picking their way back down the rocky slope. As the wind hummed and moaned over the rocks and through the upraised arms of a big saguaro, it sounded like men muttering out of the sides of their mouths—without moving their lips.

"*Bulllllshit.*"